BERLIN SYNDROME

Melanie Joosten's debut novel, *Berlin Syndrome*, saw her named a *Sydney Morning Herald* Best Young Novelist and receive the Kathleen Mitchell Award; it has since been made into a motion picture directed by Cate Shortland. In 2016, she published the essay collection *A Long Time Coming*. Her work appears in various publications, including *Meanjin*, *Kill Your Darlings*, *Best Australian Stories 2014*, and *Going Down Swinging*.

BERLIN SYNDROME

MELANIE JOOSTEN

SCRIBE
Melbourne • London

Scribe Publications
18-20 Edward St, Brunswick, Victoria 3056, Australia
2 John St, Clerkenwell, London, WC1N 2ES, United Kingdom

First published by Scribe 2011
This edition published 2017
Copyright © Melanie Joosten 2011

Typeset in 12.5/17.5 pt Granjon by the publishers.
Printed and bound in the UK by CIP Group (UK) Ltd, Croydon CR0 4YY

Scribe Publications is committed to the sustainable use of natural resources and
the use of paper products made responsibly from those resources.

9781922070364 (Australian paperback)
9781925228663 (UK paperback)
9781921942051 (e-book)

A CiP data record for this title is available from the National Library of
Australia and the British Library.

scribepublications.com.au
scribepublications.co.uk

To my parents

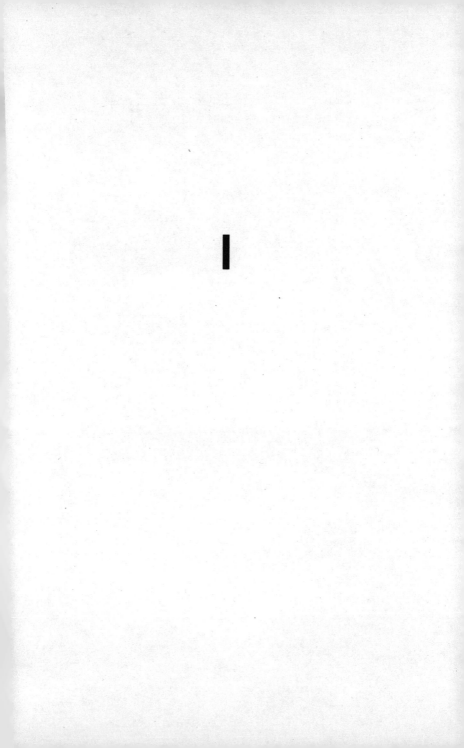

Berlin is overrun by dogs. Every evening as she waits for Andi, Clare listens to their muffled barks drift over the walls and settle in the forgotten courtyard below. She taps out a tuneless beat on her bare thigh and waits for change, for movement. Somehow it is more difficult to imagine anything happening in the courtyard than it is to imagine the unseen dogs and their walkers nearby. Running her hands across her thighs, she reads the corrugated surfaces like braille. The inflammation has retreated, the cuts have become scabs, soon they will become scars. More lines will join these ones — her legs like furrowed fields waiting for the season to turn.

The days are getting longer. Or at least it is getting dark later. Running without pause into the next, the days do not seem particularly long or short. She has turned both of the clocks to face the wall; her watch battery is long dead. An overcast sky refuses to acknowledge that it might be spring while the sun, defeated by clouds, is too diffused to track across the surfaces of the apartment.

The plant must be growing. She looks at its leaves — does it realise that time has slowed? Its foliage clings to its stem, hoping for the sunlight to return. The leaves leave in winter. The leaves are left. Left is not right. She is left here; it is not right. The words thump at her temples, demanding her attention. Refusing to be pummelled into sentences, they want to stand on their own. The longer she spends here by herself, not talking, the louder the words seem to jostle about, wanting to be acknowledged. Why does 'left' mean two things? Why can it not just be one? 'Apple' means apple. It does not mean up or down. She paces the apartment. Step, step, step, turn. Faster and faster. She tries to walk in a straight line, careful not to lose her balance, careful not to lose her mind.

In the living room, she whirls around, tries to catch the plant watching her. It must be: she is the only other living thing in the apartment. They are attracted to each other, she and the plant, of that she is sure, but she is yet to garner proof.

As she pulls on her jeans, she feels she is part of a performance. The apartment is like a stage set, ready for the same action to be played out night after night. Each item of furniture is steeped in importance, heavy with meaning and signifying something — she is determined to find out exactly what.

She takes the clock from the bookshelf, turns it to face the room. Tick. Tick. That time is still passing is a relief. Step, step, step, turn. She paces the apartment, stretching her legs as though the more distance she covers, the faster time will pass. *Come home now, come home.* At last, the key in the lock, and she hurries to the hallway.

'Andi! Andi, you're home.'

Without saying hello, he dumps shopping bags at his feet, turns away from her and shuts the door. His hair and shoulders are wet. She had not noticed that it was raining. He picks up the bags, and as he walks past her into the kitchen, she reaches out to touch his hair, conjuring up some of the absent weather for herself.

'Andi?'

'What?' He places the shopping bags on the bench and moves past her to hang his jacket on the back of a dining chair.

'You're home.' She says it quietly, but her heart bats the statement about like a refrain. He is home, he is home.

He grunts an acknowledgement and begins unpacking the shopping. She watches as he stacks cans of chickpeas and tomatoes in the cupboard and posts vegetables into the refrigerator crisper. He empties a bag of apples into the fruit bowl and flings a loaf of bread against the toaster where it sighs as it settles.

'How was your day?'

The question rolls across the floor and stops at his feet. Nothing else moves inside the apartment.

'Andi?'

He continues to put the groceries away.

'Did something happen?'

'Nothing happened.'

'Is something wrong?' She waits in the doorway.

'Nothing is the matter, Clare!' His forehead pulls at his nose, his top lip snags above his teeth. 'I've been harassed by students all day, I don't need the same from you. Just leave me alone, would you?'

She takes a step back, but he steps towards her. She is getting it wrong; she should not have asked.

'Why do I have to come home to this? You're always here, Clare! You're making me nervous, watching me the way you do.' His face is above hers: it looks like it might fall on top of her, swallow anything she might say. 'I could end this, Clare. Anytime I want. You know that, don't you?'

She nods. And she wishes that he would.

~

The first time Clare left Andi, the sun hung low in its autumn hour. Long shadows enveloped buildings, and she watched as the streetlights began to flicker and turn on, one by one.

'Do you like strawberries?'

She looked across to see a man waiting, like her, for the traffic lights to change. He was tall with curly hair, and in his hand was a paper bag.

'Yes.' With one word she acquiesced to all that was to follow. The traffic lights changed with a commanding bleep, the pedestrians surged forth around them, and she picked a strawberry from the bag.

'Do you want to seat?'

'To sit?' she asked, looking about. There were no benches nearby.

'Yes.' He nodded enthusiastically, leading her to a pink pipe that ran above the footpath.

Clare was fascinated by these pipes that wound through the city, their brutal industrial appearance softened by the most feminine of colours. Were they an art installation, leading tourists to the Museumsinsel? Without a beginning or an end, these pipes snaked about the old East Berlin — around corners, high above roads, beneath raised footpaths. They were about the size of a dinner plate in diameter, maybe smaller. The various lengths were bolted together, sometimes in strange, convoluted arrangements as though the gods had sprayed the city with Silly String.

'Why are they pink?'

'Pink? The strawberries are red, no? *Rot?*' Confusion flailed on his face.

'I mean the pipes. Why are they pink?' She banged the heel of her hand against the pipe they were sitting on.

'Ah. I do not know exactly. Because pink means nothing, I suppose.'

'Pink means lots of things — little girls, breast cancer, pride.' Pink was possibly overladen with more meaning than any other colour. Except black. Or red. Scrolling through the colour spectrum, she concluded that most colours seemed overburdened with meaning.

'True,' he replied. 'But for the streets, pink means nothing. You do not usually see pink in the roadworks, the buildings, the landscape. It is bright, so it is obvious, and it makes even the hard-hatted feel joy.'

'The hard-*hearted*?'

'Yes!' He laughed loudly. 'My accent, I suppose? Hat, heart. You see, if the pipes were red, it would be alarming, one. And two, it would be Soviet — not good. And if they were green, they would get lost in the trees. Yellow, too bright in the sun, and blue? The ones up high would camouflage against the sky!' He was triumphant. 'So that is why the construction pipes are pink.'

'Construction pipes?'

'Yes. That is all they do in Berlin these days. They build, and they build, and they build. And Berlin, she is built on sand.

Every time they dig a basement, they sink the foundations and the water comes up. So the pipes take away the water.'

It was a wonderful thing, a city built on water. She came from a country where the cities settled on dust, the water long leached away, helped by an inexorable belief in the present and an unforgiving sun. Water restrictions obliged all of Melbourne's fountains to be switched off; the punitive shutting down of such follies a reprimand to a people who had turned a blind eye for so long that, by the time they looked back, water had become a privilege rather than a right. She considered the possibility of laying these pink pipes all the way to her thirsty hometown. It would be simpler to turn the world upside down.

'Many people think they are art.' He shook his head in mock consternation. 'So where are you from, that you do not have water pipes?'

'Melbourne.'

'I see — then you are far from home.'

They paused, each waiting for the other to say something, but she broke first. Starved of company after months travelling alone, she could not bear to let an opportunity for conversation pass her by. 'You are from Berlin?'

'Yes, I am. A true local. Though I must admit I do not spend much time in this part of the city, so do not ask me for directions.'

His was a voice worth pausing for, his turn of phrase was endearing. It tripped her up and made her aware of each word — alive to what he was saying, not just considering what she would say next. He asked what it was like in Australia, and she told him — the stock-standard descriptions at first, and then the real. They talked about places they had been and others they would like to go, and she wondered at the way his brain could work in two languages while hers felt weighted down by one.

'Your English really is very good.' She plucked another strawberry from the bag, watching him closely. 'Do you always practise by chatting up foreigners?'

'Ha! You are very suspicious.' He pulled his attention from the milling tourists and turned his whole body towards her. 'I only wish I had such opportunity. But I am simply an English teacher at a high school. And so, sadly, I have more practice dealing with unruly students than women.' He held her gaze as he spoke, and she struggled to look away.

'So where are the strawberries from?' she asked. She could feel the heat of a blush wending its way to her cheeks and she bit her lip, willing it to subside.

'I grow them in my mother's *Schrebergarten*.' He looked at her to see if she understood. 'It is a little garden among many, on the outskirts of Berlin.' He gestured with his head, a throwaway nod. It seemed to indicate a place that was both close and yet very far away.

'I suppose it is really my father's now ...' His voice trailed off. 'However, I must go.' He stood up from the pipe and turned with his hand outstretched. 'My name is Andi.' His hand hovered before her, and she popped the last of the strawberry into her mouth so that she could shake it. Grasping her hand, he pulled her to her feet and kissed her with familiarity, once on each cheek.

This European gesture always took her by surprise, the brief brush of his lips plummeting her into an intimacy she had only ever found with old friends or whisky-soaked strangers in bars.

The scratch of his stubble gave her pause. In that short moment, with her own hand still encased in his, she was aware that it had been more than four months since somebody had touched her with any kind of intent.

'Clare,' she replied. The blush, too long held back, was set free, and desperate to keep him from seeing it, she leaned in and kissed him on the mouth. 'Pleased to meet you,' she said. And she walked away.

Clare is beautiful. This is a statement of fact, not an observation. Andi pictures himself in a courtroom, under oath and having to answer the questions thrown at him. *Describe her.* She is beautiful. She is small, but he expected her legs to be longer. Her smile is too wide for her face, and her hair is such a dark red it threatens to be brown. She is pretty, especially in her underwear. That, too, is a statement of fact, Your Honour. She looks so very fragile in her underwear, and he wishes he saw her like this more often. Soft and in need of protection. She cannot go out in the cold dressed like that. She cannot walk through the streets: her feet will numb, her lips will turn blue.

He watches her walk across the kitchen, take one mug at a time from the drying rack and hang each one on the row of hooks beneath the kitchen cabinets. Her legs swerve in at the knees. Ulrike had long, thin legs, but they didn't go in at the knees or the ankles. It made her seem doll-like, as though she was stuffed with balled cotton. Clare's legs do not suffer this misfortune, however, and they bend in to each other just a bit. Like a bird. When she reaches up to put the plates in the cupboard, she stands on one leg and the other flicks up behind.

He will buy her some new underwear. Something pink and flamingo-like. He smiles to himself, imagining already the delight on her face when he presents her with this gift. She loves presents. She appreciates them more obviously than anyone he has ever known. She insists on sitting down together to open any present, no matter how big or small, however serious or comedic. She will parade around the apartment, dressed in whatever he has bought, or immediately put it to use.

'What?' She turns to face him, cup in hand.

'Nothing,' he answers, innocent. He smiles at her: she looks so indignant.

'Why were you looking at me?'

'Because you look like a flamingo.'

She snorts dismissively and turns back to the dishes. He bets she is rolling her eyes at the cupboards. He is glad he did not simply say, 'Because you are beautiful.' She does not like it when he compliments her on her looks. She says it is bad manners to compliment someone on things they have no control over.

Restless, he wanders into the bedroom. When he is at work, or out shopping, or visiting his father, all he can think about is how he wants to be back here in the apartment with her. Yet when he is here, sometimes it is not quite as he remembers. In his daydreams, she wants everything he wants, does everything he says.

'Come to bed, baby,' he calls out to her.

He switches on the lamp, sits on the bed and takes off his shoes. He always thinks of his father when he sees his shoeless feet: they wear the same socks. When Andi was still living at home, they would sit together in the evenings, books open in their laps. His father's feet were large and docile, like big sleeping animals. They each liked to think they just had the television on for the comfort of sound, and that really they were immersed in their reading. Flipping the occasional page, they would furtively watch the television without comment.

'Clare?' She has not appeared in the doorway, and he cannot hear her moving about the apartment. Maybe she has fallen asleep on the couch; she is prone to doing that. And then she is grumpy when she wakes up, as though it is his fault she is so tired and he should never have let her fall asleep there. But it is not his fault. He makes sure she has plenty of time to rest.

He lets himself drop back on the bed, feet still on the floor. He stares up at the ceiling, which is interrupted by a lone globe. It used to wear a paper-lantern covering, but she removed it. She told him it was deceitful, as though it had something to hide, and that she would rather see the globe do what it was designed to do. He did not argue. He has learned when not to argue.

'Clare, baby, come to bed.'

No response. What is she doing? He clenches his fists and counts to three before pushing himself up off the bed and striding along the hallway. She is standing in the doorway of the living room. The backs of her hands are pressed against the doorframe.

'Look,' she says. She steps towards him, and her arms float up, like a slow-motion star jump. 'I can't stop them from moving,' she says, delighted. 'They just want to go up of their own accord.'

He reaches out and takes one of her hands, interrupting its ascent.

~

He was not really following her, he told himself, he was just curious to see where she was going. An anthropological study of a foreigner in Berlin. She had been reading on a park bench when he first saw her, a bag tucked beneath her head as a pillow. Something about her insouciance had caught his eye; she lay there as though she was in her own bedroom, oblivious to the square's activity — even to the school students who milled about on the steps of the concert hall, puncturing the air with their shoving and shouts. He was certain she was a foreigner: a local would have somewhere better to go, and she was not smoking.

He had stood at the edge of the square watching her. What was she doing here? What was anyone doing here? These were dead parts of the city — churches restored to eerie perfection, monuments erected to memories that had collapsed under the weight of more recent history. He felt as though the new century was hurtling forward, leaving nothing authentic in its place. He was supposed to meet his father to attend a public lecture on *ostalgie* — the nostalgia people felt for the East. As was so often the case, his father had lost track of time, had called to say he would meet Andi at the restaurant instead. Andi had been relieved: he was not in the mood to debate what was lost along with the past, and he had left the lecture hall and wandered down the street, looking for somewhere to catch the last of the day's sun. But every surface was covered with tourists clinging like brightly coloured lichen to their resting places. It was then that he had seen her, lying so still, unaware of the surrounding tumult and looking enviably content.

What would he have done if she had not liked strawberries? He had ducked into the minimart, and they had seemed the most appetising and least threatening of offerings. Never go anywhere empty-handed, his mother always said. When he came out of the store, he had experienced a moment of brief panic: the bench was bare. Spotting her nearing the intersection, he broke into a jog, arriving at her side to discover that she did like strawberries, and that she was from elsewhere — Australia. Where the people were laid back and had no worries. She even used that phrase. When she had asked where the strawberries were from, he had not wanted to disappoint her.

He followed her now as she walked down Friedrichstrasse, her hands in her pockets, and her bag hugging her back. He felt a little miffed that she did not look around, even though she did not know he was there. At Checkpoint Charlie she glanced at the hoarding that surrounded the empty lots, but must have decided to ignore its multilingual tourist information and walk on.

He should just catch up to her and ask for her number. But that would mean admitting he had followed her this far. Instead, he slowed his pace and watched as she turned the next corner and headed into a bookstore.

She had seemed to concentrate when he had spoken, to wait with a vicious intent, and he had found his English deserting him. She told him that she had been watching his city all day; an architectural photographer, she saw the city in cubes and planes, shapes and shadows. He liked the idea of her watching his city unfold, being made new again. Envying her freedom to observe, he had wanted to assure her that he, too, was an outsider looking in.

'Sometimes I like to just sit there and complicate the world.' He had watched for her reaction.

Clare had laughed, throwing her head back in a pantomime of enjoyment. Would it annoy him after some time? Would he stop trying to make her laugh?

'*Complicate*? You mean contemplate ... but it's very funny.'

He had laughed with her. It was a good choice. He had almost gone with compensate. Consummate. Concentrate. Consecrate. Complicate had definitely been the best choice.

Resigning himself to being late for his father, Andi now followed her into the bookstore. Clare stopped at a shelf of art books and dropped to a crouch. She pulled out a book, and he squinted to see. Egon Schiele. She put it back, stood and looked about, as though assessing the store. Andi seized a book and kept himself hidden behind a shelf, feeling as if he was in a British comedy. What would he say if she saw him? Pretend it was a coincidence, that this was his favourite bookstore?

Clare possessed her body as if she was the only person in the room. How was it that nobody else was staring at her? She dropped to the floor again; he was so close he could hear her knees click. They made a popping sound, like the snapping of fingers calling attention. Surely everyone in the store was tracking her every move? She pulled a book on Klimt from the shelf and sat on the carpet of the shop, legs crossed, flipping the pages and tilting them away from the glare of the lights.

Andi's phone beeped. Its vibrations felt like a small animal impatiently pawing at his hip. He put the book down, still watching Clare, who was oblivious to the people who wanted to get past her. Again he almost stepped forward and asked for her number. He wanted to yell the request out at her, to see his words slam into her face and shake her from her reverie. But because he could not be sure that she would yell back, he left the store. He did not want to play with uncertainty.

As he walked to the restaurant, Andi wondered whether his father had missed the lecture on purpose. They had such different views of the past, particularly that of the GDR. His father saw it as something separate, another world that could not be understood by those who inhabited the present. Andi saw it as an extension of today: it could not all be shuffled out of sight, or forgiven. He had no idea what his mother thought of the past, if she thought of it at all.

Stepping into the fuggy air of the restaurant, Andi saw his father waiting for him at a table. Even when seated, he was a tall man. A man whose clothes floated about his body as though they were afraid to make contact, giving the impression of much broader shoulders — of much more man — than Andi's father could lay claim to.

He wondered whether he would have liked his father if they had met as friends of the same age. Probably not. And yet they recognised themselves in each other. The same nose, the same mouth. Their teeth were disorderly, their top lips curled in a way that could be perceived as endearing or unkind. Years ago, his father would host study groups in their apartment, and Andi would watch the discussion, unnoticed as voices were raised, ideas volleyed about. He saw how his father could sneer in a manner that made students look away, or be so charming that some of them, women and men, would blush. Andi spent many hours trying to emulate his father's magnetic scowl, but it always appeared self-conscious rather than disaffected. Somehow, this failure made him dislike his father and his easy manner all the more.

As his father stood, Andi was reminded how far into old age he had retreated. They muddled through their greetings, his father apologising again for missing the lecture as Andi awkwardly embraced him and sat down too quickly. They passed their conversation back and forth across the table, questions of work and study carrying them through to dessert. He found himself watching the clock on his phone, wishing his father didn't always make him want to be somewhere else.

'Your mother would like to see you.' His father poured water into his glass as he said this, his eyes following the stream. Andi surveyed his cutlery. The stainless-steel cake knife had fine scratches all over its surface; sweeping lines from edge to edge. Cloudy marks hovered where the soapy water had dried, a snail trail of detergent.

'Why?' He watched the hurt trickle across his father's face. Andi sighed. It was not his father he wanted to punish. But he was so easy to bruise; a word flung at high speed across the table, or even a lazy drop shot, was all it took.

'You're her son, Andreas. She wants to see you.'

He thought about not even saying the words: his father knew what his reply would be. 'I don't want to see her.'

His father nodded. And they sat in silence until Andi gestured for the bill.

Clare's left foot had gone to sleep. She closed the monograph and slid it back into its place on the shelf. Jiggling her leg until the numbness began to dissipate, she hauled herself up from the floor and looked towards the doorway. Night had completely fallen: she should head back to the hostel; she should get something to eat.

She wanted to do neither of these things; both seemed like insurmountable tasks. Sighing, she picked up her bag and left the store. She was tired of creating purpose for herself and ashamed at this tiredness. Could she not just enjoy this as a holiday? She walked a few paces towards Checkpoint Charlie, telling herself to join in, to queue in the gift store for an *Ampelmännchen* tea towel and fridge magnet, and to dash off witty postcards for friends back home. Instead she walked towards Potsdamer Platz, hoping the bustle and the shiny newness of it all would shake her out of her own weary mind. She wondered briefly what the man with the strawberries — Andi — was doing that night. She pictured him holding court in a bar, his audience's rapt attention, much as she imagined his students behaving, hanging from his every word. It seemed admirably useful — teaching a language, enabling people to communicate. And though she knew that photography played a similar role, that images could parade truth in a way that words never could, her career still seemed so futile.

When she decided to take this trip, she had been overjoyed to put all of her commercial work on hold, had not even bothered to give her clients a date of return. She was tired of the smoke and mirrors or, more accurately, the mirrors and Photoshop of architectural photography. The way the architects who employed her insisted the images be more than each building was, or ever could be. That the hero shot must show the structure thrusting into the city skyline, as though it was tearing a hole in the atmosphere, despite architecture in Australia only ever being deserving of the term 'tasteful'. Wanting to see buildings that were designed with purpose, she mapped out a trip through the former Eastern Bloc. In each city and town she found these buildings, most in a state of neglect, that spoke of the utopian future that never arrived. Strictly places in which to live and to work, they were designed as an extension of a collective, rather than a personal, identity. Yet she was under no illusions about the brutal nature of communism and its socialist sisters: she remembered watching the ABC news as a child, seeing people dancing on top of the Berlin Wall, wondering whether this was the same thing as the Iron Curtain, and knowing that a display of such joy could only mean that what had stayed hidden behind that wall was merciless.

Curious to see how a society driven by an unrelenting search for the ideal could become so invalid, she had packed her studio and house into a rented storage space. Made an agreement with a gallery for an exhibition on concrete-block housing and Soviet architecture, and signed a contract with a publisher for a coffee-table book on the same. Aware that this was a project tinged with schadenfreude, she was tempted to compare the photographs to the high-rise commission housing that was dotted around Melbourne's inner suburbs. To foster a feeling of us and us, rather than us and them. But would anyone care? Did she? She doubted that the people who lived in the buildings would ever read her book — it was as much an exercise in futility as the buildings she tried to capture. She felt as though everything she attempted had been done before; her efforts to quell the emptiness just made apparent its existence.

Arriving at Potsdamer Platz, she almost laughed aloud.

The entire complex was a hero shot. All soaring ceilings and polished facades, it was a tribute to capitalism and its ability to bring people together through consumption. She was almost twenty years too late and wondered if she was ever going to catch up.

When she thinks about growing old with Andi, she is happily resigned. She looks at his profile as he watches television. The newsreader is speaking too fast for Clare to understand, and she has given up trying to decipher the words. Instead she faces Andi and tries to see him as the stranger he so briefly was. She remembers an elderly couple she once photographed, their unsteady steps held on film forever.

It was the end of winter, and she had been sitting in one of Melbourne's public gardens. The sun possessed the tiniest amount of heat as it fell through bare branches, alighting upon two men who were preparing a flowerbed for planting, arranging potted seedlings so that they fanned out from the central fountain like bicycle spokes. Lighting a cigarette, she had marvelled at the crispness of the unfurling smoke. She had been up all night working and was feeling fuzzy, yet the day placed everything sharply in focus. If ever a day was set for premonitions, this one was it. It was the sort of clear, overwhelming morning where bright-eyed people could see forever, and it was then that she decided she would leave Melbourne and see what life was hiding for her over the horizon.

The city's buildings jostled behind trees, looking as though they had been cut out of cardboard and propped up for her amusement. From a rotunda the sound of two people rehearsing a song could be heard. An accompanying cello pulled their voices into the day, retreating every time they reached the end of the chorus and, with a pause, returned to the beginning.

The elderly couple had walked by, supporting each other, feet shuffling along the sandy path. They looked at the ground and measured each step, taking no notice of the bare flowerbeds, the stunted rose bushes. The man's felt hat sat precariously on his head: 'jaunty,' women would have said fifty years ago. They seemed oblivious to the chill of the day, buttoned up in their long tweed coats.

She had waited for them to pass before standing on the path and photographing them as they shuffled away. It was a lazy shot, but when she developed it later, she could see it was better than anything she had done in a long time.

Looking at the walls of Andi's apartment, she wishes that they were covered with proper family photos, framed and legitimate, a lifetime of memories.

'Do you look like your father?' she asks him. She wonders who Andi might become as he ages.

'I guess so.' He glances up from the television. 'We are both tall.'

'What about your mother? Do you take after her?'

'No.' He switches off the television with the remote. 'Why do you want to know who I look like? I look like me.' He reaches over to her and tugs at her arm. She moves along the couch, rearranges herself to lean against him.

'Do you have any photos of them?' She wants to see his resemblance in somebody else. He doesn't answer her. 'Andi?'

'No, no photos.'

'Are you close to your parents?' She feels his body stiffen.

'Close enough. I see my father sometimes.' He nudges her away, stands up from the couch. 'Are you hungry? I might make something to eat.'

As she listens to him clatter about in the kitchen her appetite deserts her. She has not seen either of her parents in such a long time; the homesickness settles in.

~

The second time Clare left Andi, she hoped that he would follow. She had spent the morning photographing the Palast der Republik, the building dwarfed beneath the cranes being used to dismantle it. While the palace's bronze-tinted glazing remained, there was no sign of the bowling alley, the parliament rooms or the spectacular foyer dripping with one thousand bauble light fittings — nicknamed 'Erich's lamp shop', the guidebook had told her. It was the last building on her Berlin itinerary, but she wasn't quite ready to leave the city. Retracing yesterday's steps, she found herself back in the bookstore, where she squeezed past the Sunday readers perusing cookbooks and headed straight to the art monographs.

And there he was, bent over the very Klimt book she was coming to buy, his lips pursed in concentration and his shirt tag poking out, beckoning to his dishevelled hair.

Put the book down. She willed him to turn around and notice her, but he continued to read. *Put it down.* She loitered by the nearby shelves, noisily picking up and replacing a book. She was not sure what she would say if he glanced her way, but in a city of strangers she was determined to make some kind of connection. Since meeting him yesterday, she had been unable to eject him from her mind; her daydreams knew no bounds. It was just a kiss. She was lonely. But surely loneliness is as good a reason as any to talk to someone? Not quite. In need of pretence, she stepped behind him, reached for his tag and tucked it inside his jumper. Her hand brushed his neck. He turned.

'Your tag,' she said, by way of excuse.

Andi's forehead creased: the international sign for confusion. Or anger. Facial expressions are perplexingly duplicitous. She reached to her own neck, pulled at her own tag by way of demonstration.

'Ah, thank you.'

She thought he would put the book down, but he just turned back to the table. Did he not recognise her? Her face burned: the international sign for embarrassment. She wanted to tear the book from his hands, to keep its pristine pages closed against the light. She wanted to have the composure of Klimt's women and their lack of dimension. She wanted to be painted in gold leaf and empty her eyes until there was nothing left to be read in them.

'That's my favourite,' she said. Adele Bloch-Bauer, her gloves drawn up over crippled hands.

He was silent, flicked the page. A customer squeezed behind Clare, and she found herself pressed up to Andi. Sandwiched, she waited as the customer pulled a book from the shelf then stepped away. Instead of stepping back, Clare remained pressed against him, her hands resting on his shoulders. Could he feel her heart beating?

She stood behind him for almost five minutes. She said

nothing. He said nothing. The moistness of her breath caught in his clothes and clouded back at her. She could feel every part of her body where it touched his. The book and Andi were both things she could obtain, she was certain of this. Yet as the minutes passed and he did nothing to acknowledge her presence, her certainty waned. The heat of him crept through his clothes like an invitation. Her breasts perched neatly beneath his shoulder blades. The left blade poked her left breast each time he reached for a page. Her breast and each page moved in perfect unison. When he reached the end of the book, he went back to the front and began flipping the pages again. She wanted to know whether he was smiling. She stepped back, waited for him to turn to her. When he did not, she walked away.

Engulfed by her palpitating heart and racing mind, she left the bookshop, breaking into a run as she crossed the street. What had she been thinking? Why did she not act like a normal person and just say, *Hello, how are you?* But the world was ambivalent to her private anguish. The sun was setting behind clouds, shop signage asserted itself from the dusk, and the dark lifted up from the asphalt road. Unsure where she was going, she slowed to a walk. The tree-lined street soon passed parkland, and she contemplated waiting out her flush of emotions on a bench. She looked back the way she had come. Did she hope that he would follow? Or did she just want a fast escape? Envious of the cyclists who flew by, their wheels skimming the road, she fantasised about knocking one to the ground, swinging her leg over the saddle and pedalling far away. Why didn't he say anything to her?

The housing blocks gave way to a strip of bars and cafes

where punters crammed in close to one another around tables littered with beer glasses. Recalling the impassable existence of Andi's body squashed against her own in the bookstore, she pulled out a chair at an empty table and waited for something to happen.

One beer, she decided. She would wait for him for the time it took her to drink one beer, and then she would leave. But when her beer came it was slightly flat, immediately destroying any illusion that she was curating a perfect moment. He wasn't going to come walking down that street, and why should he? She thought about things too much. She wished someone would take away her thoughts, wring them out and pass them back, clean, fresh and renewed. Perhaps it was time to go home.

Clare's face broke into a smile as he approached. He hurried the last few paces, flung the book onto the table and dropped himself heavily into the chair opposite.

'I do not like Klimt, you know.' His own words were halting, as though he did not want to give them up. Around them people laughed and waved their hands about, a parody of conversation. 'I think his work is indulgent.'

'Everyone thinks that,' she replied, looking down at the book, rather than at him. 'Because you've seen his work on coffee cups and greeting cards. But when you look at it properly, you see the way his people exist on a different plane. They're real. They're oversaturated with the moment he has put them in.'

She was more than he remembered. He felt tension he had not even recognised leak from his shoes to the pavement, relief rocking in its wake. That morning Clare had appeared in his mind as a series of flashes, a stop-start animation of yesterday's meeting. The mess of her hair that clashed so badly with the pink pipes. The green stitching that skipped around the wrists of her jumper. The way she threw her head back when she laughed. And so he had walked towards the Spree rather than his apartment, crossed the river and headed back to the bookstore.

The book she had been looking at was sitting exactly where she must have discarded it the day before, and he had hesitated to pick it up. When he did, he had turned its pages slowly as though hunting for clues. He had always dismissed Klimt as being excessively decorative and flat, but looking through this book, he realised he had been presumptuous — he had never seen the artist's drawings. Thin lines depicted languorous bodies; sleeping women embraced.

'Your tag.'

And there she was. Tucking his tag into his collar, her hand fluttering over his shoulder and falling to her side.

'Thank you.' He had looked back to the book. Had he conjured her up?

'That's my favourite.'

He stopped flipping pages, and Clare pushed up against him to get out of a customer's way. Trying not to breathe too deeply, Andi had turned another page. *Put your arms around me*. He had stared down at the page, a drawing titled *Two Lovers*. The man's endless shoulders. His back a wavy line, rolling hills. The woman barely seen behind him, her body mimicking the man's. He should have returned the book to the shelf, faced her and taken her in his arms, one fluid movement. But he could not bear to move and create that momentary gap between them.

Wordlessly, she had stepped away and left the store. Why had she not waited for him to say something? Book in hand, he had followed her to the exit. The security system beeped at him, accompanied by the shop assistant's questioning eyes, and he hurriedly paid for the book.

He had walked for ten minutes before he saw her, hurrying up ahead, but he kept his distance, stayed back until she was seated.

'I think, Clare, that I am in need of a beer.' He looked away, searching to catch the eye of a waiter and, even in that moment, feeling that he was taking something from her.

'You will find, Andi, that it is flat,' she said, mimicking his own cadence. 'But I think that it will not matter.'

As the cold of the evening set in, they wielded their conversation like fencing swords. He dodged her attacks, and mounted challenges, each answer part of an adjudicated performance. When the conversation stopped, Clare looked at her watch, and he knew he could not let her away just yet.

'Shall we have something to eat?' When she nodded, he stood and offered his hand. 'How about I make you dinner?'

As she got up, he pulled her in close to him. He wanted to trace his finger along the straggling line where her hair parted. Instead he took her other hand, bringing both together so they were entirely encased between his own. He noticed that her eyes were grey, and nodded because this seemed right.

Clare wanted to postpone the inevitable. Yesterday she had met him on a street corner, today she had shadowed him in a bookstore and tonight she would follow him to bed — but not just yet. As Andi went to the kitchen for another bottle of wine, she rummaged in her bag for a pouch of tobacco. There was not very much furniture in the room. A couch and an armchair sat on a green rug as though lolling about on a grassy island. A television stood in the corner, and a nearby trestle table nursed a stereo and neatly stacked records. The floors were stripped to their boards, the walls bare. Beyond a table stacked with papers, the kitchen opened off at the end of the space, a bench forming a waist-high divide.

She crossed to the window and rolled a cigarette, the smell of unlit tobacco cutting through the room. Afterwards it would linger in the nooks but now, before it began smoking, it smelled like spring. She smoked a smoke; it smoked. What an unusually useful word. You could drink a drink, but it could not drink itself. Lighting the cigarette, she took a deep breath to the back of her throat. It was the slight dizziness of the first drag that she hankered for the most. She would be happy living on first drags for the rest of her life. Most things were like that. The first kiss, the first fuck with someone — so different from all those that came after. And yet how quickly they all became the same. A downhill slide to mediocrity. Though an uphill slide was difficult to imagine. Why did words that usually seemed so normal seem so questionable now? Aware of English being Andi's second language, she found herself scanning all her words to make sure they made sense, editing out all that were colloquial or confusing.

'Do you mind?' she asked, waving her cigarette when he came back into the room.

He shook his head and filled her glass before moving to

the stereo. She pulled the window handle, but it did not move. Locked. The night sky was pallid with the lights of the city; the television tower stood above its stunted neighbours like a candle on a birthday cake. With her head against the glass she tried to see the ground five storeys below, but the light did not quite reach, rendering the courtyard a bottomless sinkhole.

'In a desolate way, it is beautiful. You agree?' he said, coming up behind her, slinging his arms around her waist and resting his chin on her shoulder.

'Yes. Beautiful.' She blew her smoke towards the window, a futile gesture — the smoke rammed against the glass where it seemed to hang, flattened and motionless, like a bedsheet drying on a still day.

'I'm glad you like strawberries.'

Andi whispered it into her ear, his breath tickling at her neck and sending a buzz down her spine. As she turned to face him, he plucked her cigarette from her hand and dropped it into his wineglass on the windowsill. Stripped of its distraction, she felt combative.

'Do you really grow them?' she asked, ducking her head to avoid his kiss. Passing the linden tree in the first courtyard earlier, its last leaves clinging to the branches, had reminded her that it was the tail end of autumn. Could strawberries be coaxed from the ground at such a time of year?

'Does it matter?' He kissed her, his arms creeping beneath her shirt, vanquishing all thoughts of strawberries.

In the bedroom, they fumbled and clawed at each other's clothes, falling to the bed as they tried to undress without letting each other go.

Then, just as suddenly as he had begun, he leaned back, his

hands withdrawn to his hips. 'Wait.'

Her body was singing, crying out to be touched, but he climbed off the bed, leaving her lying there. She shuddered, like machinery too quickly shut down, and in response he lifted a finger to her, requesting pause. Bending to the bed, he unzipped her boots and pulled them from her feet. Trailing his hands up her legs, he slid his fingers beneath the waistband of her undone jeans. She reached for the yoke of his shirt, wanting to lift it over his head, but he shirked away. Nullified, she dropped her hands to her side. She was so entranced by Andi's purpose that it suddenly seemed ridiculous to reach out and grab at his body.

She lifted her hips in compliance, and he guided her jeans to her knees, tugging at one leg at a time until they came free. He kneeled astride her then, pulling her into a sitting position and relieving her of her shirt before letting her fall back to the bed. She reached to touch him, but it was as though her arms were not long enough.

'Be patient.' He smiled at her, bending down to kiss her stomach.

She felt like she was on an operating table, surrendering her body to the responsibility of others. Goosebumps broke out along her side as he ran his hand up her bare leg. From toe to fingertip she could feel her hairs standing alert, and as he got up and finally began to shed his own clothes, longing broke out across Clare's body like spot fires. She wanted him, and his composure only fuelled her impatience. She had been expecting the usual instantaneous give and take of these situations, real-time gratification dissolving the inevitable doubt that accompanied a one-night stand, not this kind of enforced hesitation.

Undressed, he walked across to the doorway and turned off the light.

'No, keep it on.' She did not want to tell him that she had a fear of the dark. That unable to see where she was going, she worried about never being able to go anywhere. She would rather see him, see what they were about to do.

'You know exactly what you want, don't you, Clare?' he said, silhouetted in the doorway.

And because she knew it was expected, and because it was so immediately true, she replied without pause, 'You.'

He flicked the light back on and returned to the bed. They fucked as though it was a test to later be examined on, composure abandoned along with their clothes. She felt deeper in the bed than she possibly could be; that it was Andi who was both holding her down, and setting her free — a bubble rising to the surface. Yet when it was over and they pulled apart, she could not help but feel relieved. The thing they had danced around all afternoon was done; she had nothing owing.

His voice broke the silence. 'It's funny, don't you think, that we come to this?'

She wished she was already asleep and not obliged to take part in this dissection. 'How do you mean?' These conversations that happened afterwards had once intimidated her; she always felt as though her answers were delivered off-key. But now they simply irritated her. She did not want to discuss what they had done; not yet, when they had just finished the doing.

'Well, yesterday, there you were reading in the square, and now we are lying here naked.'

'But we are still strangers,' she said, casting her mind back, then realising. 'You saw me reading? Where? Near the concert hall?' She lifted her head to look at him.

'Of course. That's why I came to talk to you.'

It made sense, but she detected a flutter of apprehension. She had assumed he just happened to be standing beside her at the intersection, strawberries in hand. This revelation meant something, she knew, but sleep beckoned and she hoped he would say no more. Cold, she reached to pull the quilt up.

'No, wait.' Andi grabbed her hand in his own.

'But I'm freezing.' She reached for the sheet again.

He grabbed her wrist, held it beside her body. 'No, really. Wait. When you get very cold and then cover up, it is even better.' He looked at her. 'I promise.'

'Okay.' A shiver crept up her leg, ready to pounce. She tried to imagine that it felt exquisite, but she could sense her body slowly becoming stiff. She tensed her knees, not wanting to move too much and stir the air around her. She released her kneecaps and the left one began to twitch uncontrollably as though it was jogging up and down to keep warm. She clenched her knees again, trying not to think about how cold she was, resulting only in thinking about how cold she was. Finally she gave in, curling her body to huddle against Andi's. But he gave off little warmth, just enough to remind her that the rest of her was cold. She reached for the quilt and pulled it up.

'So, what is next?' His voice was borne through the air to one of her ears, travelled as vibrations through his chest to the other.

'You will turn off the light, and I will fall into a deep sleep?' Please, please let her sleep.

'And after that? What then?' He shifted her off his chest, and slipped out of bed to switch off the light. 'What about love?'

His disembodied voice floated from the end of the bed, trailing behind him as he climbed back in beside her. Did he really say that? He could not be serious.

'Love?'

'Will it come next, do you think? For us?' He slipped his arms about her as he spoke, and despite the warmth, she thought about getting out of bed, dressing and leaving. She closed her eyes and waited for sleep to take her.

One of Clare's breasts is larger than the other. It droops a little more. Her left one. His right. He is watching her move through a series of stretches, and it's making him feel lazy. She raises her arms above her head, grabs the elbow of one and holds the pose. As she does it, her breasts lift and come together, but even so he can tell one is slightly larger. Perhaps it is because she is right-handed. Is she right-handed? He tries to picture her reaching for something, or eating, but he cannot recall her hands. He does not think he has seen her write. Is it that she has nothing to write on or nothing to write about? He feels he knows her body better than he knows his own, yet he does not know whether she is right- or left-handed. If he bought her a notebook, would she make it into a diary? Document each day they spend together, muse about the future? Would she mention him at all?

'You have one breast bigger than the other.'

She looks at him. Says nothing. Drops her arms and then lifts them again, grabbing the other elbow. She is wearing a pair of his boxer shorts, and each time she stretches her arms, he can see how she has rolled them over at the waistband to keep them from falling down.

'The left one.' He wonders whether it has always been that way. He has not noticed it before. It sits lower than the other one. Just a little. Not much. Enough to notice if you're looking closely. He likes to scrutinise her; there is so much to see. She is like a new person every day.

'I know.'

'Oh.' He thought he was telling her something new.

'Most women do, you know.'

'Really?' Now it is she telling him something he did not know. This is why he will never tire of her. She asks him sometimes when he might get sick of her, and no assurance he gives ever seems to convince her that it's just not possible. 'So you are not symmetrical.'

'No. No one is.'

He contemplates this.

'Is that a problem?' She sits herself down on the ground, one leg placed straight out from her body, the other bent, and reaches for her toes. She looks like she is preparing to go for a run. She says it is one of her favourite things to do, and he thinks maybe he should buy her a treadmill — she would like that.

'I'm not sure.' He wonders if the perfect woman would have the same-sized breasts. Clare is strangely removed from her body. Sometimes when he sees her crash her hip into the table or misjudge the distance between herself and the bed, he wonders whether she is aware of her body at all. It is only when she is doing something like this — stretching, or yoga, or handstands — that she seems to pay her body any attention. Even then she treats it as a machine, something to be serviced.

'Would you like me to do something about it?' She stands

in front of him, her left breast cupped in her hand, questioning.

'Perhaps.' He wonders what she could do. 'But it might be what makes you perfect.'

'I could lop it off, like an Amazon warrior. They were rumoured to cut off a breast so they could fire a bow and arrow more accurately.'

'Really?' It makes sense. Breasts would be in the way. But it seems a lot of effort.

'Well, probably not. They probably just bound them.'

'Bound them?'

'Like Chinese women's feet. Broken up and packed away.' She comes over to where he is leaning against the windowsill and mimics his stance. The sill thrusts her hips forward, an invitation. 'So which one?' she asks as he turns to her.

'Huh?'

'Which one would you cut off? The small one or the large one?'

'Neither. I like every bit of you equally.'

When he kisses her, he feels her breasts flatten against his chest.

~

The third time Clare left Andi, the moon was sliding from the sky. As she extracted herself from the bed, Andi breathed on through his dreams. This was what she loved each day, this moment of possibility before the rest of the world caught up. Naked, she could be anyone right now. A businesswoman perhaps, about to slip into pantyhose and a suit that would crackle with static assurance as she trotted confidently down the stairs. An athlete about to attack the day, prove what her body was capable of.

She walked across the dark hall to the kitchen, a room so incidental with nobody in it. She recalled her grandparents' kitchen, dominated by a long table that could seat ten, more if you squashed into the reclaimed church pew that pressed against the wall. When all of her aunts and uncles were home, the kitchen was raucous, a battle zone. Younger cousins would slip beneath the table when they finished their lunch, clamber out from beneath the forest of legs and escape to the openness of the backyard. She would often wish she could do the same, feeling trapped as her family talked on through the afternoon. Instead she found herself sitting still, smile fixed, utterly bereft.

As she stood in this stranger's kitchen, wondering which cupboard held the glasses, that same feeling came crashing down upon her, landing with a thump in her chest, nausea making her reach for the sink. She drank from the tap, letting the water run about her face and neck, the indifferent smell of the metal calming her twitching stomach.

Back in the bedroom she watched Andi, his arm flung above his head, his lashes shivering on his cheeks. He was beautiful. It was pride she felt at having slept with him, a feeling she would never admit to another. She tried to dress quietly though every movement seemed to call out for attention. She never liked waiting for men to wake up. She would rather leave and be a memory that could be returned to. If she stayed, she would become her own bad habits, her stale morning breath, her repeated stories. It was all so very ordinary. She took her boots to the front door, bent to put them on. Would he stir? Call out her name, beg her not to leave? And if he did, would she stay? She liked to think she was strong-willed, but knew that if he woke, she would not walk out that door. Embarrassed by her neediness, she would not let him see it.

Down the stairs, two at a time, and she was swishing through the courtyard leaves that masqueraded as snow in the faint morning light. The air was sharp, winter just around the corner. Once on the street she pushed out her stride and her legs thanked her for it. Perhaps later today she would go for a run, sweat out the excesses of last night.

Connecting the dots on the metro map, she headed back to the hostel and gathered her things. She had been in Berlin almost two weeks and had photographed everything she wanted to. It was time to move on.

Once she had showered and packed, the day had started for everyone else. Trotting down the U-Bahn stairs she tried to keep out of the way of closed-faced people heading to work. The man at the hostel said all trains to Dresden left from the Ostbahnhof, so she found herself repeating the morning's cross-city journey in reverse. She was glad to be on her way.

When Andi woke, she was not there. He threw back the sheets, scissoring his legs, as though he might find her snuggled like a cat in the warmth at the end of the bed. The water pipes were silent; he could hear no footsteps. He held his breath, warding off a false reading. She was gone.

Pulling on yesterday's clothes, he could smell the sex and sweat that clung to him. Still buttoning his shirt, he stood in the doorway of the living room. Was it only last night that he had been right here, wineglasses in hand, watching her roll a cigarette? He had wanted to climb inside her mind, to understand exactly what she was thinking. She had moved so quickly about the apartment; he was certain that if he took his eyes off her she would cease to exist. And so she had. He had found himself following her as she moved from couch to bookshelf to window, a street mime copying her for cheap laughs. She had kept edging ahead of him, throwing her voice over her shoulder like a cape, and he found he could not quite keep up with her, as though the language delay was translating to the physical.

He grabbed his jacket and slammed the door shut behind him, fumbled with the keys in his hurry to lock it. Where would she have gone? Did he have any hope of finding her? The courtyard was too cramped a space to break into a run; he skidded across it and threw himself against the entrance doors. On the street, people marched by on their way to work, and he fell into step with them. His heart was beating so fast it felt as though it was growing inside him: it threatened to break out of his chest and scatter the morning commuters with its bloody shards.

He tried to commandeer his thoughts. Where was Clare planning to go today? She had told him of her travel plans, and he had listened in the way people do when the information does not concern them. Had he not actually thought she would be going anywhere? Or had he not thought he would care? He picked up his pace, headed towards the city. She could not be too far away. What time had she gotten out of bed?

Dresden. He broke into a run. She had said she was going to Dresden, that she wanted to photograph the buildings that had been put back together like a puzzle. Which meant she would be taking a train from the Ostbahnhof. He could catch one, too, he could follow her to Dresden and … And what? What was he doing? He could not chase her down; he would never find her. But still he ran, his feet slapping against the ground, a stitch stabbing at his side. At the station he barely waited for the doors to slide apart. He burst onto the concourse, conscious of his heaving chest, his expanding heart. He stared blindly at the departures board, the letters swimming about in a code he could not recognise, before running across the hall, dodging the travellers coaxing their wheeled bags. Stopping at the first platform, he looked out across the tracks. And there she was, waiting for him.

'Don't leave.'

The morning after the night before and there he was again. As he came lurching up the ramp to the platform, he looked more bedraggled than she remembered. Her stomach was burning — his presence or sudden hunger? She never could differentiate between her mind's attraction and her body's needs.

'Come back with me.' He delivered his plea with the now familiar jerk of his head, indicating somewhere both nearby and far away. She waited for the question mark, but it did not appear.

'No.'

'Why not?'

'I can't stay, Andi. I've got things to do.'

'Like what?'

'My photographs. The exhibition. The book.' She was touched, and certainly tempted, but she wasn't going to stay — this wasn't part of the plan. She shrugged, apologetic, and tried to change the topic. 'Don't you think train stations just cry out for drama?' Annoyingly, her voice wavered, and she tried to bring the situation back under her control. 'Always scenes of parting. And desperation. Like Anna Karenina wanting to stand back up at the last moment.' The soaring ceilings, the architecture that acknowledged these places as gateways to worlds of more possibility. Flying had appropriated the romance of travel, and budget airlines had killed it.

'Not always,' he replied.

He looked despondent, standing so close yet so separate, and she felt responsible. She knew nothing about this man, she didn't want this connection. And yet she waited for him to reach out and take her hand, to make her stay. But he just pushed his hands deeper into his pockets, and she strengthened her resolve.

'Just stay for a while.' He sounded like a whiny child, and his eyes, which should have been pleading, were accusatory. 'Last night … it was fun.'

With that, her compassion dissolved. It was hardly a declaration. She turned away, wishing that the train would arrive. She wanted to kiss him goodbye and climb aboard. *Clickety clack, don't look back.* It was getting messy, this liaison. It was taking on too many locations.

'So let's leave it like that, Andi.' She refused to look at him, to play his games. Fuck, she was so hung-over. She could feel the station leaning in on her, an overbearing parent waiting for her to confess to some playground crime. Why didn't he touch her? It was disconcerting; it was as though he was not real.

They stood there in silence, each refusing to look, to hold, to walk away. Each wanting the other to force the decision.

'Come back with me, Clare.'

He moved to hug her, and she thrust out her hand, wanting to force him into an awkward goodbye clasp. But he reached higher than she expected, grabbing her upper arm and squeezing. She could feel each individual finger pressing down. Later that night she would look at the bruised imprint of his fingers on her skin and wonder if he needed to be quite so forceful.

'I want you, Clare. Stay.'

'But I want to be away.'

It was the idea she had clung to from the moment she left that crowded kitchen of her childhood. That kitchen drenched with so much sunshine and goodwill that it dripped down the walls and pooled on the floor, causing everyone to slip and slide and crash into each other. She could see them all still there, grabbing at each other for support, laughing as they fell over, helped each other up and fell over again until they were all in a heap. All of them like pick-up sticks not ever wanting the game to be over.

'Everywhere is away from somewhere else.' He squeezed her arm again, the pressure pulling her into the moment.

The sun was cutting through the glass beneath the awning; she felt as though it was chasing them up the platform at speed. Her hangover headache pounded at her skull, teasing her heart to beat faster.

'Please stay, Clare. I really *like* you.' His emphasis on the word made them both blush like teenagers. 'I want you.'

Who could argue with being wanted? In a blaze of clarity,

she saw how simple it was — he would care if she left, and there was no one in Dresden to care if she arrived.

'Okay.'

And in response came that smile running across his face like an incoming tide. When they kissed the taste of him shocked her with its familiarity, so much so that she wondered whether it was, somehow, exactly the same taste as her own.

'Let's go.' He took her hand, pulling her up from beneath all the other pick-up sticks, and not one of them moved.

As the leaves begin to unfurl on the city's trees, Clare keeps her eyes closed and pretends to be asleep. She breathes long, deep and even, listening to Andi go about his morning rituals. The sound of his frothy spit falling into the basin, coffee bubbling on the stovetop. She wonders whether he looks at her as he goes in and out of the room, to the bed, the bathroom, the kitchen. She doesn't dare open her eyes to check. Intent on the order of things, he is conservative in his morning movements, as though he may be taxed on too many trips between sink and breakfast table, fridge and bathroom.

Just before he leaves, he comes to the bed. She hears him pause by her side then feels his grip on the sheets, and they are pulled down to her ankles. The cool air licks across her back but, lying face down, she does not move. With one knee on the bed, he rests his palms on her shoulders before laying himself down upon her, mimicking the length of her body. His knees jut into the backs of hers. His hips are cushioned by her bottom. Despite being much taller than her, he seems, at these moments, exactly the same height.

Flattened beneath him, she feels more present than at any other time during the day. She can feel him along the length of her body, and the weight of him, the stillness of him, calms her. Like this, he cannot hurt her. She can hear his breathing. She wonders whether the earlier smells of coffee and toothpaste were real, or whether they were imagined precursors to this. He bites softly on her earlobe. The goosebumps sing up and down her arms.

'I'll see you tonight,' he whispers, then gets up, takes his bag from the floor and leaves, closing the door behind him.

She lies still on the bed. With his weight removed, she feels light. In this way, every morning she is her very own zeppelin.

When she does get out of bed, she switches on the television. The deep voices of the newsreaders, who never seem to get too excited about anything, encourage her to feel that today is going to be significant. Something is going to happen, they assert with a firm nod. She watches the abbreviated news stories scroll across the bottom of the screen, the English words waving at her like old friends, while the German words slowly become familiar. The multitude of capital letters no longer make her feel as though she is being shouted at. From the newspaper, she cuts out individual letters to make ransom-note poetry. Poetry about the kitchen sink and the grey shrinking view from the apartment window. About the wide land back home, and grass that is never greener on either side. When the ink becomes too smudged to make out the letters, she cuts out more. She can only use the headlines because the other print is too small.

In the long afternoons, she reads the poetry aloud. Demanding the attention of absent crowds, she performs it in bombastic ways that she would not dare to attempt if other people were present. In Budapest she spent a night in a tiny bar listening to poetry. She understood nothing of the language, allowed the unfamiliar sounds to rain down on her until she was slick with the musicality of it. It was not a spoken-word night as she knew it; there was no underlying desperation to remind the audience that poetry as an art form was entertaining, relevant, important. Instead, it was proud literary cabaret: the darkened room, people gathered round the tiny tables, perched on bentwood chairs, smoking, drinking and wallowing in the sea of words. She performs her poetry as though she is back in that room, as though no one can understand a word she is saying, but they do not care, wanting her sounds and listening with rapture.

In the evening, he goes through the sheets of paper, smoothing their curled corners. He reads closely, asks questions. At first, she thought he was making fun; her answers then were curtly monosyllabic. She cringed at the way he enunciated each word, the way he repeated each line with a different emphasis. But she continues to cut out the letters, to shuffle them about into constructions, to glue them in place and dry them by the radiator.

She dreams that there are no more words left in the world. That the authorities have come to her door, knocked, and politely informed her that she cannot use any more letters. Told her that there will be no more newspapers — the population is getting too upset at all the bad news so they will not be printing any more. They tell her that she must recycle her recycled poems, and she does, cutting them up and gluing them down until the letters become ghosts on the page, haunting her with reminders of what has been lost.

~

'Can we walk back along the Wall?' Clare called out to him, pointing at the strip of graffitied Wall that ran beside the river. Andi had paused outside the Ostbahnhof to phone the school and plead that he was too ill to work. He was almost disappointed that the receptionist took his excuse without question. *Actually, I met someone*, he wanted to tell her. *It all started in a bookstore. No, in a park.* But the receptionist just wished him well and hung up.

'It's not really on the way.' He hitched up Clare's bag — the straps were cutting into his shoulders.

'There's no rush is there?'

Of course there was. He wanted to be fucking her. To have her back in his apartment, where they would not have to consider anybody else.

'I just want to get you home. Far away from those mischievous trains that want to whisk you away.'

'I thought you might want to show me your city,' she said, waiting for him to catch up to her and taking his hand. 'I am a tourist after all.'

'There will be plenty of time for that.' He squeezed her hand and could barely believe it when she squeezed his back. He began walking towards his apartment, refusing to let her go. 'Anyway, that bit of the Wall is not real.'

'How do you mean?' She stopped. 'I thought it was the last bit of the Wall still standing.'

'Well, it is. But it's not what it was really like, not how I remember it. There were two walls, with the death strip in between. This bit of wall was on the East side; you could never graffiti it — it was kept completely blank. All those paintings are from after the Wall fell. It's not what it really looked like.' He tugged her arm, made her keep walking.

'How old were you when it came down?' she asked.

'Twelve.'

'What was it like, living like that?'

He shrugged. He never knew how to answer this question. Nothing he could say ever seemed to be the truth. It couldn't encapsulate how normal it was, how definite. How East Germany was a world built on ideas rather than money, that, beneath all of the bad, there was some good. People from outside could never see that.

'It was just how it was. When I was born, the Wall had been up for twenty years. Everyone thought it would be up for a hundred more. It was just the way things were. But it all changed faster than anybody expected.'

'It's odd,' she said. 'Most people feel as though their childhood happened in a world so far away that it doesn't exist anymore. And yours actually did.'

'I guess. In a way, it was like a childhood for everyone — the government was like a parent.' He walked faster, knowing that she was only just keeping up but aware that every minute they were out here, she might change her mind, return to the station. 'Not that parents always know best.'

'But they usually have their children's best interests at heart.'

'True,' he agreed. 'They wanted to produce a society that was as perfect as they knew how. But in the end they screwed it up — just like parents do to their children.'

'You can't blame parents for everything. We all have to grow up at some stage, don't we? Childhood will always hold the attraction of innocence, but it's not a way of living. I suppose the Wall coming down was like a massive teenage rebellion.' She pulled her hand from his and stopped walking as she swept her hair up, tied it with a rubber band from her wrist.

His own hands twitched, impatient. He wanted her, wanted to be home.

'Don't you wish you could just go back to being a child though?' he asked. 'Someone else making all the decisions for you?'

'You're like Peter Pan. The boy who never wanted to grow up.' She grabbed his hand; now it was her pulling him forward. 'I can't see you in green tights though.'

Laughing, she lifted his hand to her lips and bestowed a kiss, which he returned. He remembered the story well enough; it was one of his father's favourites.

Finally, they reached his building, and he led Clare once more through the courtyard and up the stairs. As he unlocked the door, she pushed him aside. 'Race you to the bed!'

Hours later, standing naked in the lounge room, Clare pointed at the television tower. 'It's kind of weird, isn't it, to know just about everyone in the city has the tower in view.'

'It's not what I'm looking at.' He came up behind her, ran his finger down her back.

'It's kind of like a lonely pervert. Looking into everyone's living rooms.' She stepped away from him, leaned a hip against the window frame and began rolling a cigarette. It was as if she didn't even notice she was naked, yet that was all he could see.

'Have you been up there?' she asked.

'Not since I was little.' He remembered waiting in the queue, and then the elevator operator standing between him and his father, the material of her dress tickling his face. He had squatted to the floor as the elevator climbed, and his ears felt like they were going to burst.

'Let's go now,' she said.

He didn't want to leave the apartment. That he had to work tomorrow burrowed at his consciousness. If they went out there, it would take time. Time to go up the tower, to come down again, and to come home. And then once the time was all used up it would be tomorrow, and he would have to leave Clare and go to work. But her enthusiasm was infectious, and soon he found himself at Alexanderplatz, queuing for the lift, tickets in hand.

'It is only going to disappoint you, Clare.' Standing beside her, he twisted a lock of her hair around his finger, marvelling at how each strand was a different shade of red or brown. 'It will be full of tourists and screaming children.'

He was wrong. When they arrived at the top, it was busy but hardly overwhelming. They circled the deck slowly, and he pointed out landmarks. From here, it looked like any city. When he had last visited, the Wall dominated the view, a gash across the city stitched together with guard towers and raked sand. At some places, the gap between the Wall was over a hundred metres wide; at others, it looked as though you could leap across.

'It could be the end of the world, couldn't it?' she said.

The setting sun cast elongated shadows across the city, the twilight emphasised by the observation deck's tinted glass. At the bar he ordered drinks. A portable radio crackled through top-forty tunes, and he was bewildered that, despite being inside Germany's biggest aerial, the reception was so bad. Clare must have felt sorry for the barman, who kept trying to tune the radio, and she distracted him by ordering elaborate cocktails in her tourist German.

By midnight he was drunk on Japanese Slippers, and even he could tell his conversation was nearing incoherence. They fell into the lift, and as they plummeted to the ground, he wished there was a gentler way. The train home rattled his insides, and he was relieved to be back on solid ground as they walked the few blocks to the apartment.

Up five flights of stairs, Clare behind him, out of breath as he searched for his keys. Pocket after pocket. They kept eluding him, and he couldn't remember which pockets he had checked and then he had to start his search again. Clare leaned against the wall, raised her eyebrows, and once more he felt the panic that if he didn't find them soon she would be down the stairs and on a train. There. He pulled his keys out at last and let them inside.

In the kitchen he filled two glasses of water and swallowed them both down before refilling them and taking them to the bedroom. He could hear the shower running. Kicking off his shoes, he lifted his shirt over his head, tossing it on the floor on the way to the bathroom. He drew back the shower curtain. She was so blank. Immediately, he went hard. Colour flushed her body where the hot water struck.

He had never fucked in the shower before. Pulling her to him, he did not know if he would be able to hold her up. She wrapped her legs around him, he pressed her against the wall. Her skin was hot beneath his hands, against his chest. He pushed. She pushed. He pushed harder. Every move of hers was a challenge to him.

He could feel her resistance and he wanted to reach her there, where she stopped being soft. He grunted and pushed. The water was deceiving; it slid between them, taunting. Just as he felt like he was getting closer to her, he would find himself further away. And then it was over. Clare, her back against the tiles, slid down until her feet hit the ground. He let go of her, his knees shaky. He could not feel the water on his face, only the sweat forming beneath it. He turned the taps off, leaned back on the wall beside her, and they stood there, dripping, not touching.

Catching his breath, he reached for her hand and pulled her to him. 'I wish this moment never stopped,' he said. She was warm on his front, the tiles were cool on his back. 'If I could have one wish, that is what it would be.'

She kissed his neck, and he felt her hot breath creep over his shoulder. 'I would wish to never want to be anywhere else.'

The words muffled in his ear, confused, and he tightened his grip as though to squeeze their meaning out of her. '*To never want to be anywhere else*,' he said. 'So you want to always be here?'

'No.' She pulled away from him, kissed him and stepped out of the shower. She seemed so composed, yet he could only just keep standing. Surely she was as drunk as him? 'Well, in a way. But what I want is to live in the moment. Don't you think that would be amazing? To never be wondering what will happen next and whether it will be better than this?' She passed a towel to him, took one for herself. 'I wish I always wanted to be wherever I am.' She started vigorously drying her legs, her arms.

He watched, transfixed, her words piled in his mind. He wanted to fuck her again, to have her never stop talking, to keep on drying herself as long as he stood there. The room shook in time with the movement of her towel.

'But maybe we are always looking forward to something else,' he said. He followed her out of the shower, concentrated on keeping his balance. 'I don't think there is anything wrong with that. Not if there are things to look forward to.'

'It is impossible to be present in the present.' Her words floated out from beneath the towel and eventually her face followed. She threw the towel at him, and he caught it.

'I suppose,' he replied, shaking his feathery head.

'Which is exactly why it is the one thing that I always want.' She grabbed his hand, pulled him into the bedroom. 'Apart from sleep.'

When she woke she lay still, hoping the throbbing in her head would be alleviated by her inaction. It was. She opened her mouth, stirred her bloated tongue. Reluctantly, she opened her eyes. The bedroom window was translucent: it presented a muted swatch of sky, giving only a hint of the weather and the time. She became aware of the weight of the blankets, the sheet twisted around her shoulders, and she pulled back the covers, inviting the cold air of the apartment to clutch at her bare skin. Relief. She did not remember going to bed last night. Sitting up, she swung her feet to the floor. Her hair was matted — she must have slept with it wet. Remembered the shake of the shoulder, the kiss on the cheek, and a promise to be home no later than four.

God, they must have drunk a lot. She recalled scenes like a game of memory, tried to match them with sense. The views from the television tower observation deck, Berlin laid out like a distant galaxy. That barman who kept trying to woo her with lines from songs, his voice sailing above the static of the radio. Andi surveying the barman's attempts, smiling beatifically. *Ugh*. No wonder she felt rotten: cocktails.

Head pounding, she walked to the bathroom. The apartment had retired beneath a grey shroud. In the shower, more vague memories of last night returned. She soaped her body all over. She felt tender — they must have been so drunk, gone at it hard. Was the steam from the shower beneficial? Or was it making her feel dizzy? She turned off the water and, as she stepped onto the bathmat, she remembered: they had sex in the shower last night. She grinned. No wonder she was sore.

Feet wet, towel tight around her, she walked back to the bedroom. Aware of every movement of her body, she tried to dodge its demands. She wanted orange juice. An apple. She needed to feel cleansed on the inside. She would go for a walk, get some air. Maybe buy something for dinner. The regular little housewife.

She dressed and liberated her jacket from last night's clothes. Without Andi's presence, the apartment was numbingly impersonal and, considering her current state, she was glad. Being unable to tell what kind of person lived there meant she did not have to make judgements on her own presence. The books and records gave a clue, but most of the surfaces were bare, the recipients here and there of everyday possessions. Used wineglasses. A cigarette lighter. A newspaper. There were no photos, not even free cafe postcards stuck to the fridge. In the bedroom, her own belongings crept out across the floor, attempted to colonise the space.

She swung her camera bag to her shoulder, checked that her wallet was inside. Her phone battery was flat, and she debated whether to leave it charging, but the only people who had her number were on the other side of the world, sleeping. She imagined all the people she knew sharing one enormous bed. Sighing, shifting their weight, searching for the cool creases of untouched sheets, surrounded by the rustling of polite dreams. It was a relief to toss her phone back on the bed. Friends texted occasionally to ask her where she had been, where she was going, but somehow her answers never seemed to match the colour-saturated anecdotes they wanted to hear, and the messages dried up.

In the kitchen, she checked the fridge and hunted out a string bag from the drawer. Cutlery always in the top drawer, kitchen utensils in the next. Tea towels in the third and bags and cling wrap in the fourth. An organisational system as universal as the Dewey decimal.

She was at the front door and reaching for the handle when she realised she did not have a key. Damn. She couldn't go out; she couldn't get back in. A rushing in her ears. The silence was — what was it? Not quite encompassing. It was absent. It was almost suffocating, as though the noise had left, taking the air with it. She wondered why she had not noticed before. There — the hum of the fridge. Her heart slowed, she was holding her breath. The creak of the building shifting. Her own shifting weight. Her head hurt. Perhaps she should go back to bed. It was the sort of day when, if she wasn't forcing herself into the studio, she would usually call a friend, drink a pot of tea and while away the afternoon until the ache subsided.

Fuck, this was really annoying. She took off her jacket: she was sweating. She tried to open a window but could not. In the bedroom she kicked off her shoes and flopped onto the bed. The sheets had already taken on the familiar, sour smell of intimacy. She wanted to be angry with Andi for not thinking of her need for a key. But she expected he felt as hung-over as she did, and he'd had to go to work. Poor thing.

She lay on the bed for a while then moved to the couch. The apartment did not seem so very spacious and light anymore. The ceiling dropped, the walls shuffled in. She closed her eyes and imagined she was far away.

She remembered being in the car when she was young. Waiting with her sister for their mother to come out of the supermarket. Clare's sister had unbuckled her seatbelt, climbed into the front passenger seat and shut the vents. They weren't supposed to touch them. Everything on the dashboard was off limits. In fact, being in either of the front seats was off limits without Mum or Dad about. Her sister locked the passenger door then reached across the driver's seat and did the same on that side. With two hands she pulled on the window handle, winding it up.

'If we make it airtight, it will be like space,' she had said. Clare had pictured the dark night sky, constellations she could never identify. 'Zero gravity. If we have no gaps we will be able to float, like in space.' Her sister nodded her head gravely.

'Pass me the tissues.' Her sister pointed at the tissue box on the parcel rack. Clare did not move. She recalled so desperately not wanting to be involved. Her sister rolled her eyes and climbed over into the back seat where she grabbed the box of tissues. Back in the front seat, she began stuffing the tissues into the air vents.

'You'll break them,' Clare had said, concerned. She hated it when things broke. It was not the being in trouble that she minded. It was seeing the broken thing in front of her, useless.

Her sister ignored her and, taking a gulp of air, lifted her arms from either side of her body. Clare almost expected to see her float up to the roof, to bounce lightly off the windows. She didn't.

'It doesn't work.' Clare felt it was her duty to pronounce this, to allow the experiment to be over before their mother came back.

But her sister just looked at her with annoyance. 'It will.' She began stuffing the tissues around the windows.

'Don't waste them,' said Clare. That was what Mum always said when they used too many tissues. Her sister continued to ignore her, determinedly stopping the gaps.

She could not remember how it actually ended. They didn't float, she reasoned. Mum probably came back and bawled them out for using all the tissues, laid down new rules for being left alone in the car. Always the reassessing of rules.

She wished there were more rules now. A rule that Andi had to be back at a definite time. A rule that if he went out he had to leave a key. Relationships established their rules quickly: the permissible and the unthinkable were soon separated, the latter quarantined until further notice. And when the rules were broken, the relationship was weakened. Snap, snap, snap, until it fell over. So maybe a relationship without rules was not so bad. No rules to break, no way to end. The logic was astounding. She opened her eyes, tried to shake the overly earnest thoughts from her head. She found that her mind always raced when she was hung-over, while her limbs trailed behind. It was no use: she needed to get outside.

Maybe there was a spare key somewhere. She stood up from the couch and began hunting. There weren't many places to look. She rummaged in the bowl by the bedside lamp. Nothing in the drawer of the bedside table — some papers, two buttons, three condoms, a paperclip, some tweezers. The bathroom held only bathroom things. The kitchen, too, lived up to its name. She walked along one of the floorboards in the hall as if it was a balance beam in gymnastics class. In the bedroom she took four small steps from the door to the end of the bed, where she flopped down again, defeated. The foot of the bed. Why was it hands but not foots? Feet but not hend? What the fuck was she going to do all day?

'Don't just lie there.' As she said it, she could almost hear her mother's voice. She got off the bed, put her shoes back on, and picked up her jacket and bag. She had not really thought about her mother in years. Not in this way, the memories colliding into one another like dodgem cars. And she didn't want to think about her mother now; she just wanted to be here, no future, no past. Fuck it, she would just go out. If she stayed out long enough, Andi would be home from work when she got back.

The front door was locked. She twisted the latch and pulled, but the door did not open. Perhaps there was a trick to it. She pulled again, but the door did not open. She was confused: she had no trouble leaving yesterday morning. And then she saw, lower down on the door, the second lock. A deadbolt. Had he locked her in?

She felt slighted, wanted to kick something. She gave the door a half-hearted nudge with the toe of her shoe. It was one thing not to be able to get in. But not get out? How could he have forgotten she was here? How could he have locked her in? She kicked the door again, harder, and a scuff mark appeared like a rebuke.

It was not even one o'clock. At least three hours until Andi came home. She let out a groan of irritation and resigned herself to waiting. He was going to be so embarrassed when he got home. In the kitchen she mixed up a bowl of muesli, made a coffee in the stovetop percolator, oily and dark with use. If it did this to stainless steel, what did it do to her insides? She took her coffee to the living room and tried to concentrate on choosing a record, but all she could think about was Andi. His smile, the way he mooched rather than walked. He haunted her like a pop song: she couldn't get him out of her mind. How did he forget her long enough to lock the door? It was almost insulting. Annoyed at his oversight, she still smiled when she thought about how mortified he would be when he returned. Sipping her coffee, she turned the pages of the Klimt book. It was just a door, she reminded herself. A simple door, in a regular apartment. It was not Fort Knox. Where was Fort Knox? If Andi had a computer, she would Google it. It sounded American. It must be something to do with the Civil War. A short, strong American name. Square. Democratic. It was a quarter past one. Hours of confinement to go.

Andi watches ribbons of rain flap against the window frame. The bulb of the television tower is lost in fog; the lights announcing its tall presence flash faintly, like hovering UFOs.

'I'm bored, Clare.' He looks over to her. She is lying on her back, reading a book he gave her, her feet pressed up against the radiator.

'Clare?' He can hear the whine in his voice. He is jealous of her ability to get lost in a book. Whenever he buys her one, he feels like he is giving her permission to ignore him. 'Clare, what can we do?'

She doesn't answer him, so he walks over to the stereo, flips idly through the records. The tips of his fingers seem extra sensitive, the record sleeves tickle. He bounces on the balls of his feet. It's the being cooped up, the closed walls. His father is the same, cannot abide small spaces. They used to head to the country on weekends. Go hiking through woods, across fields. It should have been idyllic, a father-and-son outing in bucolic isolation. But Andi remembers it being so suffocatingly purposeful. They would get off the train at whatever station his father had chosen and begin walking. When they ran out of roads, they would tramp through fields, animals shuffling away from the path. Andi would try to keep up with his father's long strides by settling into a quick trot. But as the day wore on, he would drop further and further behind as his father disappeared into the distance.

When eventually he caught up, his father would be laying out their packed lunch beneath some shade.

'You made it!' he would say, ruffling Andi's hair. He always seemed so pleased to see him, making Andi wonder why his father had worked so hard to leave him behind. After lunch they would walk back to the train station together, at an easier pace. His father would point things out. The names of trees, the different types of clouds. He would ask about school, his favourite subjects. He would tease Andi about when he was going to find himself a girlfriend. On the train home Andi would sleep uneasily, and when the rolling carriage jerked him awake he would see his father staring out the window. As dusk crept by and turned everything navy, it seemed his father was shrinking. He would slump lower and lower in his seat, his bony knees jutting further into the aisle, his eyes never closing.

'Here we are then,' his father would say, as the train pulled into their station.

They would walk back to the apartment in silence: Andi, his father and the week ahead.

'Let's make something.' Clare has tossed her book aside, rolled onto her stomach. Her feet dangle in the air, misshapen in a pair of his socks.

'Like a cake?'

'No. You bake a cake. I mean … I don't know. Like a house or a model. A structure!'

'But what with?'

'Well,' she says, standing up, ready to take charge. 'What about newspaper?'

Following her instruction, he begins rolling the weekend newspapers into thin tubes.

'I used to do this as a child.' She tells him about the house she grew up in. The fruit trees in the backyard, the swings hanging between tall gum trees. The track she and her sister wore into the ground from riding their bicycles around the yard in circles. How they would build jumps for their bikes and rollerskates from brick and scraps of plywood. Build them higher and steeper until one of them eventually hurt herself enough for their mother to come outside and tell them to stop.

He tells her about how he once wished for siblings. His memories are all of school and the Young Pioneers. Of organised sports and camping. He spent so much time with his friends and classmates he was never lonely, but he mainly remembers activities that were supervised and always for the good of something other than himself.

'Even then it never felt real,' he says. 'It was always mediated, as though even childhood had to be commandeered to the socialist cause.'

The afternoon trundles on. They compare more childhood memories, sing jingles from advertisements and ABBA songs. The rain falls, and their newspaper tower rises. He doesn't recognise his fingers, busy and smudged with newsprint. He cannot remember the last time he spent an afternoon making something.

'It's more Pisa than Eiffel, isn't it?' he observes, as they flop onto the couch later to admire their handiwork. The tower is made of tightly rolled tubes, taped together to make a pyramid base. As it got taller and thinner, it had started to bend; despite the reinforcements, it seems to be performing a curtsey to them. The peak is decorated with a splay of newspaper, its fronds falling open like fireworks. Impressive for an afternoon's work.

He runs his hand up and down her thigh — it gives beneath his touch. Forgiving. He feels like he could endlessly knead it and it would keep bouncing back like yeasty dough. He wishes she was not wearing jeans; he wants to feel her skin. The metal button at her waistband carries the heat of her body, and he slips it from its buttonhole. She lifts her hips, tugs her jeans to her feet, and his hand is on her skin. She lifts one socked foot and then the next from her discarded jeans while he continues stroking. Inky fingerprints mushroom across her thigh. She keeps her legs pressed together, a neat valley forming in her lap; the reddened lines that cross her legs like highways on a road map are hidden from view. They do not need to be mentioned. She lays her head on Andi's shoulder; he knows she has closed her eyes, is leaving him for somewhere else. He picks up one of her hands and places it on his own leg. Directs it up and down. When he stops, so does she.

'Don't you like touching my leg, baby?'

He feels her tense beside him. She does not like being told what to do. But he wants to feel her hands on him, he wants to be covered with her newsprint fingerprints.

'Of course I do,' she replies. Her hand recommences its brushing back and forth.

~

As he taught his way through the day, Andi resorted to a mantra: *she is home, she is waiting for me*. He repeated the phrase to himself under his breath, over and over, breaking only to give instruction to his classes. He wished he did not know his students' names, that they would appear only as an indistinct sea of pimples and petulance. He felt exposed, all of his inadequacies on display. She did not need him. She would not be there when he returned home. When he left the apartment that morning, he had wanted to run back up the stairs, make her promise not to go anywhere, to be there when he returned from work. But she would have thought him desperate. Was he? He herded students through grammar exercises, corrected pronunciation. His answers were concise. *She is home, she is waiting for me.* The students nodded in agreement: his explanations of the nominative case made sense to them. They laughed at his jokes and didn't groan at the amount of homework he gave. When the final bell rang, he bolted. *She is home, she is waiting for me.*

Peter called out to him as he collected his things from his locker in the staffroom.

'Are you coming for a drink, Andi?'

He tried to avoid Peter's expectant gaze, did not want to explain about Clare, not yet. 'I've got to get home.'

'Come for a drink with us. We have something to celebrate.'

Jana appeared by his side, nodding encouragement.

To celebrate? He did not want to know, did not want to share in anyone else's joy.

'Sorry, I really have to go. We will celebrate soon, okay?' He clapped Peter on the shoulder and hustled his excuses ahead of him out the door.

When he realised he had forgotten his scarf, he did not go back. What if she wasn't there when he got home? He stopped walking and leaned over the gutter: he felt ill, his body punishing him for last night's cocktails. What if she had already left again for the station and he had not been there to bring her back? A woman passed by, her dog sniffing around his ankles. A cyclist threw him a dirty look, not sure if he was about to step out into the street.

He started walking again, hurried down the steps to the station platform. The air was dry and heavy. People shuffled about like pigeons, heads down, retreating from the day, a sea of brown and black and denim. Would she at least have left a note, her email address? He willed the train to go faster, cursed the slow opening and closing of the doors at each stop. A man sat down beside him and bit into a kebab. It squelched like a kitchen sponge, the smell of garlic sauce filling the carriage.

It was a relief to finally head out into the open, to cross the road to his street. There was no way she would still be there; she could not possibly feel this way about him. She did not seem to need him in the way he needed her, in a raw, irrational way. She liked him. She wanted to fuck him, of that he had no doubt; her body met his with possessive audacity. But was that enough?

He opened the door. She was still there. The relief bucketed down on him like a practical joke. He had been running this scene through his head all day, readying himself for the disappointment of her absence, and yet here she was, she was waiting for him.

'You locked the door, Andi! I've been stuck in here all day.' Hands on hips, she stood her ground like a child.

He had locked her in? He looked from her to the door to the keys in his hand. Ran through his morning routine — and realised.

'Oh, Clare! I'm so sorry! I did not think. Why did you not call me?' He rushed towards her, grabbed her hands, a literal begging for forgiveness. He had locked the second lock as he did every morning when he left. What was he thinking?

'But I don't have your number. I was stuck here. It was like being a prisoner.'

'I am so sorry, Clare, I really am. I did not even think about it. It was routine.' He was horrified. He could not believe he had been so careless.

'At first I thought I wouldn't be able to get back in. Then I realised that I couldn't even leave.' She shook off his grasp, attempted to assert her annoyance.

'And I spent all day just trying to convince myself that you were real and would still exist when I got home.' He reached for her again, squeezed her arms as if they were a pair of soft toys, almost expected a responsive squeak. 'I *am* sorry, Clare. I really am.'

He wrapped her in his arms, rocked her from side to side. He wanted to have her right now, to feel her bare skin against his, but when he moved to kiss her she pushed him away.

'Stop!' She was laughing as she batted away his needy hands. 'Let's go out — I need to get out of here.'

'Of course you do.' He wished she did not. 'Shall we go and get something to eat?'

Her assent was a lingering kiss, which he savoured while she went to gather her things together. He ducked into the bathroom, his heart bopping in his chest. *She is here, she is here, she is here*. He splashed his face with water, sluicing away his too obvious relief and trying to dampen his desire.

'Ready?' She appeared in the doorway as he dried his face on a towel.

He rubbed doggedly, taming the corners of his smile, which wanted to jerk up in triumph at every opportunity. *She is home, she is waiting for me*.

Andi suggested a Turkish restaurant around the corner, but she did not want to sit down just yet; she needed to walk off the day's confinement. As they crossed the railway lines she packed away her bad humour and tried to concentrate on what he was saying. She was surprised when the River Spree came into view, and they walked its banks towards a mammoth sculpture of three men who looked like they were about to embrace. As with Melbourne, where the Yarra runs like a mud-brown afterthought, she never thought of Berlin as a river city.

With relief, she felt time begin to slip. They crossed a turreted bridge that an artist had engaged in an endless neon game of rock, paper, scissors, and left the main road to head into parkland. She always found herself so very aware of time — of its passing, of its residue, of its promise. It was one of the things that initially attracted her to photography, the way it managed to hold time still. There was a peacefulness about the final image that belied any urgency to capture the moment. When pressing the shutter button, she felt as though she was protecting her subjects from their future, allowing them to stay at their best. Trying to explain this to Andi, she was aware of how unintentionally worthy it sounded and she let her voice trail off.

'But what is wrong with the future, Clare?' He did not look at her as he asked, gave her the space to answer. 'Are you afraid of what might happen?'

'Not afraid,' she replied too quickly. He would think she was lying. She had never needed to be afraid, never been in any kind of danger. 'But just so very aware of it.'

She tried to speak as Andi did, selecting each word carefully to isolate its meaning. 'The future crowds out the present. If I knew the future would be no different from now, I would just enjoy it. But I never know, so I can't ever stop wondering.'

'It's enjoyable enough if you ask me.' He pulled her into a kiss then stopped. 'Why do you close your eyes?'

She opened her eyes to find him scrutinising her face. 'I don't know.' She had never thought about it before. If she had, she would have assumed that the person kissing her was closing their eyes also. 'Because your face is too close to focus on?'

'But don't you want to see?'

'I already know what you look like.' She kissed him again, her eyes closed. She opened them. He was staring at her, and she broke away from him, laughing. 'It's distracting! I need to close them so I can concentrate.'

Abruptly, he let go of her hand and began walking up the path. Was he angry? She was not going to run after him. She stood still, unsure of whether she had just made a decision or whether he had.

'Come on. I want to show you something.'

Walking backwards, he beckoned to her. She hesitated, then hurried to catch up. They walked past the memorial, caught only glimpses of the heroics of the Soviet soldier, saved child in arm, swastika crushed beneath boot.

'Look,' he said. A Ferris wheel peeked from behind the bare trees, autumn's fall bringing it into view. 'There's a whole theme park here. It's been closed for years.'

They came to a tall picket fence, and he gave her a leg up. She scrambled over the top and let herself down the other side, her feet sliding without purchase on the slippery wood.

'Are you sure this is a good idea?' she said, as he landed heavily beside her.

'Shhh.' He put his finger to her lips. 'It's patrolled by security guards.'

The forest was completely overgrown. The last of the daylight struggled to drip through the canopy; bracken snapped beneath their feet. But even in the murky light of dusk, she found the park's incongruity becoming. A Viking ship tipped in a deep curtsey at the foot of the Ferris wheel; a herd of swan-shaped pleasure boats crowded the chestnut trees like the gathering of a lonely hearts' club. Further on she stifled laughter at the sight of toppled dinosaurs and little cars that must have once travelled on tracks, their passage now halted by the impenetrable undergrowth. The cars were shaped like moustached men, their windscreens decorated with painted spectacles and their roofs sporting brightly coloured hats. Above, purple egg-shaped capsules hung from a track that wound through the trees, ivy anchoring each one to the ground and, just beyond an enormous big top, a rainbow cat's gaping mouth welcomed the tail-end of a rollercoaster. He led her into the big top where the red and yellow canvas reined in the last rays of sun, bathing the circus ring in an apocalyptic orange dusk.

When it was so dark she could hardly see Andi's silhouette, let alone his expression as she mimed amazement at each neglected ride, she let him lead the way through the jungle-like scrub back to the fence. It was only when they were safely on the other side that she looked at him and burst into laughter.

'It's amazing, Andi! I can't believe all of that is right here. I have to come back in the daytime with my camera.' Her words ran on, tumbling out of her mouth in her excitement. 'It's like a dedication to all the fun that people are not having. Those little cars were so adorable! And the swans, they're so forlorn.' She paused, waited for him to tie his shoelace. 'But there's something kind of hopeful about it all, don't you think?'

'Perhaps.' He took her hand, and they began to make their way towards the city. 'But not for the owner. I think he was done for drug-running in Peru.'

And for some reason neither of them could stop laughing at the misfortune of the funfair owner, even when it started to rain and they had to sprint through the park and across the bridge. Splashing through the streets, Andi pointed out favourite places and endeavoured to make his neighbourhood her own, and briefly she dared to think that perhaps this was what life had in store for her. Under the influence of such unfettered happiness, she wondered why she had not believed in fate all along. Was it too sentimental to start now? As the rain pattered in fat drops, they slunk into a bar and, legs pressed up against each other's, fingers entwined, they participated in their own private call and response deep into the night.

She wishes she had fresh flowers, but the ones Andi bought last week had browned and drooped within days and were consigned to the bin shortly after. It is winter in Berlin: no flowers are growing anywhere nearby. She guesses the ones he bought were imported from Africa, cut, refrigerated and flown to Germany. They were probably in shock, the blooms no longer sure what season it was, whether they were supposed to be open or closed. It was little wonder they only lasted a couple of days. She strips the bed and makes it with clean sheets, tossing the dirty ones into the laundry hamper in the corner. In the living room she clears mugs and glasses from the coffee table, slips records back into their covers. She takes the broom from beside the fridge and sweeps the floors. They need to be mopped, but she does not have time today.

In the kitchen she takes milk, eggs and butter from the fridge; flour and sugar from the canisters on the shelf. She wants to make a cake for Andi's birthday but must do it by guesswork and memory — she didn't want to ask him to translate a recipe and ruin the surprise. As she measures and stirs, she is assaulted by memories of her mother doing the same. Each birthday, Clare was allowed to choose a cake from the *Women's Weekly* children's cake book. She and her sister would crowd over the book, turning each page slowly and considering the merits of each cake. There were trains and aeroplanes, dolls in full skirts, pirate ships. The swimming-pool cake, with its chocolate log walls and blue jelly surface was a favourite, as was the racetrack in the shape of a number eight, decorated with Matchbox cars. One year, Clare helped her mother make a cake for her father. It was shaped like a guitar: the strings were made of strips of liquorice, and the tuning pegs were chocolate bullets. He was so impressed, he had not wanted to eat it; he even got her mother to cut it up. 'Would you look at that?' he kept saying, shaking his head. It was his last birthday. He died three months later, a car accident on the way to work, and when his next birthday came around, none of them knew what to do, or whether to do anything at all.

For Andi, she will keep it simple. His kitchen doesn't have an electric beater, and by the time she has creamed the eggs, butter and sugar her hand is aching. She sifts in the cocoa and flour, adds the milk and keeps stirring, tasting as she goes. She lines a pan with baking paper and pours the mixture into two shallow trays, which she places in the oven. Once it has baked and cooled she will slice the cakes and shape them into a letter 'A'. She knows that he will be pleased.

When the timer goes off, she takes the cakes from the oven and leaves them to cool. She was surprised to find icing sugar when she hunted through the kitchen cupboards last week, and she mixes it with water, crushing the lumps against the side of the bowl. She slices the cake and arranges it on a chopping board. The two cakes did not rise the same amount, so she has to cut one down. It's fiddly work, and she is running out of time — it all took a lot longer than she expected. When she starts applying the icing, she finds the cake crumbs get caught up in it. The cake looks nothing like the professional surfaces of her mother's. She scoops on more icing, and it drips down the side of the cake, pooling on the board, but finally it is finished. Exultant, she places the cake on the dining table. She has achieved something at last; her day has been worthwhile.

~

Andi's weight lifted from the bed, dropping her deeper into the mattress. Shivering, she tried to move her body beneath the covers, but her arms were too heavy, they could not grasp the blankets, and she gave up, curling her body to warm herself. Her limbs were aching. She was so incredibly tired; she felt as though she had danced all night. Her head was soft, and still she could not open her eyes. She slept. When she woke she could hear Andi's footsteps about the apartment, and she pictured him following close behind. Step, step, step. He opened the bedroom door.

'Andi?' Her voice did not sound like her own. 'Did you leave the key?' She felt his lips on her forehead; she supposed it must be a kiss and she forced her eyes apart, tried to find his face in the dull light.

'Here it is.' His face was closer than expected, and she pulled away as he flashed a silver key at her, putting it on the bedside table. 'I will see you tonight.'

Her mousetrap eyes snapped shut, and she tumbled back into sleep.

When she woke again, her mouth felt chocked full of cotton-wool clouds. She must be coming down with something; she probably caught it in the rain last night. Coughing a papery cough she retrieved her knickers from the floor and pulled on one of Andi's t-shirts. If she were a Hollywood star she would look fresh-faced and fabulous. The t-shirt would hang from her shoulders like haute couture. Instead, it looked large and misshapen. Her breasts lounged ungracefully without a bra.

It was cold in the apartment, and she hunted out a pair of Andi's socks, not wanting the uniform of her own clothes. The floorboards became a skating rink under her feet, and she glided easily across the hallway to the kitchen. As children, she and her sister had wanted to ice-skate, yet Australia was not a land for ice and snow. A rink was set up in a marquee by her town's lake one winter, but it proved a grey, crowded disappointment. The ice was lost beneath a watery sheen, making the whole thing appear an oversized puzzle, and skaters moved about the rink stiff with awkwardness, trying not to see themselves in their neighbours' discomfort. She and her sister had more fun at home slipping about on the polished wooden floor of their playroom in socks, yelling out 'red' or 'green' and trying to catch each other out as they stopped and started.

Now the heft of her body tried to pull her to the floor, but she resisted. At the living-room window, she pressed her face against the cool glass. Below, the courtyard was unkempt, the concrete cracked and uneven. The veneer of the building opposite was crumbling. Andi had told her that the whole building was deserted — a property developer owned it and was planning on renovating it. The practical side of the apartments faced her, pipes like varicose veins and mean, frosted bathroom windows.

The television tower rose above the city in a timeless parody of itself, unconcerned by gravity. It was one of those literal, concrete reminders of the past that she had been photographing, trying to capture within her lens the proud socialist hope for a future already lost. It reminded her of last night's fun park — she would try to get some decent photographs there this afternoon. Reluctantly, she peeled her face from the windowpane. She felt rotten; she should shower. In the bathroom she was careful, as was appropriate in a stranger's abode. She was learning the rules. She didn't want to upend a bottle or let a jar go clattering loudly into the sink. She didn't want to leave pubic hairs on the soap or a wet puddle by the shower. The water plunged from the shower rose, fat and dull, and the steam seemed to fill her as it expanded, pushing her unwilling mind against its peripheries.

Her head spun when she got out, and she let herself sink to the floor. Her eyes drooped of their own accord, and she sat on the bathmat in a cocoon of darkness, waiting. After a few minutes she pulled herself upright and, towel wrapped around, stumbled back to the bedroom. The sheets were cool as she fell into them, and for a moment she thought that might be enough to keep her awake, but then she pulled the blankets over her, drew her knees to her chest and let go.

'Clare?'

She rolled over to see Andi in the bedroom doorway.

'Why are you still in bed?'

Irritation dragged her away from sleep. His question made her feel like a posing teenager. 'I was tired.' She pushed the sheets away, the towel still clung damply to her. 'What time is it? Did you come home early?'

'No, it's almost six. Are you okay?' He sat on the edge of the bed. She watched him reach out to her and saw him hesitate. When he did touch her his hand was cool, like a doctor's.

'I've just been so tired. I think I might be getting sick. I haven't slept that long in ages.'

He tossed the towel to the floor and lay down. She experienced a disorientating moment of déjà vu. Had he lain down clothed beside her before? From here she could see only one of his eyes; it blinked rapidly as though wondering where its partner was.

'It's nice to come home and find you in my bed, Clare. It's like a gift.'

Watching his watching eye, she moved her face closer to his, kissed him on the lips. Lifting the blankets up, she let him into the bed and shifted her body around his. The cool of the outdoors drifted from the creases of his clothes, and she felt him shudder as she slipped her hand beneath his shirt.

He appraised Clare's body with his hands: they swept up and down her length. Like a store mannequin, her body dipped and curved into stillness. Her hot hands crept beneath his shirt, and it was the confirmation that he needed. She wanted him just as much as he wanted her. They tumbled about the bed, and her body seemed to slip through his fingers while her hands grasped at his clothes, simultaneously pulling them off and holding them tight as though she might drift away.

Later they sat at the dining table, and he watched her eat, his own food lying untouched on the plate. He was holding her camera, and as he scrolled through her photos the buildings formed a flip book of Soviet history.

'So did you go out at all today?' He held his breath, waited for her answer, knew what she would say.

She wrinkled her forehead at him, turned her attention back to her food. 'No, I told you. I was exhausted. I slept all day.'

She had decided not to leave. He continued scrolling through her photos. He was right.

'Why buildings?' he asked. He wanted to hear her voice, the unfamiliar accent rippling out across the table, filling the space of his apartment and reminding him that he was not alone.

'Because buildings can lie. People think that they don't — and that photography doesn't lie. But they both do. They manipulate perspective, influence memory. They hide things in shadows, draw your eye away from detail.' Her fork swivelled in her hand like a conductor's baton, pausing to wait for the next beat to continue on.

'You can only be in one bit of a building at a time and a person's eye can only focus on one thing at a time. I like playing on these presumptions. There's so much going on out of the shot, but people refuse to think about that. They think photography is the whole, captured truth.'

Looking through the photographs of the buildings that skirted the cities of Riga and Vilnius, he was surprised by how similar the setting of his own childhood seemed to these places. It was the level of decay more than anything, the crumbling frontages between the uniformly sized windows. These same buildings had already been renovated in East Berlin or were waiting to be revealed, hidden behind builders' scaffolding, their facades being plastered over like the faces of ageing matinee idols.

And then he saw it, why the images seemed like postcards from an indiscriminate time: there was evidence of human habitation but not a single person in any of the shots.

'There are no people.'

'Exactly!' She put her fork down, pushed the bowl away. 'Do you know how long I had to wait to photograph some of those places?'

He scrolled back through the photos; his revelation had made them seem unsavoury, as though they were documenting something that was over, not a place where life was still happening.

'But why? People live here. They use these buildings every day. That is what makes them important. Otherwise they are just shells.'

'But they're not. Buildings make us do certain things. I wanted to cut out all the people so the viewer can't humanise the buildings.'

'What is this one?' He passed the camera to her. It looked

like a manipulated photograph, a stately nineteenth-century building framed by a black border with letters cut out of it.

'It's the Terror Háza in Budapest. A museum for victims of fascism and communism. It's not for the exhibition, but it's kind of interesting, don't you think?'

She described how the black blades cantilevered out from the building's roof to form a verandah, and how the sunlight fell through the letters, casting the word 'terror' across the museum.

'The Nazis and the Soviets used the same building to torture and imprison their enemies. Don't you think that's strange? Buildings matter more than we know.'

'They have them here, too,' he said. 'The former Stasi offices, the prison in Hohenschönhausen, they are all memorials now.'

'What I love about buildings is that they signal civilisation. When they're standing, all is well, and when they're destroyed, it's the end. Knocking them down is a way of deleting history, so those very buildings that people were terrified of at one stage become the ones people visit to face their fears. Have you been to the prison?'

He shook his head. He had never contemplated going to Hohenschönhausen. It was another world, another time. It did not belong to him. Clare frowned at him. He had disappointed her.

'You know what's fascinating? Every city throughout the former Eastern Bloc seems to have them. Museums of terror, of occupation, of genocide, of deportation. And they are often in the very building where the KGB had their offices. Even when the people are gone, the buildings remain. It's sad that these places exist, but necessary, don't you think? So that people know?'

He could hear the urgency in her voice, the ownership, and something about it put him on edge. 'But don't you worry that it's not your story to tell?' It was not her history. 'You can exhibit your photos, put together your book, but it's not your story, you were not there.' He watched the hurt spread across her face. This is what he wanted. Because he felt like she was lecturing him — she did not know what it was like. She knew nothing about him.

'I'm not trying to make it mine, Andi. I'm just taking the photos and putting them out there. I don't want to speak for anyone — I don't think I am.'

'The buildings will not tell you anything, Clare. It was the people inside who were responsible. People did things then that they would not usually do. You'll never know what it was like.'

She shrugged. 'People can do terrible things to each other. We'll do it again and we'll use the same buildings to do it in. I guess I just want the buildings to tell their story, that's all.'

He focused his attention on the screen, scrolled on through the images. 'There are no photos of you.'

He lifted the camera and pointed it at her, pressed the button. Captured her in that moment just before she smiled, as though her expression was waiting to be issued the command to show him happiness.

'Why don't you have any tattoos?' he asks her.

He runs his fingers across her back as they lie in bed, marvelling at the foreverness of her skin, so white and pink.

Not pink — beige. No, it is something else, a white over red, her greedy skin hoarding the red pumping moistness of what lies beneath. White with a blush, like that of a pig's carcass hanging from a butcher's hook. He pictures a fluorescent pink stamp marking her, stating what she weighs, how much she is worth.

'Because everyone has tattoos.'

'And if everyone says the sky is blue, do you say it is red?'

She furrows her brow at him, purses her lips. 'And tattoos always fade and bleed into blurriness,' she says, refusing to bite. 'Why don't you have any?'

He watches his own hand stroking her back. When he spreads out his fingers, he can cover quite a bit of her. He could draw a line around his fingers, tattoo his handprint onto her skin, where it would wave at her in the mirror every time she undressed for a shower.

'I don't know.' He pictures the tattooist, a stranger, holding his skin taut. 'I have always been too worried that I wouldn't love the design forever. Imagine waking one morning and realising you hate it but you are stuck with it for the rest of your life.'

'It's like cattle branding, isn't it?' she says. 'A way of identifying who owns what.'

'I suppose it is nice to belong to something.' He lies down beside her, pulls her body to his as he nuzzles into her neck. She does not resist — she is a rag doll. 'Isn't it?' he says.

He had wanted a tattoo for a long time. The same permanency that attracted him made him afraid to commit. He recalls sitting in a park, eating an egg sandwich, mesmerised by an elderly man's tattooed feet. At the time, he was studying in London, always amazed as the office workers stripped their clothes off in the public gardens, worshipping the weak sun in their lunch hour. The man's suit jacket was discarded beside him on the grass; his shoes were unlaced and placed neatly together, the socks laid on top. His feet were almost luminescent in the sun; the blue ink of the tattoos seemed to have melted into all of his crevices. It had taken Andi some time to figure out what the two figures — one on each of the man's feet — were. A rooster and a pig. He had been fascinated: the age of the man, the unexpected discovery of his decorated feet. Later he found out that they were sailors' tattoos, mired in superstition. A pig on one foot and a rooster on the other was a guarantee of a sailor's life: both animals feared drowning so much that they would ferry the sailor to shore as quickly as possible, if only to save themselves.

The more he discovered about sailors' tattoos, the more he wanted one. The anchor that marked a voyage across the Atlantic, the shellback turtle that indicated a crossing of the equator. Twin swallows on the shoulders that told of the crossings of the tropics of Cancer and Capricorn. He did go to a tattoo parlour once, determined to get a swallow tattoo of his own. Desperate with homesickness in the droning buzz of London, he had thought it particularly pertinent. Swallows always come home. But sometimes people do not. In the end, he learned so much about the tattoos that he respected their meaning too much to get one. He was not afraid of drowning, but it seemed like tempting fate.

'Maybe we should get tattoos,' he whispers into her ear. There's no longer any fate to tempt. For a long moment she does not answer.

'There was a couple I knew,' she says, finally. 'They each had a star tattooed onto their wrists, with a tail trailing behind. When they held hands, it looked like the stars were jumping from one arm to the other, round and round in circles like they were being juggled.'

He skims his hand up her arm, sees a jet stream in its wake. 'I have a better idea.' He goes into the hallway and comes back with the satchel he takes to work and searches around in it until he finds a pen. 'Now, don't move.' She is lying on her stomach, and he sits astride her, smooths his hand over her lower back.

'Oh god, not there!' She tries to roll over, laughing, but his weight is too much. He feels her squirm but sits firm, pinning her to the bed. 'I could never get one there! It would be like getting two dolphins swirling around my belly button.'

'Ah, the ironic tattoo position? Hmmm …' He reaches behind, grabs her calf. 'What about here?'

She kicks her foot. 'No!'

'I know.' He grabs her hand and holds it above her head. Straightaway she seems taller. The hair beneath her arms is strawberry blonde, a washed-out version of the hair on her head. Still straddling her and holding her hand aloft, he begins to write, just below her arm, towards her back.

Her skin gives beneath the pen; he has to press down to get the ink to catch. She doesn't move — is she holding her breath? *Meine*, he writes. It looks like a tattoo immediately, apart from the inky blob on the tail of the final 'e'. The ink takes and holds: it looks like it is embedded within, rather than written on, the skin. He should have done it in red pen, like a meat stamp. *Meine liebe.*

'What is it?' She squirms about, impatient.

He lets go of her hand and throws himself back onto the bed. Spread-eagled, he stares at the ceiling. Happy. This is what happy is. His face feels flushed, his palms are sweaty. He forms the words silently, in English, hoping that she is looking at him. He feels how first his front teeth touch his lower lip, and then his tongue touches his front teeth. Then his lips close and seal shut, before bursting open: *I feel happy.*

She is sitting up in the bed, her arm in the air, trying to see the tattoo. She tries to pull her breast out of the way with one hand, the other dangling uselessly in the air.

'What does it say?'

He says nothing.

'Andi, what is it?'

'I'm not telling,' he replies, grinning.

'You're a shit, Andi.' She gets off the bed, pads down the hall to the bathroom.

He hears the click of the light switch. He rolls to the side of the bed; he can see her elongated shadow across the hallway floor.

'*Meine?*' She comes out of the bathroom, forehead creased. 'Does that mean "mine"?'

He laughs. 'Of course it does, sweetie.'

'I'm not yours, Andi.' She comes back to the bed, pouting.

Fuck, she's beautiful. 'Yes, you are.' He reaches for her hands and pulls her down to the bed. He kisses her, wraps his arms around her back. Squeezing, he hopes the tattoo is printing a mirror image onto his arm. 'Right now you are, little sparrow.'

~

Once again, Andi had left by the time she woke. Her life was falling into a pattern, and she needed to hoist herself out. She showered; her muscles felt tight from lack of use. Back in the bedroom, she looked at the bedside table. It was empty: no key. She checked the floor. Nothing. The room suddenly seemed airless, as though it was holding out on her, knew more than she did. Still wrapped in a towel, she went into the hallway, the living room, the kitchen, scanning every surface. Her camera sat on the table where he had discarded it last night. She trailed down the hall to the front door and half-heartedly tried to open it. She already knew. It was deadlocked.

He must have left the key for her somewhere. He could not possibly have forgotten again. She went back to the bedroom and dressed, straightened the sheets on the bed, prolonging the moment before she would have to start searching in earnest. Knowing already what she would find. Kneeling on the floor she looked under the bed, the sea-grass matting digging into her palms and knees. Nothing.

In the kitchen she glanced about for a note, something to remind her that Andi had not forgotten about her. But it seemed she was trespassing in his life; there was no acknowledgement of her existence. He had simply forgotten to leave her a key. Sighing, she opened the fridge. Everything looked slightly different from what she was used to. As she tried to decipher the various labels on the condiments, she noted how much she relied on language. Without the words to guide her, to remind her of what she liked and disliked, she had to think carefully about the distinctions between cheddar and edam, raspberry and strawberry jam. Slicing bread, cheese and an apple, she arranged a breakfast plate, spooned out some of the condiments on the side. She attempted to conjure up Andi but could capture nothing other than a snatch of smile, the feel of his hands around her waist. It was so easy to forget — all she knew about him was so quickly in the past; in the present his absence pushed itself to the fore.

After she had eaten, she tried the front door once again. She felt a rush of anger towards him: how could he be so absent-minded? Somewhere between the bed and the stairs, did he just forget her altogether?

In the living room she flipped through the records, scanned the bookshelf. All of the titles were in German, which struck her as odd for an English teacher. She turned on the television, flicked through the channels. News and music videos. She turned it off, flinging the remote onto the couch. The air in the apartment seemed stale: while she knew this was only in her imagination, she wished she could open a window. She tried each one, yanked at the handles with increasing frustration, but none of them would cede. Nothing moved in the courtyard; she could not tell if it was windy outside. The sky had stripped itself of colour, presenting a uniform grey that offended no one. It was at least six hours until Andi would come home.

Stillness shrouds the morning. She wraps her hands around her coffee mug, shoulders hunched, her coffee uninviting and lukewarm. Who was this man, Luke Warm? A man of tepid personality, dull as dishwater? She is reminded of her childhood baths, splashing around with her sister. The same sister who would be wondering why she has not sent her any postcards. Does she, too, remember the baths? Turning into prunes, they used to say, holding up their puckered hands as the bathwater cooled. Clare is still always quietly relieved when her wrinkled skin smooths and returns to normal after a soaking.

She curls up on the windowsill. The glass is hard against her cheek and shoulder. An exhibition she had seen in a science museum as a child had suggested that glass was a liquid, falling with gravity as it performed its task of transparency. Its motion slowed to the point of being indiscernible to even the most attentive of gazes. She wishes that it was true, that eventually the glass would puddle on the sill, letting the outside in.

Unthinkingly, she picks at one of the scabs on her legs, letting her fingernails catch underneath it. She teases it, gently at first, then more and more insistently until it lifts free. The blood is sticky beneath her always dirty fingernails. When she goes to bed her nails are clean, yet she wakes to find dark moons beneath them, as though she has been gardening in the night. Andi's nails are always white and a regular length, but hers are ragged, the skin around them dry and cracked. Years ago she would blame it on the darkroom chemicals. Now it is just a habit; she fidgets, picks and pulls. Sometimes Andi comes up behind her, wraps his arms about her, and she examines her fingers in comparison to his. His fingers are thicker, his palms wider. Her fingers look spindly next to his, the ends red and angry.

She watches the blood trickle down her thigh. Blood down a leg runs much slower than rain down a windowpane. She likes it when he is not here and she can see her body, blood sliding to escape. She will dress properly before he comes home, and when his hands run up her legs at night he will not say anything.

Leaving her sentry position by the window, she puts a record on the turntable. She lifts the arm and lets it drop; it bounces a little when it hits the record before settling in. The needle holds still as the vinyl spins. She is the needle. She is the constant in this equation. She holds herself straighter. She is the strong one — she is providing an essential service. She changes this world from being grooves on a disc, illegible to the casual observer, to being a symphony, a full house of sound and meaning.

In the bathroom she considers her reflection in the mirror. Her skin is pale, her face is tired, her hair is lank. But she is the needle. She raises her arms above her head. She can see the rosy blush of bruises on her upper arms. They look like splodges of paint. An abstract interpretation on her skin. She lowers her arms and, as her shoulders release their load, she feels the blood rush back to her hands.

If she is the needle, what does that make Andi? Is he the record, turning around and around? She imagines him spinning, arms outstretched, giggling like a child. No. He is the arm, holding her out over the world. He is grasping her tightly and letting her fingers drag along the surface. He is keeping her still and steady and just far enough away that she does not get hurt.

But she is *terrified*. The word hits her in the chest. She steps away from the mirror. Her reflection does not appear terrified, only glum. She moves back to the living room. Looking down at the turntable, she can see the blur of her reflected face. What if he lets go and she tumbles into the black whirling continuity of this record world? She imagines trying to stand up and being knocked back down, caught in a rip as the tide of all she knows goes out. If she is flung off the record, her body will hit the wall, slide down to the skirting boards. She will be left there, unnoticed, swept under the couch. She will become friends with the balls of dust, the lost change. Perhaps there is something to be said for being the needle in all of this.

~

She registered his shadow, a passing cloud bringing inclement weather.

'Clare?'

She was not even sure she heard her name, but she watched his mouth form the shape. The stereo was turned up loud, his voice lost in drums and double bass. He ducked his face to hers, kissed her on the forehead, then crossed the room to the stereo and lifted the needle from the turntable.

'How was your day?'

She stayed lying on the couch, did not turn to face him. 'It was pretty boring, Andi.'

He didn't say anything, and she pulled herself into a sitting position, waited for his response. And when there was none, her words flew out, angrier than she expected.

'You didn't leave me a key! I've been here all day again.' She could not help their force, her fury as pent up as herself.

'But I did leave you a key! It's in the drawer of the bedside table.'

The immediacy of his words stunned her into action, forced her to her feet. 'What?'

'I left a key in the table by the bed.'

But she checked, she was sure of it. She marched to the

bedroom, opened the drawer. A silver key sat amongst its contents. 'I'm sure I checked there.'

She remembered pulling open the drawer, lifting the papers to see if there was anything beneath. Didn't she? But there was the key. She faced him, embarrassment rising.

Andi leaned against the doorjamb, his top lip curled into the slightest of smirks. Pushing himself from the doorway, he lifted his shoulders in an exaggerated shrug as he walked towards her. 'Maybe you did not look hard enough.'

They spent the evening in bed, Andi occasionally going to the living room to change the record. When he did, she slid open the bedside-table drawer, checked to see that the key was there, and closed it again. She did this three times before she forced herself to stop, tucked her hands under her body to bar them from reaching for the handle.

Andi was in the shower when she woke. She pulled on one of his shirts, took the key from the drawer and slipped it into the chest pocket. In the kitchen she began making coffee; she could hear him singing in the shower.

'Hey, what are you doing up so early?'

'I just wanted to see you in the daylight.' She handed him a cup of coffee, hoisted herself up onto the kitchen bench.

'You will see me all day tomorrow. It's Saturday.'

'I know.'

He slurped some coffee before shrugging apologetically and pouring the rest of it down the sink. 'Sorry, I'm running late. I've got to go.' He rinsed out his cup, the drops sounding dull pings against the metal sink. 'Now, the key is in the drawer, okay? Make sure you lock the door from the outside after you leave — it's better that way.'

He pulled her towards him, placed her legs about his waist. She could feel the sharp edges of the key digging into her breast as he kissed her goodbye. She hoped he could not feel the same. His tongue jutted into the corners of her mouth, and desire darted between her legs.

'I will see you tonight. Have fun exploring the city.' And he was out the door, key turning in the lock, and his footsteps ringing down the stairs.

Sliding off the bench, she tried to ignore the wave of loneliness that threatened to engulf her. Perhaps sticking around in Berlin had been a bad idea; she wasn't looking for this kind of dependency.

She slowly made the bed, picked clothes up from the floor. She should do some washing, contemplated lugging her clothes down to the nearest laundromat. But life had slipped too far into domesticity already, so she took off Andi's shirt, pulled on clothes of her own, and headed to the front door.

The key did not fit in the lock. She tried it again. Not even the tip would go in. Maybe it was just stiff because it was newly cut. She manoeuvred the key every possible way. It was the wrong key.

She let her bag fall to the ground and ran back to the bedroom and wrenched open the drawer. No key. She pulled the drawer out from the table and upended it on the bed. Nothing.

Shit.

She ran back to the front door, tried the key again, but it did not fit. Why didn't she leave with him this morning? She knew something was not right, she just knew. Back in the bedroom she picked up each item from the drawer and shook it as though the proper key might appear, the rabbit from the hat, but there was no magic there.

'Fuck!' She threw herself back on the bed. 'Fuck, fuck, fuck!'

This could not be happening. It must have been a mistake. Andi had just left the wrong key: there was no need to panic. But it was more than that, she knew it was. She needed to speak to him but she didn't have his number. Why hadn't they swapped numbers? Maybe she could call him at his school. What was the name of it? She was sure he'd mentioned it; there must be a telephone directory she could look it up in — she would recognise the name when she saw it. This thought propelled Clare from the bed, and she grabbed her phone from her backpack. It was still flat, so she rummaged in her pack for the charger, pulling it out through the tangled mess of clothes. She plugged it into the socket, impatient for the screen to light up with its welcoming note, its friendly chimes and helping hands reaching across to each other. With soothing familiarity it did all of those things — then flashed a stop sign at her. *Insert SIM card*. Shit. She flipped the phone over, pulled its casing apart. The slot was empty.

Surely he had not taken her SIM card? There must be some explanation. She removed the battery, took out the memory card, shook the phone as though to force sense into it. Maybe the card had just fallen out somewhere. Maybe she had taken it out. Maybe he took the card because he wanted to swap it for a German one, wanted to be able to call her more cheaply. But as her excuses got more convoluted, the facts stubbornly refused to change. He had left her the wrong key. He had taken her SIM card. She was locked in an apartment, and nobody knew she was there.

She sat on the floor and dropped her head in her hands. What the fuck was she going to do? She thought back over the last couple of days, sifted through her memories for some kind of sign, something to say she was warned, that Andi was not all he seemed. But the more she thought about it, the more ludicrous the situation became. Andi would not do this! It could not be deliberate. There must be some kind of misunderstanding. It was just the wrong key. She needed to calm down. Yesterday she must not have looked hard enough; she must not have opened that drawer. She had only herself to blame.

She felt like she had spent a lifetime in the apartment. She had slept all of the day before yesterday. And the door was locked the day before that. Three days she had spent here alone: it was too many for coincidences.

Her head was thumping, and she lifted it from her hands, looked about the room, wanted it to melt away. As she stood up from the floor, her vision blacked and she swayed, tried not to fall. Sweat broke out in the small of her back and at the nape of her neck, and her stomach twisted and rollicked as the thoughts swarmed unhindered through her mind. He saw her reading and he offered her those strawberries. He was there in the bookshop reading the book she had looked at the day before. He found her at the station and he wouldn't let her leave. But even as she made this list, she knew that it was not the whole truth. This was Andi! She had come willingly. She had left and come back again; she had not been forced to do anything. And she liked him — she was a good judge of these things. But the facts would not leave her alone. She had slept with someone she barely knew and now she was stuck.

Fuck this. She ran to the front door and banged on it with her fists. 'Andi! Let me out! Can anybody hear me? Let me out! Please!'

What was it in German? Did it matter? Was 'help' universal? It should be. Like Control-Z. Undo. She wanted to go back a level to a time when flirting with an attractive stranger on a street corner was okay. Because it still felt like a game. Surely it was some kind of game?

'Fuck you, Andi! Let me out of here! Let me out!'

When she stopped pounding, she heard the silence. There were no shuddering pipes, no footsteps above. No television or radio murmurs from the neighbouring apartments. Up five flights of stairs and not a sign of life. No open doors, no blue television light, no music, no neighbours. Nothing.

Shit. She leaned back against the hallway wall, its cool plaster surface held her up for a moment before she fell in an ungainly heap on the floor, and it was here the tears overtook her.

'Why me?' The question bobbed, a lone duck amongst the sobs pooling in her mouth. She was pathetic. She was the most hopeless she had ever been. She gulped down her sob, wishing Andi was there to comfort her. This was why this could not be happening. It was just a series of weird coincidences. This was Andi; he was not that type of man. And she was not that kind of woman.

In the living room she crossed to the window. Leaves huddled along the courtyard walls, too tentative to venture into the expanse of the yard. One of the windows, no, two of the windows of the apartments opposite were broken. The building was falling apart. What the fuck had she gotten herself into?

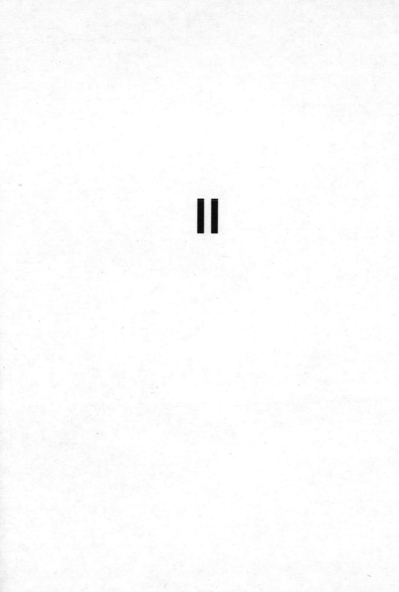

'Clare?' He calls her name out to the apartment and braces himself for her response. Nothing. But she must be here. He hangs his jacket on the hook in the hallway and walks into the living room. 'Clare?'

The glow of her cigarette in the darkness gives her away. He switches on the light, and there she is, sitting on the windowsill, hugging her knees, her face turned away from him.

'You didn't leave me the key.' She doesn't look at him.

He takes a measured breath. He must approach this with care. 'I left you a key.' There, that's not a lie.

'It was the wrong key.' She is not accusing him: she is simply stating facts. This is a good sign — she does not blame him. 'And you've taken my SIM card.'

He had hoped she wouldn't notice — her phone was flat. It is just a precaution until they work out an agreement.

'I wanted to make sure you would be here when I got back.' He crosses the room, watching the smoke rise from her cigarette. It climbs the window, curls towards the blinking television tower.

'I would have been here.' She stubs out her cigarette. She doesn't seem too upset.

Encouraged, he steps forward and tentatively pats her arm

before enclosing her in a hug. 'I just wanted to make sure, Clare. I couldn't bear the thought of coming home and you being somewhere else.'

Bringing his lips to her hair, he feels her shoulders stiffen. He tightens his embrace, but she shakes him off, forcing him to take a step back. Released, her legs swing free from the window ledge, knocking the ashtray to the floor with a clatter. She grabs the sill fiercely as though to stop herself from attacking him.

'Where was I going to go?' She looks at him, accusing. 'I was here because I wanted to be here. I wanted to be with you. But you can't *make* me stay — you have to let me go.'

She uses the past tense. His mind races. He was right — she would have left today if she could. He knows her, the way she works.

'I just thought it would be easiest, Clare. I did not want you to get lost in the city. I was worried about you out there alone.'

She looks at him as though she does not recognise him. As though he is an annoyance she wants to kick away. She launches herself from the windowsill, and he tenses, prepares for her to shove him. But she comes up short in front of him, and this is worse, this not touching. It is as though she has already removed herself from the room.

'Andi, if you had left me the right key I would have gone out, I would have walked around the city, taken some photos and I would have come back. That's all. But you have totally fucked it up.'

But what if she had not come back? What if she hadn't realised that this is where she is supposed to be? It was too big of a risk.

'And now I have to leave.' She shrugs. 'Don't you get it,

Andi? I don't even have a choice. You've ruined it.'

She stands in front of him, waiting. She wants an apology, an explanation, and he is relieved. This he can do. She is still here; he can make it right.

'Clare, I'm really sorry. I should not have done that. But you can't leave. You need to be here. You need to stop running away from things.'

'Running away? What have I ever run away from? You don't know me at all!'

'I'm just trying to help. I'm giving you a place just to be yourself. In the moment, not looking to the future. That's what you said you wanted, isn't it?' He is doing this for her. Why can she not see that?

'That was just talk, Andi! We had sex — people say all sorts of things when they go to bed together. But you can't lock me up and tell me it's what I want. You're fucked up!' She crosses the room to her backpack, which is leaning against the wall like a portly companion.

She cannot leave. What they have is more than sex: he cannot believe she is denying this. Surely she doesn't mean it? As she heaves her pack onto her back he has an undeniable urge to run across the room and push her over, to make her stop saying these things. But he won't; he won't hurt her.

'Clare.' He tries to keep his voice steady, reasonable. 'You know this is not just about sex. We have more than that. You could have got on that train, but you stayed. Don't leave now.' He hears his words rushing together — he is starting to panic. What if she leaves him? What will he do then?

'And wasn't that a fucking mistake.' She stumbles under the weight of her pack and grabs her camera bag. 'You need to get help. You're lucky I don't report you to the police.'

She storms out of the room, her shadow a stooped packhorse wobbling down the hallway wall behind her. He hears her try to open the door. He should unlock it. He should let her go.

'Unlock the fucking door, Andi.'

He can hear the terror in her voice.

'Andi! Unlock the door!'

He does not move. If he does not move, she does not leave.

'What the fuck is your problem?'

Her voice is cracking; he can hear the sobs crowding in her throat. His heart is beating loudly, and he swallows as though to placate it. He wants to comfort her, but still he does not move. If she did not try to leave, she would not be so upset. He is trying to make things better, but she is making it so much worse.

'Andi!' She strides back into the room, stops in front of him. Her face is red, and she is terrified. He has never seen such obvious fear in someone before.

'Andi, please. I want to leave. I want to go now. I don't want things to be like this. I just need to go.'

She is crying. Her cheeks are wet, and he wants to reach out and touch them. He cannot let her go. He cannot let her leave in such a fragile state. He has caused this; he is the only one who can make it better.

'Clare, I can't let you go. I need you here. As soon as I met you, I knew that this was something important. You and me, this is what we are.'

'This is not what we are! We're strangers. We barely know each other. We slept together and that's it. You have to let me go!'

'But I can make you stay.'

Her face falls. His words have had an immediate effect. He is impressed with the tangibility of them. They are still hanging in the air, and the fear, the despair, every emotion has dropped from her face.

'No, you can't.' Her voice stumbles — she is beginning to understand. Andi watches the redness clawing up her neck. 'You're not allowed to do this.'

'Clare, trust me. It will be okay. This means nothing is going to get in the way of what we have.' He is pleased with how sensible he sounds.

'But I don't want this! I want to leave!'

'No.' It is easier than he thought it would be. He will not let her leave. He will keep the door locked, and she will stay. She does not need to go anywhere else.

He watches her chest heave. She noisily draws in air through her nostrils, pushes it out in quick little bursts. She is shaking. He doesn't like to think that he has frightened her, but perhaps he has.

'I'm sorry, Clare. One day you want to stay and the next you want to leave.' He keeps his voice even, soothing. His thoughts are making sense now; he can see the way they're heading as though their route is marked on a map. 'You are inconsistent. You don't know what you want. But I just want the same thing, the same thing every day. You. And in time you will understand, I promise. You will want to stay.'

It is so clear to him. They will make their world here in his apartment; they will not be affected by the decisions of others. They will be very still in their own moment, and there will be nobody else to make things different. No one can enter. No one can leave. And no one can tear down the walls and push them out. It is so obvious: he doesn't know why it has never occurred to him before. It is easier than he thought to take control. It must be because he did not know Clare before. She gave him this.

'Andi, this is madness. Unlock the door. You can't do this. You can't keep me prisoner. Just let me go. I won't tell anyone. I'll just walk away, you'll never hear from me again.'

'I can't let you go, Clare. I'm doing this for you. For us. You know that, don't you? That is why you did not get on that train. It's why you came up to me in the bookstore. You knew.'

He steps forward and lifts her bag from her shoulders. She does not protest, and he lowers it to the floor where it sways for a moment and then topples. He almost expects it to spring back up like a weighted children's toy. He embraces her rigid body, and she does not hug him back — but she does not break away.

'It will be okay,' he says.

'It will be okay,' he tells her.

His arms are tight around her, and she squirms, wrenching herself free. She wants to wipe the smile from his face, quite literally. To reach up and smear it aside, leaving nothing but a bristly expanse. Instead she reaches for the handle of her bag and drags it along the hallway to the front door, which she tries to open again. Locked. Without a key she is going nowhere. She props the bag against the wall and slumps down beside it, her head in her hands. This is fucked. This cannot be happening. She hears Andi's footsteps fade, listens to the sound of domestic banality as he moves about the kitchen and begins to cook dinner. This *is* happening.

No one is expecting her to arrive anywhere. No one will come looking for her. She closes her eyes and counts her breaths. Tries to breathe in strict time, as though the imposition of order on this one act will bring everything else into line. *One, two, three, four*. She inhales. *One, two, three, four*. She exhales. And nothing has changed. *Three, four, locked door*. She tries to ignore the rhyme, but it will not go away.

Where is everyone she knows? How can she tell them she is here? Isn't the world supposed to have shrunk with the glut of instant communication? But her phone is useless, and she has no online profile to be neglected. She has successfully cleared the decks of her life, and now she is quite alone. Andi goes about his evening as though nothing is amiss. She sits in the hallway, her arse numb against the floor, disbelieving that time is allowed to pass under these circumstances.

'Do you want something to eat, Clare?' He appears at the end of the hallway, a tea towel in hand.

She tries to look into his eyes but he is in shadow, his face a smudge. She does not reply.

She listens to his cutlery tap out his presence as he eats. He moves back to the kitchen and washes the dishes. Then a series of noises she cannot identify. She hears him walk across the living room and wonders what record he will put on, holding her breath in anticipation as though he might offer her a clue. But no music eventuates.

She does not leave her plot by the door. She doesn't know what she is waiting for, but what else can she do? She leans against her backpack, her legs across the hallway. He must open the door soon. It's some weird fucking power trip, but he will have to realise how ridiculous it is. This can't go on forever.

'Are you coming to bed, Clare?' He crouches down to speak to her as people do to toddlers.

He is going to bed? As though this day is ready to end? He looks concerned, his eyes brimming with care. She does not answer, yet he stays staring at her, swaying on his unsteady feet. What is going on? She wants to scream at him, to cut through whatever this is and find Andi underneath, but the words don't come, refusing to believe that they are needed.

With a pneumatic sigh he lifts himself and goes into the bathroom. She hears him use the toilet, brush his teeth. Such normal things. He comes out and pauses in the doorway. His shadow stretches towards her. A chain glints around his neck and from it hangs a key. He reaches for it, drops it inside his t-shirt. They look at each other, and he goes into the bedroom.

Fuck. She still cannot believe this is happening. But she must. She has to stop thinking about how unlikely, how impossible it is, and just concentrate on getting out. She needs to steal the key while he sleeps. But how? He will wake if she tries to remove it, surely? She will have to knock him out. With what? A book? A frying pan? But it all seems so laughable. She has never actually hurt anyone before. How would she do it? How would she bring that weight down upon his sleeping head? What if she killed him? Even in her mind it all seems like an overreaction, let alone carrying it out. Surely this whole thing is a misunderstanding. If she hurts him, it will become real.

Her legs aching from inactivity, she pulls herself up from the floor and tries the handle of the door. Locked. She walks into the living room and stands there, making out the shapes of the furniture in the dark. There is nothing she can do; she cannot bear the thought of doing anything. She takes her shoes off and lies down on the couch. She wants to sleep, for all of this to go away. To be able to think clearly, for something to happen next.

She wakes shivering, reaching for the bedclothes before remembering where she is, that there are none. She stands stiffly from the couch and, without switching on the light, finds her way through the apartment to the bedroom. She pushes the door open, and the darkness rolls out towards her. When she switches on the hall light, she can make him out in the bed. He looks the same as before — the Andi she knows. In small steps, wishing she was anywhere but here, she approaches the bed, seeks out the chain from around his neck. She will just yank it off; even if he wakes, it will take him a moment to react. And he will realise, won't he, how ridiculous this is? She will run; she will be out the door, and this will all be over. The chain is warm from his skin; it sits lightly across her fingers. She tugs it.

It doesn't come free. The pull is made sluggish by Andi's weight, and as the chain jerks back his eyes open. Her hand retracts as though burned. She should have pulled harder. She knew it even as she did it. But she couldn't; she couldn't quite believe what she was having to do.

'Clare?' He reaches out his hand and grabs her wrist. His touch is warm. 'Come to bed.'

She looks at the space beside him; her pulse is beating loudly in her head. *Three, four, locked door.* She just wants to sleep. She wants it all to be over, to be normal again. He lifts the covers, shuffles aside to make room for her. His breathing is regular; he is unperturbed, as though this is just a little disagreement and he forgives her if only she will stop sulking. And when she slips into the bed, his heavy limbs envelop her. *One, two, three, four*. She breathes in. *One, two, three, four*. She breathes out.

It wasn't as though he planned it outright; he wasn't trying to trap her — he's not like that. Clare rolls over in her sleep, and Andi loosens his hold. When she has settled, he slides his hand around her waist, interlaces his fingers with hers. She does need him, she keeps coming back to him: that much is clear. The bookstore, the train station. The first time he had locked the door it was an accident. Habit ruled his life; every morning as he left the apartment he pulled the door closed behind him and turned the key in the second lock. It was a near-empty building: he dreaded coming home to find his apartment burgled, his stereo gone.

As he battled through his classes that first day, his hangover washing over him in waves, he had been certain that Clare would have woken and left, a breezy note on the kitchen table all that would remain. His despondency had trailed him home where he found her, an unintentional prisoner. She was not meant to leave him, not yet. He believes in fate. How impossible not to.

The other night, after the fun park, he could not quite believe how lucky he was to have met her. Still damp with the evening's rain, she lolled against him in the booth of the bar. She seemed too real. As though her body took up more space than his own. Her presence seemed to push the air about, to increase the pressure so that he could feel each moment pushed up against him. She made him feel immediate, and he did not want it to end.

As they drank and talked their way through the night, he had watched Clare closely. *Stay with me*, he wanted to say. But he knew too well the effect of those words. The way they would mute her desire, replace it with a skittishness that would let her eyes slip from his face to the door. The women he had known were always too willing to leave. The moment they discovered his need for them, the depth of his want, they started making excuses. Watching Clare's large laughing mouth, her shadow-puppet hands, he knew that he could not say the words, but he could make her stay.

It is not such a big thing, to lock a door. The turn of a key, that is all. He has been locking the door every morning when he leaves for work, and when he returns it is as though his time outside the apartment has not happened. Clare is still there, just as he left her. He doesn't want to keep her captive forever; he's not cruel. He just wants to limit her options so she can see that what they have is something unique — nothing from the outside world can compare.

He *had* gotten a spare key cut for her. But when he kissed her goodbye and went to leave the key on the bedside table, he just could not do it. The thought of her posting the key back under the door as she left, never to return, disabled him. He slipped the key into his pocket, walked down the hallway and out the front door, locking it behind him. He would deal with it when he returned; he would explain everything. It was all so normal. He knew he was crossing a line, but it didn't *feel* wrong. Not in the way that coming home to an empty apartment would feel wrong. The wanderlust that had brought her to him would eventually take her away, he knew that. But not just yet.

Clare turns over in her sleep again, moves away from him

to the edge of the bed. He shuffles his body a little closer, takes a handful of her hair. He wants to wake her, show her how he feels, how much he adores her. But he will not; he will let her sleep. He will let her do whatever she wants.

When he had returned to the apartment that evening, she did not hear him unlock the door — the music was too loud. In the bedroom he slid a key from his key ring and put it in the drawer of the bedside table. He convinced her it had been there all day, that she had not looked hard enough. And when he left the apartment this morning, he knew she would not be going anywhere. He had left the wrong key.

He has spent the day thinking through all the possibilities for their future, and the result is always the same. If she has the option, eventually she will leave. If she doesn't have the option, she will stay. He sat at his desk after teaching his last class, and listed all the pros and cons on a sheet of paper. But it is far simpler than that. He can keep her here, or he can let her go. He moves closer to her, mimics her body with his own.

She tries to go back to sleep; she cannot. She opens her eyes and lets the grey static of the morning scramble into position and assume the shape of Andi's bedroom.

She gets out of the bed. Her clothes belong to yesterday and feel hostile, angry at her for wearing them all night. She walks down the hallway to the door and tries to open it.

Locked.

'Is that you, Clare?'

His voice floats in from the kitchen, and her heart flips: familiarity or apprehension? How can she not know?

'Who else would it be?' She follows his voice to where he stands in front of the open fridge, regarding its contents.

'I'm just going out to grab a few things. Is there anything you want?' He looks at her, almost a smile, and she hates him for this confusion, for acting so normal.

'Can't I come with you?'

He closes the fridge door, grabs his wallet from the bench. 'You don't have your shoes on.'

He moves past her to the hallway, and she grabs at his arm. Her fingers latch onto the weave of his knitted jumper, but he keeps walking, jerking her arm in its socket, and she is forced to let go, fingers burning.

'I'll be back soon.' He marches down the hallway, and she bolts after him.

At the door she hooks her arm through his as he turns the key. 'I'm coming with you. I don't want to stay here.'

'Clare!' He tries to wrench his arm away, but she holds tight. If he opens that door she will escape.

'Andi! Let me out! I can't stay here!'

'Yes, you can.' Yanking his arm free, he pushes her roughly away; she is amazed at the strength of him. He twists the key in the lock, opens the door. She lunges forward, tries to squeeze herself between him and the door, but he is too quick. He wedges himself into the space, slams the door shut behind him, forcing her to throw her hands up so that her fingers won't be crushed.

'Andi! Let me out! Andi!' She grabs at the door handle, hears the smooth click as the lock slides into place. 'Andi! Stop being such an asshole! You can't do this.' She beats on the door with tightly closed fists, her fingernails digging into her palms, her knuckles singing out in pain. When she stops, his footsteps have already faded away, and she is alone again. This is no dream.

She must get out. She needs to think about this rationally. She puts on her boots, ready for flight. Her bags are still packed and waiting. In the living room, she tries the handle of each of the windows. Locked, locked, locked. Methodically, she goes through each room in the apartment and tries every window. They are all locked. She hits her hand hard against the glass, and the thud is dull. The windows are double-glazed: a vacuum traps any sound she makes. Would it be possible to break the glass? And then what? She looks at the facade of the building opposite. There is nothing to cling to; she could not climb down and five storeys is too far to drop.

She moves through the apartment searching for clues as though she is in a puzzle book, certain that there must be an answer to her dilemma. As she opens every cupboard and drawer, she does not find anything to give hope. She comes across a blister pack of tablets in the cutlery drawer. Their pharmaceutical name means nothing to her: neither English nor German, it is a language of its own. That they should be sitting here amongst the forks and teaspoons is strange, but she cannot see how they might help her and she drops them back into the drawer, slamming it shut. She runs her fingers around the doors, the windows. Everything seems so solid. She has never thought of walls as something to keep her in before; they have always been only shelter, a means to keep intruders out.

She has not eaten since yesterday afternoon. In the kitchen she chews on bread, but her mouth refuses to make enough saliva to let it slide down her throat, and she spits it into the bin. She needs to think. From a pot in the fridge she spoons some yoghurt into her mouth; slices an apple into small, undemanding pieces. She contemplates the knife in her hand. It's the only way. She will have to ambush him. When he comes in the door, she will take him by surprise, knock him over and run. She will leave her bags, her camera, everything. She can come back with police. She will make him pay.

She opens a kitchen drawer, looks at the other knives lying there. Could she actually stab him? She imagines the motion, her arm drawing an arc through the air towards his heart. But it is like hitting him over the head with the frying pan — it seems too extreme. But it's not, is it? She is trapped in here. He would do the same to her. Is that what he's planning? Is this going to get worse? Thoughts of rape, of murder flit through her mind, but she cannot hold on to them; they don't belong. She weighs the knife in her hand: is it easier to stab someone with an underarm swing or overarm? What does she aim for? Could she actually get close enough to hurt him without him overpowering her? She feels so inept; she is not prepared for this. Will she be able to stick a knife into him, push it through his flesh into what lies beneath? How deep would it need to go? Would he die instantly? Or would she have to stab him again and again? But she doesn't want to kill him. She really doesn't want all of that. He is a confused madman, a modern-day fool, but she does not want him dead. And who will believe her story?

She hears his footsteps trip lightly up the stairs. She can do this. As the key is slid into the lock, she runs down the hallway. She hears the bolt slide across and sees the handle turn. The door swings towards her, and she drops her head and charges, knife held tight in her fist. She will get out! It is only three steps, and she knocks Andi towards the wall with her shoulder. He is steadier than she imagined and he holds fast to the door. His hand blocks her way and pulls the door into her shoulder. The pain ricochets through her body, and she drops the knife. She is jammed between him and the door, and her head jerks forward then back.

She screams. It echoes down the stairwell, and she is desperate to follow, her body lunging at Andi, her feet kicking. He lets go of the door, shoves her back into the hallway, and slams the door shut. She hits the wall, her knee buckles, but she will not give up — the door is still unlocked. She slams her elbow into his back, tries to push past him to the door. But he turns and grabs hold of her arms, twists her away from him, and seizes her in a tight embrace.

Shit. She took him by surprise. Holding her against his body, he uses his free hand to slip the key into the lock and turn it. She's wrestling to get away, but he won't let go until he has the key in his pocket.

'Fuck you, Andi!' She pelts him with the words as she twists herself free of his grasp. She sounds like she hates him. The knife spins out from her stomping feet, sliding into the skirting boards.

Was she going to stab him? She wants to kill him? He does not hear what she is saying. Her face is red, slick with tears, and the sounds cascade out of her mouth. She is waving her arms about; her hands hang loose at the end of them, as though they might fly away, until she grabs at her hair, tethering them to her shouting face. She is pure sound, no language — her words like panicked animal calls.

'I want out, Andi! Can't you let me out? I don't want to be here. Why do you want me here if I don't want to be here?'

He watches her hands tear at her hair and wonders if it hurts. He does not want her to be in pain.

'I hate you, Andi! What are you doing? Why are you like this?'

She is race-calling the words: there is no emphasis or phrasing. He reaches out to her; he wants to make her stop. He pulls one of her hands free of her hair and brings it to his chest, as though to protect it. She keeps shouting, and he takes his other hand to enclose hers. He is holding her hand in prayer, and still the noise does not stop.

He coos her name, and her hand jumps, tries to wrest itself free. He cannot hear her words; he can just see her mouth opening. Up, down; up, down. When he pulls on her little finger, it yields far more easily than he expected. He thought he might have to tug it, entice it with his whole body weight. It pops like a still-green twig, unwilling to give up the fight but helpless to do anything about it.

For a second there is silence as her legs collapse beneath her. She drops towards the floor, but he will not let her give in. He holds her up, wraps his arms around her, and she screams. It is an unreal sound, haggard and splitting, yet amongst it he recognises one word.

'Andi!'

His name fights out of her mouth between the anguish and surprise. It is propelled by pure desperation — he can hear that, too. She does need him.

And then her scream breaks, and she folds in on herself and moans. He tries to lift her, but she is too heavy, her body leaden, and he moves her awkwardly down the hallway and into the living room where they stumble to the couch. She collapses onto it and curls herself into a corner where her moans become sobs.

He has dislocated her finger; he did this to her. What sort of person is he? Looking down at her crumpled body he tries to feel, but his emotions are absent. He should feel remorse, he knows he should, but it is crowded out by satisfaction. He is in control. This is the way things have to be. They are in this together now.

'I'm sorry, sweetie.' He crouches down to her. 'I'm sorry, I really am. I had to make you listen — you were only going to hurt yourself.' He puts his hand on her shoulder. Her sobs are slowing.

'Let me take a look at it.' He draws her hand towards him. The little finger sticks out awkwardly, dislocated. Her whole body is quivering. His heart is racing; he will make it better for her.

'I'm going to fix it for you.' He takes her finger and swiftly moves it back into position. It makes the same pop, and she shudders.

'Just hold it like that, Clare.' He puts down her hand and goes to the bathroom where he finds a bandage. Gently, so as not to hurt her, he binds her little finger to the others. He makes a mitten of her hand.

Her finger is throbbing. Dulled pain butts against her skin as though it has somewhere else to go. As she watches the second hand limp around the clock face, she wonders whether her finger's throbbing is keeping truer time. The pain is taking cues from her heart, her pulse feeding the signals and reminding her that something is not quite right. She lifts her unharmed hand to her chest, seeks out her heartbeat with cold fingers. She cannot find it. Somewhere beneath the cushioning of her breast it beats, but on the surface all is still. She drops her hand to her lap and regards its bandaged partner with suspicion. What is it doing here? What does it want from her? She stands up from the couch, surprised at how holding her hand so stiffly close to her body affects her balance. She needs to do a little skip to keep herself upright and then she is stable, her feet planted on the green rug.

Knowing she will find no way out, but still obliged to search, she steps from the rug. Her socks are loose about her feet, and she walks slowly across the floorboards, careful not to slip. She circuits the living room, so rudely familiar, and tries to see it with fresh eyes. White pipes run above the skirting boards connecting radiators. Furniture convenes with the walls. A bookshelf idles between the two locked windows; a sideboard keeps watch from the far side of the room. Four chairs press up against the dining table, holding vigil upon the untouched breakfast. Fruit performs a still life on the kitchen bench; Andi has left the milk out by the refrigerator. Opening a drawer, she reveals the cutlery resting in its bays, but she closes it quickly, jumping at its rattle. Nothing seems to mean anything; she cannot understand what it is all for.

In the bathroom everything is cold. The tube of toothpaste is clammy in her hand, the bar of soap appears dry, but when she takes it from its dish its bottom is soggy to touch. Surely the soap is useful; she could rub it against something, make something come loose, and take her leave. She returns it to its dish. In the bedroom her socks catch on the matting, and she opens the wardrobe, hoping for a Narnia escape. But the wardrobe holds only clothes; her imagination is not rich enough for this situation.

She lies on the bed, her bandaged hand stretched out and quarantined from harm, and closes her eyes. But the smell of the sheets is unforgiving; she feels the tears cooling on her cheeks before she realises she is crying. She pulls herself up from the bed, not bothering to wipe her face. She tries once more to open the front door, but it is still locked.

The television tower peers in at her through the living-room window, stoic as a prison guard. She thinks about drinking gin slings, she thinks of fun parks and bookstores. Why did she never think of this? Sun glints off the tower; arching an eyebrow, it is sceptical of her excuses. She curls into a ball on the couch, her toes digging into the cleft between the cushions. She is too scared to cry.

Andi takes three books from his locker and puts them in his bag. There is no one else in the staffroom. He does not want to go home, is not ready to face her just yet. He puts the books back in his locker, one at a time.

He has tried to make everything as normal as possible. After bandaging her hand, he had unpacked her bag, made room for her belongings amongst his own. Her clothes are so small in comparison to his. They had been twisted and folded into little bundles, and when he shook them out they released tiny clouds of her scent. These clothes know Clare better than he: all day they cling to her skin. He realises he cannot actually be jealous of clothes, but he feels something very similar, and it makes him uncomfortable.

He had gone to a hardware store and bought a tiny safe in which to keep his keys and his phone. The safe has a six-digit combination, and its simplicity pleases him — it makes him more certain that nothing will go wrong. He does not want to make this harder on either of them; he wants all of the possibilities to be erased and for normality to settle. He is amazed by how easy it has been to complete each step. To lock the door. To not leave a key. To take the SIM card. Each of these things is just a tiny action, but each one allows him to breathe a little easier.

When he leaves the apartment every morning for work, he places the safe in the stairwell. He does not want Clare cracking the combination in his absence, does not want to think about her trying. But at the moment she is not trying anything. It has been days since she last spoke to him, not a word since she hurt her hand, and he has given up hope of anything changing. The apartment is becoming a bell jar; there is no sound or movement between them. They could be living in completely different spaces, parallel universes, for all the attention she pays him. This is not how he wanted it to be. He is worried she might vanish completely and he does not know what to do.

'Andi! How are you? What's news?' Peter weaves his way through the field of chairs and tables to his own locker.

Andi looks at the book in his hand. He cannot remember if he wanted to take it with him or leave it here. 'Not much.

What about you?' Andi puts the book in his locker. He cannot concentrate enough to read it at home.

'Oh, you know, it's been pretty hectic.' Peter opens his locker and grabs his bag. 'Did you hear? Jana and I got engaged.'

'Congratulations!' Andi puts down his bag, shakes Peter's hand. 'I'm really happy for you both.'

'It's good, hey? We just thought, you know, that it was time.'

'It's great news.' And Andi realises that it is, because it's the excuse he needs to avoid going home. When he returned last night, the apartment was dim. Clare lay on the couch, facing away from him, and she did not move for the entire evening. Not when he patted her back, not when he asked her how her hand was. 'Do you want to go for a drink to celebrate?'

'Sorry, Andi, I can't. We have dinner with Jana's parents, and I'm already running late.' Peter gives him a grin. 'You know what it's like.'

'Of course.' He has no idea. He imagines dinner with Clare's parents. Does she even have parents? 'Well, another time. Congratulations, Peter.'

'Thanks.' Peter hurries to the door. '*Tschüss.*'

Andi takes up his bag and trails Peter out into the deserted corridor. He wanted to tell him about Clare, to share his news, but how can he? It would be the beginning of too many questions. What has he done? He cannot keep her locked in his apartment. It's ridiculous. And criminal. But what is the alternative? He cannot let her go. He just cannot. It's going to be alright — he knows it is.

He recalls Clare as she was, that very first day, reading in the square, and he is consumed by unadulterated pride. She is his. *She is home, she is waiting for me.* He pictures her bent over in laughter after their adventure through the theme park. The way she pulled him into the shower; her naked body on his bed. He thinks of bandaging her hand: how useless it was, lying there damaged. She needs him. He needs to be with her.

Each day while Andi is at work she unwraps the bandage. Holding her injured hand in the other as though to keep from dropping it to the floor, she turns it this way and that, inspecting it from all angles. She cannot quite believe that he did this to her, but the proof is irrefutable. For the first couple of days it was hideously swollen; it looked as though something inside was fighting to get out, and she wondered whether some part of her was permanently broken, not just displaced. But the swelling has receded, and she can see that it is not going to remain misshapen. She will be fine. Absolutely fine.

How can her body betray her like this? As the bruising fades, her hand reproaches her. *I'm doing okay*, it seems to say. *Why aren't you?* She finds herself bumping her hand on the tabletop as she walks around the apartment, looking for a way of escape. She lets it graze against the wall, knocks it against the windowsill, satisfied only when the pain asserts itself.

He had taken her hand. He had held it to his chest as though to comfort her. He had entwined his fingers with hers, as lovers do. She had tried to pull away. She wanted him to let go, to let her be. And that's when he had tugged down: her finger just gave way, like it was colluding with him. She had not experienced such pain before. It shot up her arm like fire, it stabbed into her belly, it shook at her knees. And just before she shut her eyes tight, white diamonds dancing across her eyelids, she saw his face. He was smiling. Wasn't he?

What went wrong? When should she have made a different decision? When they met? When she accepted the first strawberry? Of course, but she knows that she would do that again. When she stood behind him in the bookstore, was that it? Did he think her so alone that she needed this? Or when she went home with him, when she drank, when she undressed, when they fucked? But all of these she would do again, every single one of them. She racks her memory, but there is nothing there: not a single moment that acted as a warning that he was so unhinged. For this is what he must be.

But he cannot be. This is Andi — he is so ordinary. His way of taking her hand, his easy stride. He is like any other man. If it wasn't for the door ... It's there at the end of the hallway. Like a third person in the relationship: the one who watches, the only one who knows what's going on. With Andi at work, she finds herself drawn to the door. She lays her hand against it as though to discern a pulse, but it gives nothing away. Everything in this apartment is so resolute.

She thinks back to the days, so recently, before she met Andi. Everything seemed normal. She was tiring of travelling — she didn't like the way it made her feel as though real life was always happening elsewhere. But this is so much worse. When he leaves the apartment for work, she has to stop herself from calling out to him. *Take me with you*, she wants to cry. After the sounds of him have gone, she lifts herself from her bed on the couch and makes her routine tour of the apartment. She tries the door and each of the windows. She opens drawers and cupboards, stands in the centre of the living room turning slow circles and contemplating every object that she can see.

There must be a way, something he has not thought of.

She switches on the television, waiting to see a news report on her mysterious disappearance accompanied by a grainy photograph supplied by her mother. But the newsreaders carry on speaking in their low, sensible voices as if nobody has gone missing. As if she is nobody. She listens to the radio, wonders if there is any way of making it send out signals rather than just receive them. She wishes she knew more about how things worked. Locks and combinations and radios. The German voices seem to be taunting her — they drone on and on, refusing to be understood — and it is a relief when she finds a station that plays nonstop pop songs. It is the kind of music she would never have listened to before, but its familiarity soothes her. It is music from cafes and clothes stores, and she knows that out there other people are listening to it, too.

She bangs on the front door, creating a monotonous rhythm, interrupting it only to jolt the potential listener into action. She puts on her boots and kicks the door, again and again and again, resting her head against her arms, her foot swinging like a toy woodpecker. When this brings no results, she hits out the same beat with a spoon on the radiator. She thinks perhaps the sound will carry along the pipes, leak into someone else's apartment, and they will come upstairs to complain. But Andi says the building is empty, the other apartments uninhabited. If only the apartment faced onto the street: she could break a window, call out, wave until someone saw her. But the apartment is set well back in the block, far from the street and passing traffic. No one ever appears in the communal courtyard, and Andi's are the only footsteps ever heard in the stairwell.

She recalls a famous photograph from 1961 of an elderly

woman hanging out of the window of an apartment building on Bernauer Strasse. On one side of the street, the buildings sat in the East, but stepping out of their front doors meant entering the French sector of the West. Weeks after the barbed wire went up, marking the path of the future Berlin Wall, people were still trying to escape to the West from these buildings. The doors of the Bernauer Strasse apartments were blocked first; eventually the windows would be bricked over. In the photograph, a crowd waits on the cobbled street, a bedsheet stretched taut amongst them, ready to catch the desperate woman, while East German police try to haul her back in through the window. Clare does not know whether the woman survived.

Throughout the day, she tries to open the door, but it is always locked. It just keeps being locked, and nothing will make it change. She paces in the living room, or stares out the window, or sits crumpled in the corner of the couch. She pretends the door is not locked. That she is just sitting in her boyfriend's apartment, waiting for him to come home. The longer he is away, the more surely her disbelief in the situation dissipates in the apartment's close air; as Andi is reduced to vague memories, the good clouding the bad, she begins to wonder whether she has made the whole thing up. Yet when she fingers the bandage on her hand, her thoughts come to a teetering stop.

He thinks that Clare might be fading. She is becoming less herself, more like a stranger. He notices it when she lies on the couch, with only the top of her head visible to him above the armrest. Her hair looks like a neglected toy that has been dragged out, limp and matted, from behind a cupboard somewhere. He feels guilty; he is not looking after her properly. He has told her that she can use anything she likes in the apartment — what's his is hers — but she does not seem to touch anything. She eats when he is not there, at least he thinks she does, but she must take only tiny bites from everything, leaving little trace. She does not answer him when he talks to her. She has started to sleep on the couch, blankets and clothes woven around her like a nest.

He thinks about what to give her and what to take away. Are knives dangerous? Surely to confiscate those would be going too far. He wonders about keeping his laptop at school but instead guards it with a password. And pens? Should he get rid of those? He fears what she might write down, what kind of memories she will create for herself if she keeps a record. He tiptoes around the apartment one night, gathering them together into a rubber-banded bouquet that he dumps in a bin on the way to school in the morning. Better safe than sorry.

He removes the sleeping pills from the cutlery drawer in the kitchen, but knows he may need them again, so he takes them to school to store in his locker. When he had given them to her after their night at the fun park, he'd had no particular plan: he just knew that he did not want her exploring the city on her own. He had crushed up the pills, four of them, and stirred them into her cup of tea. When her head had begun to nod, he had undressed her and helped her to bed. She had slept through most of the next day, was still in bed when he arrived home. That was when it first began to seem possible: he could make sure she would always be there.

She has not spoken to him in almost a week when one evening he finds her cross-legged on the couch, the safe in her lap. With her bandaged hand she holds the metal box steady and with the other she punches in numbers.

'Why are you doing that?' She does not look up. 'Do you know how many possible combinations there are?'

She does not answer him; he does not expect her to. He walks over to her and takes the safe. She does not hand it to him, but she offers no resistance; it is as though the safe glides from her clasp to his.

'Don't touch it again.' Worrying that he sounds too gruff, he strokes her hair. He almost expects it to come away in his hands.

She shudders at his touch. He feels the movement race through her and he gently presses down on her skull, tries to stop it from leaving her body and entering his own.

'Clare, please. Come on. Talk to me, sweetie. We can talk about this.'

He has taken to delivering monologues in her direction, trying to make her understand. 'It's not that I want to keep you here,' he explains. 'It's just that I'm so worried that you will leave. It's not a punishment — you have not done anything wrong. It just removes the possibility of you leaving. It means we can concentrate on what we have together right now. And I'm just as much tied to you as you to me. I must return to the apartment every day to care for you, to bring you what you need.'

He wishes things would go back to the way they were, but they do not. You cannot always have what you wish for. He goes to bed alone and lies awake, desperate for sounds of Clare moving about the apartment. But there are none; the nights trade in the very same silence as the days.

When he talks to her, a chorus starts up in her head. *Don't listen to him, Clare. Don't talk to him.* She can hear the voice of her mother, and that of her sister. The voices of the architects she used to work with, the student she took on as an assistant. They talk over one another, raising their voices; some become louder and more adamant, others talk quietly but steadily. They all tell her to keep calm, to not get upset. She tries to isolate any one of them, but as soon as she identifies a voice, somebody else speaks up, drowns the first voice out. Once they start, she cannot hear a word that Andi says, and for this she is thankful.

'It's for the best,' he is saying now, and the voices begin, telling her she will be okay, she just has to think. There must be a way out. She watches him speak at her, and she has no idea who he is.

At night, after Andi has gone to bed, the voices turn on her. *What have you done?* they ask. *How did you end up here? What were you thinking? How could you be so stupid?* She tries to apologise, to explain that Andi seemed so normal — she was not to know. *You went home with him*, they scorn her. *You didn't have any idea who he was. How could you?*

She is unable to sleep; it is as though her body has no need for it. She wraps herself in blankets, burrows her head into the corner of the couch, a pillow jammed on top, hoping the heat will lull her. Instead she sweats, her skin crawls, and she throws the blankets onto the floor until the chill sets in. Her body will not let her sleep; it keeps dragging her back, forcing her to continue with her thoughts.

She is not used to being so sedentary. During the day she walks the apartment, up and down the hallway, a circuit of the living room. She wants to climb atop the furniture, throw herself at the walls. She feels as though her skin is too small for her. Her limbs have forgotten how to swing in time; her feet knock against each other. She flicks the fingertips of her unbandaged hand repeatedly. She cannot be still, and yet she is sure she is not moving. When she sits, she finds herself rocking back and forth, her eyes refusing to focus on anything. It doesn't matter how deeply she breathes, she feels she is not getting enough oxygen. Her lungs seem to have shrunk to nothing, like they know they will never inhale fresh air again. She sits by the pot plant and concentrates on her breathing, willing her lungs not to give up. All she wants is to give up.

On Saturday morning, he makes her breakfast, setting out the cheese and fruit, slicing things onto her plate. But she won't join him at the table, and his lone chewing is the only sound in the room. When he puts the stereo on, he notices that she waits until he goes to the bathroom then switches it off. He is reminded of breakfast with his father, both of them with their heads bowed to the newspaper, their eyes tracking across the page as their hands ferried food and drink to their mouths. When his mother had been there, breakfast was different — she would take slices of cheese from his father's board when he wasn't paying attention, slap his wrist in jest when he tried to do the same to her. She would pour herself the powdered orange drink that stood in for juice but never drink it, reaching only for the coffee and complaining about the taste. And she could peel the eggs faster than Andi or his father ever could, even when they had just been lifted from boiling water.

But Clare does not touch her breakfast, and soon his anticipation for the weekend is curtailed — he had been looking forward to them spending time together. Still, he is sure she will start to speak to him soon. Hemmed in by her indifference, he busies himself around the apartment. He plays records and changes them after a single track. When he scrubs the kitchen and the bathroom, revelling in the sharp smell of the bleach that makes his eyes water and his head spin, she turns off the stereo, leaving him to hum his own tunes.

After the apartment is clean, he sits on the arm of the couch and tries to reason with her, but she leans away from him, her eyes closed, nursing her hand in its grubby bandage. It is as though he is not even there. He has a sudden urge to form his hand into a fist, to punch it into the door that has caused all of this trouble and to feel its unmoving response reverberate up his arm and assure him of his being.

'Maybe we should take that off?' He reaches for the bandage, and she shrinks back, their hands performing an orderly tease, all the yearning leached away. The dressing is stained and it smells like wet dog, a pungency that makes him think of the U-Bahn in winter.

'How about I put a new bandage on for you?' He is ashamed of his pleading voice and overcomes it by defiantly reaching for her hand. This time she does not resist but nor does she help. He is touching her. As her fingertips brush the palm of his hand, he is reminded of the way she would hold his face when they kissed. It feels like so long ago. Watching her face for signs of pain, he slowly unwraps the bandage. It has frayed at the end: the outer lengths of it are grey and tie-dyed with water marks as though she has been measuring rising tides in his absence. Her fingers are wrinkled, and shadows of yellow and indigo bloom from her palm.

'Oh, Clare!' He strokes her fingers; he can feel the bone through her skin where it gathers at her knuckles. He rests her hand in her lap and goes to the bathroom where he soaks a washcloth and rubs it with soap. Bringing it back, along with a towel and a length of bandage, he cleans her hand, dabbing between each finger. He wraps her hand in the clean bandage, binding her fingers back together for safekeeping.

'All done.'

At this, she takes possession of her hand and places it in her lap. He breathes the ripe, unwashed smell of her and wants to strip her of her clothes, take her in his arms. But he knows she does not want this; he is afraid that she will let him.

Her silence eventually drives him to action. He opens the safe, takes his jacket from the hook and slips out the door, ashamed of his relief as he locks it behind him. On the street, people are gaily partaking in their Saturday afternoons. Long lunches, bicycles balanced with groceries. He thinks of paying a visit to his father; they could drink beer in the weak afternoon sun and talk about … They have nothing to talk about. Except his mother, and she's not there to correct them when they get it wrong. He imagines his mother joining them at the bar near his father's house. Would she laugh at their jokes, try to impress them with tales of her travels? He cannot remember her voice, has no idea whether she speaks through her mouth or her nose. In his mind, she has become like the mother of a *Wessi* girlfriend he once had: her skin taut, her hair shining and not moving, her jewellery banging on the table as she reaches for her drink.

He is looking for a free table at his favourite cafe when he sees Ulrike. How long has it been? A year? Longer? As he debates walking on to a different cafe, she notices him then looks away. She stares at the newspaper propped against the napkin canister in front of her, and he waits for her to look up again. When she does not, he walks over.

'Ulrike.'

'Oh. Hi, Andi.' She picks up her knife and a piece of bread then puts them both back down.

'How are you?'

'Good, thanks. And you?'

'Good, thanks.' He waits patiently for her to ask him another question. Eventually she does.

'How's work?'

'Not bad.' Surely there is more to talk about? In the past, he had spent hours in his apartment waiting for Ulrike to return from nights out with friends, dinners with her sisters. Hours of just waiting and wondering what she was doing every minute that she was away from him. And now he cannot think of a single thing that he wants to know about her.

'Um.' She looks at the empty chair that sits opposite her. 'I'm expecting someone.'

'Oh.' He moves aside, and the sunlight reaches Ulrike's face, causing her to squint. 'Anyone I know?'

'No.' She looks back at her breakfast board, takes a bite of bread. 'It was nice seeing you though.'

He notices how the sun picks out grey hairs amongst the

brown; she is looking more like her mother than ever, and he wonders whether he should tell her this. He should not. He decides to eat somewhere else.

After lunch he walks until he finds himself in the busy anonymity of Alexanderplatz, as people rush around him. Now that he is away from Clare he misses her; he wants to be back in the apartment, things as they were. He thinks about returning home and opening the door, leaving it open and letting her walk away. But then he would not see her again, and he cannot bear the thought of that. What would she do, if she left now? She would report him to the police; he would end up in jail. He imagines his father coming to bail him out, the way they would not embrace, his father would ask no questions. But he doesn't plan on keeping her trapped forever; it's just until she understands. And then she can come and go as she pleases. She will want to return. It just takes time. Time and effort and things will come right.

He will buy her a book. This thought cheers him. But what? The Klimt monograph sits unopened on the coffee table, though he suspects she looks at it when he is not there. In the first bookstore that he encounters, he loiters by the art section, continually looking over his shoulder as if to find her there, waiting for him to take her home. He moves to the photography section, flips through a book on the Bauhaus school. But he cannot tell if the photographs are good or not, and he does not want to get it wrong.

He overhears a customer ask for the English book section. Perfect. He will buy her a novel, something she has not read before. He follows the man to the back of the store, and they stand side-by-side, their heads craned, reading the titles on the spines. But he has the same problem: he does not know what she likes or what she has already read. They do not know enough about each other yet; there is so much to learn.

He has almost scanned all the titles when he comes across it on the bottom shelf. *Anna Karenina*. Something about it seems just right. Has she mentioned it? But of course. That's how he found her, knew that she was not quite ready to walk away. He went to the train station because she had told him how she loved the directness of train travel, the way the journeys have a distinct beginning and end, the tracks leading the way and the train dutifully following. And that day she had not been ready to leave — she is still not ready to leave — so he had trailed behind, a lonely caboose, and brought her back.

At the time, her easy assurance rankled him. Her impudence. As he dashed across the streets trying not to roll his ankle on the cobblestones, he was furious at her for leaving without saying goodbye. Yet as soon as he saw her on the platform he realised: she did not say goodbye because she knew that he would follow, that they were not done yet. She stood there so composed and in charge while he was jerked about, a marionette without a stage, embarrassed at his heaving chest, yesterday's rumpled clothes. She just knew.

When they fucked for the second time, she whispered fiercely in his ear, 'Harder, Andi, harder. I want to come all over at once.' He was wary at first, the simultaneous resistance and yielding of her body made him uneasy, but then he gave in, pushed harder and harder, wanted to do exactly as she said. He followed her directions.

And now she waits at home for him. He buys *Anna Karenina* and leaves the store feeling light. He will go to the market, take his time to choose food she might like or that she may not have tried before. *She is home, she is waiting for me.*

The bandage on her hand is clean and tight and, reluctantly, she admits that this makes her feel a little better. Hopeful. She hears the familiar sounds of Andi returning. The key shifting in the lock, the open and shut of the door, the key in the lock again. Precise and without ceremony. Andi's footsteps coming down the hallway. She looks out the window. *One, two; one, two.* The lights on the television tower blink steadily. *One, two; one, two.* They don't hesitate. She hears him coming up behind her. *One, two; one, two.* She imagines him doing a quickstep through the lounge room. Sweeping her into his arms, through the door and down the stairs into the courtyard, the leaves now brown and soggy beneath their feet. It feels like it has been months; it has only been a week.

When he places a book in her lap, she instinctively picks it up and then wishes she had not. She wants to remain in control, but all the books in his apartment are in German — their content unavailable to her, they have become objects, more like building bricks than stories — and her eyes go straight to the book; she cannot help it.

The greatest love story ever told, the cover declares, and she almost laughs: if that is the case every potential lover in the world should give up now. She wants to thank him, an automatic politeness, but she is not ready to speak. Her tongue feels heavy and useless in her mouth. It slouches against the crevices between her teeth. Why is he being so nice to her? He hates her; he is keeping her prisoner. As he sits himself beside her on the couch, her heart quickens. She wishes it didn't, but it does. Why does her body keep betraying her like this? For it is not fear that she feels but anticipation. She knows because she waits for her stomach to begin its tricks, for the disgust to rise in her throat, but it does not. She feels like she is lying in a bathtub, her ears underwater, the noises amplified. She wants him to explain everything to her, and she wants to listen, to believe him and then to take her leave.

'All happy families are alike ...' he says. He reaches out his hand to her as if to stroke her cheek, offers her a grimace of shared understanding.

Surely he cannot be thinking this applies to them? Who the fuck is he? Her stomach leaps, and she follows it off the couch, throwing the book on the floor.

'That's love, Andi!' She points at the book. 'Not this. I'm not a character. You can't make me be the person you want. Just let me go!' She turns to face him where he is seated on the couch, one leg tucked beneath him, his hand drawn back as though he has been burned.

'I want you to be happy, Clare.'

'I am happy!' It's a sentence never made to be yelled, and in the silence that follows she thinks that this is it, he will let her go. But he says nothing, and she stretches to fill the quiet. 'I was happy. I don't want to be here, Andi. Can't you understand that?' Her voice shrinks as she ends the sentence — she has never felt so forlorn. But he does not understand. He has no idea.

He gets up from the couch, offers her a shrug. 'You came here, Clare. You could have left, a number of times, and yet you stayed. We have been so happy together. We will be so happy.'

She wishes she had something to throw at him but instead she hurls herself, drumming at his chest with her fists, pain stabbing at her injured hand. She wants to hurt him, she wants to beat him down until he is nothing.

'Just let me go, Andi! Let me go!'

He grabs at her arms, tries to turn her from him, and she reaches for his face, wanting to scrape away that mouth, those eyes. But as his fingers squeeze at her arms she springs away — she cannot bear his hands on her.

'Don't touch me!' She faces him. Her chest is heaving.

'Clare —'

But she cuts him off, shakes her bandaged hand at him like a talisman, warning him to back away. 'Don't you say my name. Don't say anything to me. I hate you for this, Andi. You disgust me.'

His face crumples at her words, his slack hands pulling at his shoulders as if they were guy ropes. She runs from the room, but there is nowhere to go. She's furious at herself for reacting; she's back at square one, feels like she has missed a turn. She does not want him to make her feel like this; she does not want him to make her feel anything at all. She stands in the hallway, wanting to throw herself at the walls, to break something, to scream, but all she can do is stalk into the bathroom, slamming the door. Dropping to the floor she wants to sob, but the tears do not come.

He opens the book to the title page: she didn't even see the dedication. *Liebe Clare, To romance and forever, Andi*. Why does she not see he wants only what is best? Reading it now he realises how stupid it sounds, how inappropriate, and he tears the page from the binding, crumples it in his hand. What has he done?

He can hear her crying in the bathroom. His chest contracts, and he locks the door behind him and charges down the stairs. In the courtyard he takes greedy breaths, free of her cigarette smoke that deadens the air. She hates him. How did it come to this?

He walks the streets trying to keep up with his thoughts. He should let her go; it was a stupid idea; what was he thinking? But if he lets her go, he won't be able to make it right. She will be lost to him, and he will be without. She is so obviously alone in the world. She needs him. She has put him in an impossible situation.

He thinks of Peter and Jana, the way they fight and taunt each other. He remembers Ulrike: how desperate he was for her to leave each morning; how he would sit in the bathroom with the shower running for half an hour, hoping that by the time he came out she would be gone. When it was finally over he had gathered her belongings, squeezed her clothes into a duffle bag and stacked her books into boxes he had pilfered from the grocery store across the street. Glad of something practical to do, he had gone through the rooms, taking down anything that was hers and packing up their shared memories — the requisite holiday photographs, gifts she bestowed upon him. It was all neatly lined up in the hallway when she returned, climbing slow-footed up the stairs, and he had retired to the couch with a beer. He heard the door open, waited for Ulrike to appear.

He remembers making out the low hum of voices, the

scuffling of boxes being lifted, the footsteps in the stairwell. He thought she must be packing her car first, would come in to say a final goodbye when she was done. He would give her room, let her move at her own pace. It was only when the door closed the second time that he realised she was leaving; she must not have known he was in the living room, waiting for her. He ran to the stairs, could hear her down below.

'Ulrike?' His call did not even bother to echo. It dropped down into the centre of the stairwell, where it must have reached her ears, for her footsteps paused.

'Ulrike? Aren't we going to say goodbye?'

Her footsteps had resumed. He heard the outer door swing open then shut.

'Ulrike?' He called out her name again as though her real self might be wavering, waiting behind as her ventriloquist footsteps continued their journey.

But there was no response. She had not even thanked him for packing, and he was genuinely surprised by this — it was not like her. He was the one who had done the right thing. He had realised the relationship was going nowhere and he had let her go, let both of them free.

Walking faster now, he finds his thoughts swinging back to Clare. To let her go would be to put their relationship on the same level as what he'd had with Ulrike. The way Clare stood so closely by him in the bookstore, how she patiently waited on the platform for him to arrive: it is no accident that they met. This relationship is like nothing he has ever known. But knowing this truth does not make it any easier.

When she leaves the bathroom, the apartment is empty, and the front door is locked. When Andi has not returned by midnight, and desperate for the kind of enveloping sleep that the couch denies, she considers sleeping in his bed. But she does not want to be there when he comes back. Surely he will come back.

The springs of the couch make themselves known as she rolls from one side to the other. The morning light, as insipid as it is, offers her a new day, and she watches the darkness lift and form the shapes of the various pieces of furniture that will accompany her through this day as they have each one before.

'Andi?' She creeps from the couch, stepping quietly so as not to wake him.

His bed is empty. It has not been slept in. She does not know what to think about this — her mind refuses to engage. She tries the door. Locked. She eats some cereal, the only food she seems to be able to keep down at the moment. Quickly spooning the flakes into her mouth, before they become soggy, she can feel the milk trickling down her chin. She doesn't wipe it away. It will drip to her t-shirt, just as it did yesterday, where it will dry into a cloud shape, nestled like a pendant between her breasts. In the lounge room, she puts on a record. Edith Piaf's voice is familiar enough to buoy her against her surrounds, but it is not right; it makes her think of summer nights, iced tea with gin, and other forms of restless happiness. Instead she puts on an album by Air — the thin music says nothing to her — and she rolls a cigarette and waits. But Andi does not return.

She does not want to see him again yet she is on tenterhooks for the sound of his key in the door. What will happen if he never comes back? *I want him, I want him not.* How is it possible to desire something she does not want? For him to never return, while dreading that he will not.

If he does not come back, she will die. She surprises herself with feeling nothing for this outcome, and she prods the thought repeatedly as though to assure herself she is actually thinking it. Does she not feel anything because she does not believe it? Or because she knows she cannot do anything about it? Or — and this notion interests her more than those of death — is her body tired of reacting to her feelings, insulted by her recent ignoring of its alerts? She feels physically ill when she sees Andi, yet she longs for him to come home. Perhaps her body has given up on her, is refusing to play the necessary charades with her mind to interpret her emotions. She tries again to reflect on whether she feels anything at the thought of dying. Her body is silent, and she taunts it with details, trying to get a rise. How long will it take? Three weeks? Four? Because if he does not return, it will happen. There is no way out of this apartment, no one to hear her calls, no way of reaching the outside world. She will starve to death.

Will she allow herself to do this? She imagines her body might refuse. Why should it be so punished by her decision to accompany Andi home in the first place? It just came along, it participated, but it did not lead. But even if her body refuses to die, it could not continue living, not under the circumstances. She suspects that at some stage she would break a window and drop herself from it. Not having eaten, her body would lightly drift to the ground, swinging from side to side on stray gusts of wind, her mind following like a parachute.

Maybe that's what Andi is doing right now, sourcing something to kill her with. What would he use? An axe? A gun? The words are too small for the horror of the required action.

And the whole possibility seems too messy to be probable. How would he dispose of her body? The difficulty of this task gives her hope. Because the body is never properly disposed of: it is always found. And if they find the body they find out who did it — this is a truth of modern science. But by then it would be too late to save her. So why is she not more afraid?

She leaves her cereal bowl in the sink. Andi will wash the dishes; he does them every night. And for this reason it seems unlikely that he will not return, or that when he does, he will kill her. He is a normal person: he does the dishes every day. What to do next? She should take a shower, but then she would feel like she is preparing to go somewhere, so she does not.

Sitting on the windowsill she wonders whether many people use the binoculars on the observation deck of the television tower. Can they see her? She waves. She could make an SOS message, a tale of despair written on a bedsheet and hung in the window. But she doubts any of the tourists up there would take any notice — she is too far away. She certainly didn't. She was too busy cracking witty one-liners, lavishing Andi with charm and being thankful that he did not let her get on that train.

How did she let it come to this? She made him fall for her: why has she not made him change his mind? She hears the arrogance of this belief, but recognises its accuracy. She did not force him to be captivated by her, but she did set out to beguile. It is like a game, that first attraction, and she knows how to play. She fed off his enthralment and made a conscious decision to win him over. To place all of the blame on Andi for this situation would be disingenuous. Staring out at the building opposite, she plays this thought back through her mind again, reconsidering each of its parts. Yes, she wanted him to want her. And now here she is, wanting him not to, wanting only to be away.

So why has she not yet made him despise her? She puts those earlier thoughts aside and picks up this one, shaking it out. It is like trying to fold a fitted sheet. First, she has to find the corners and then she must wind the thought over on itself. And if it comes out too lumpy to be shelved, she must shake it out and begin again. Why has she not made him let her go? She has gone about this the wrong way. She should have been wailing and complaining for hours on end, making her entrapment as uncomfortable as possible for him. But she has been silent. As though she does not want to bother him. Is it because she harbours hope that this cannot continue for much longer? Or that she does not quite believe that this is happening? But she knows these are not the reasons. It is because she cannot purge herself of the knowledge that she is partly responsible for being here and something in her feels obliged to see it out. And with this, her body finally unites with her mind. Her stomach churns; she is disgusted with herself.

Darkness has settled long before she hears the key in the lock, and her trembles involuntarily begin. She draws her knees to her chest and seizes her ankles, futilely trying to smother her bodily quake. Her body's every reaction is so prominent, as though to remind her of its renewed presence. And yet, still it feels as though it belongs to someone else, that it is on loan to provide her company through her static days. She hugs herself and knows: this is when it is going to happen. Either way this will be the end, and she braces herself for the horror that is to come.

'Are you still up?' Andi sticks his head through the living-room doorway.

She freezes in her armoured pose, waits for his steady steps across the room, waits for a blow, for pain to spread from a point of impact and to encompass every part of her. But his footsteps retreat, the bedroom door closes, and she lets herself go. Her legs splay and drop towards the floor, her arms flop at her side, and her whole body quivers, a soundless harp.

When Clare finally speaks, her voice falls out into the quiet of the apartment. 'What are we going to do?'

It takes him a moment to find her in the room. He is so used to her silence he is not sure where her voice is coming from. Then he sees her feet hanging over the end of the couch, and when he doesn't give her an answer her head lifts from the cushions. She sounds just as he remembers but she looks different. Different from what? From how he sees her in his mind, he answers his own inquisition. From the real Clare.

'What are we going to do?' She repeats the question. She is facing him but she is looking above him, addressing some part of him that is standing behind, and so he stands.

'What do you mean?'

In response, she sighs. Her hair looks greasy and squashed to her head. He is ashamed that he has not been paying her more attention. He feels cheated. Why did she not tell him that she would change if he was not looking closely enough? She has become like an indifferent house pet, not noticing when he comes or goes. It wasn't how he expected things to be, but he found comfort in the quietness of each day. It never seemed necessary to make a decision about the future.

Since her outburst when he gave her the book, she has said nothing. More than two weeks. That night, he had stayed at his father's apartment, half-heartedly trying to return to his childhood and fervently wishing his present was not happening. Why had he locked the door? Why could he not unlock it now? He had hoped that when he returned to the apartment the next day things would be different, had even hoped that she might have somehow escaped, leaving him miserable yet relieved. But everything remained the same. She went back to not speaking to him, not doing anything when he was in the room. The last fortnight has been an uninterrupted collection of Clare's silence and his own pleading monologues, both tinged with the dullness of familiarity.

But when she speaks, she is anything but familiar, and he waits, breath held and not wanting to put a foot wrong, for her next words.

'Well, what next? Now that we're here, what's going to happen next?'

There *will* be a next. Faced with this revelation, he realises he has no idea. He has given no thought to how this will be. 'Nothing will happen. This is enough, isn't it?'

Her voice has drawn him across the room to the couch where he squats in front of her. Her mustiness huddles around them both, daring him to touch her. He reaches out a hand and places it on her knee, which twitches in response. Is she trying to pull away? Her leg is cool. It begins to jerk up and down beneath his hand. She is shaking — her whole body is blurry. Tears begin to run down her nose, trailing into her mouth; it is a watercourse they know well.

'Don't cry, Clare.' He can feel the tears pricking his own eyes; it pains him to have upset her. He can feel something rising in his throat. Can a weight rise? Would it not sink? He can feel it aching there. He swallows. Why won't everything just be normal?

'Don't cry, sweetie. There's nothing to cry about. I'm here. I'll look after you. There's nothing to be afraid of.' He lifts his hand from her knee and puts it on her shoulder. It feels improbably large, and he raises it a little — he does not want to be holding her down. He understands the clichés now: a burden is a terrible thing to bear.

She looks at him. What does she see? He squeezes her shoulder. Her eyes are large and growing as though they will suck him whole into her gaze. She needs him, and her desperation pulls him forward. He wraps his arms around her, dispelling her stale smell. She is tiny, so easy to break. 'It will be alright. It will be okay.'

Beneath the unwashed body, she is the girl from the bookstore. His throat aches as her body folds into his own. The record on the stereo comes to its end; he hears its futile spinning as the needle swoops away. Her shaking has stopped — or is he simply holding her too tight? He loosens his grip, registers the ache in his knees. His neck is craned too far forward to be comfortable, but her arms are clasped around him.

'Come on, Clare, let's clean you up, shall we? You will feel better, I promise.' He disentangles himself and pulls her to her feet by her good hand. The stereo speakers hiss static at them as they pass. In the bathroom he makes to release her hand, but she holds his firmly. With his free hand he unwraps her bandage, and as it spirals to the floor, he sees the bruising has disappeared. He lets go of Clare's hand to help her take off her clothes, but she clutches at his arm, trying not to lose her balance when she steps out of her jeans. He moves around her, reaches in and turns on the shower. Only when she is underneath the water does she completely let him go.

She places both hands on the tiled wall as he rubs her body with soap. Her legs seem shorter than he remembered. Her torso is longer. He has forgotten her body, and yet it feels so familiar. Her skin has a yellow tinge to it. Waxy, like potato but softer. He washes her all over. He squirts shampoo into his hands and massages it into her hair. Still fully dressed, he feels his wet sleeves cling to his arms. A trickle of cooling water runs down his side. The foam slides out of her hair, along her body and swirls about her feet. She brings her hands up to her face, rubs away the soap, combs fingers through her hair.

'Hold me,' she says.

And he steps into the shower, his black socks alien next to her sea-shell toes, his head at rest upon her shoulder.

She pulls on a woollen jumper that has been discarded on the floor by the couch. The apartments on either side, above and below, are empty. Unheated, they don't act as very good insulation, and in the mornings it takes the apartment time to warm up.

When she was thirteen, her science teacher told the class that if you had enough cups of hot coffee you could heat a room. That the steam they gave off would be enough to keep you warm. At the time she wondered why the teacher didn't simply use hot water as an example; she had been too young to know the great significance of coffee in adults' lives. Even now she never can tell what is good coffee and what is not. She just agrees with whomever she is drinking with.

She takes a cup of coffee now and wraps her hands around it. It is too hot to sip. She puts it on the floor then pours a second cup. She puts this one by her feet as well. She is careful not to spill. They have seven cups in the apartment — it should be enough. She places the percolator back on the range and feels the steam from the two cups on the floor kiss at her ankles. She wonders how many it would take to warm the apartment and where the cups could be stored during summer. She is glad she drinks her coffee black now. If she had to add milk, it would cool them down considerably. Though maybe it wouldn't. Maybe the milk would act as an insulating layer, keeping the heat of the coffee in. Who can say?

She places a third and a fourth cup of coffee on the floor, but notices the first two cups are looking cool. She crouches down and puts her hand over them; she cannot discern any heat. She feels like a paramedic looking for signs of life. If she had a small mirror she would hold it to the cup, as to a dying person's mouth to see if there is any breath to steam up the mirror. No mist; the coffee has passed. She tips it down the sink and pours from the pot again. It might well be a fruitless task, but she will persevere. There is a pub near her old house in Melbourne called The Perseverance. Right across the road from The Labor in Vain. She remembers long afternoons spent on The Labor's rooftop garden, dodging the sun from beneath canvas umbrellas and hoping against reason that Monday would fail to roll around. She wonders whether she shall ever go back there.

After two hours and twenty minutes of trying many combinations (half-filling all the mugs, arranging a newly filled mug by an older mug, and so on and so forth), she gives up. She is a little warmer than before, probably from all of the bending and crouching. And at least she is closer to the end of the day. She could spend her whole life doing this; she could measure out her life in coffee spoons. Her hands pouring the coffee down the sink are so pale: the freckles have faded; she is losing her detail. When she stands on tiptoe to put the percolator back on the shelf, her feet wobble with the effort. She clenches her knees, tries to keep steady, but her muscles waver and let go. Perhaps her body will just give up — so little is required of it here.

She continues with her exploration of the apartment. She has taken it upon herself to investigate every single thing in the space, to look in every cupboard, open every jar. She has completed the circuit twice now and while so far she has found nothing unusual, she continues unperturbed. The explanation will be hiding somewhere. Beneath the kitchen sink, she finds a bag of tealight candles from IKEA. Holding the bag's slack weight in her hand, she contemplates how, at the beginning of the year, she was holding an identical item. The two bags would have come from the same factory, one ending up in her house in Melbourne, the other stowed beneath Andi's sink. If only she could be sealed up in a bag and delivered without ceremony back into her own life. It seems unfair that these inanimate objects can travel the world while she is so confined.

She rips open the bag and takes a handful of candles. She puts them in a row along the bookshelf, another along the windowsill. As she lights each one, the flames rise up towards the ceiling. She thinks of her old house. It featured similar high ceilings, except the walls were broken about a foot from the top by picture rails, and she had spent many rainy weekends trawling op shops for prints to hang from them.

The walls of Andi's apartment are bare. When she asked him why, he laughed. 'I've got you to look at. Anything else would be a distraction.'

His open admiration of her is unnerving. But it also brings her comfort: it means she is safe, he does not want to hurt her. His arrival home each day seems to afford him great relief, which she comes to share. His reluctance to leave each morning is painful to witness. His Lost Boy eyes make her feel guilty for putting him through this. She has to wait until he is busy, tiptoe down the hallway to the front door and attempt to open it, reminding herself that she is the one in danger, that he holds all of the cards. Yet every time she touches the door, panic sets in, eased only by consoling herself with how much Andi needs her and that surely he will not hurt her.

She watches, mesmerised, as the flames flicker, cheered by movement that is not her own. She lays out more candles, creates dashed lines of fire through the apartment, relieving the dark of the winter afternoon. The candles look cheesy, like strewing rose petals all over a marital bed, but there is no doubt that they are beautiful. Andi will like them; she hopes he returns soon. She stretches her arms to the ceiling, watching her shadow grow taller, her hands waving like foliage. In the candlelight her belly button is a bruise of shadow across her stomach. In the window glass she sees her charcoal snowman eyes.

He leaves his father in the kitchen drying each utensil and piece of crockery with a tea towel, scorning Andi's suggestion to just place them in the rack. It has been snowing all evening, and despite having run out of things to say, he does not yet want to face the icy trek to the station and home. Clare is speaking to him again, but things are still not right. Sometimes he asks her a question, and she stares at him blankly — his words don't always register. Late at night she crawls into his bed and curls there, not touching him. He finds he cannot sleep without her there, stays alert until she leaves her nest of blankets on the couch; sometimes daylight is already nudging at the window. In the morning he lets his arm rest across her back, so awake he feels he will never need to sleep again. He comes to his father's to escape his own anxiety, until the pervasive loneliness pushes him back home.

On the pretext of looking for some cherished childhood treasure, Andi heads to the spare room, a city of cardboard-box towers that wait for attention, unlabelled and unpacked.

It is only after he has opened a few of the boxes that he realises: they are his mother's belongings. He had always thought the room was full of his childhood possessions and the excess of his father's library. Seeing all of the boxes there makes him furious. His mother didn't want these things — why does his father keep them? And if she was so willing to be rid of her husband and her son, why didn't she just fold them up, squeeze them into one of the cardboard receptacles, and tape down the flaps?

He picks at the tape of another box, and it comes away with barely a whisper. Inside are paperback books — their pages yellowed — and records, which he pulls out, flicking through each one. The Puhdys. Karat. City. Silly. The names haul him straight back to his childhood. They were bands that seemed to disappear as soon as the Wall came down, or hung around as overnight has-beens. And despite his anger, he laughs to think of his own mother once listening to these records. He pictures her playing air guitar in the kitchen, letting loose, her black hair flying about her face. He will take the records home to show Clare; she will have never heard anything like it.

Looking through another box he comes across a camera. Its clunky body is surprisingly light, the button making a satisfying click when he presses it down. Somewhere in the boxes will be its spawn, the albums full of Polaroids, stuck down and captioned. His father would dutifully bring the camera out at every birthday and Christmas, Andi's smile frozen throughout the years. The only time his father appeared was in the occasional shot taken at an awkward arm's length on one of their hikes, his father's mouth caught in the top of the frame, level with Andi's curly hair.

Without telling his father, Andi takes the camera back with him to his apartment. Now every day before leaving for work he takes a Polaroid of Clare, which he stows in his work diary. He stands close enough to her so that the frame is filled with her face; he is amazed by how different she looks each day. He finds himself glancing at the photograph throughout the day, flipping through his diary in class, using her image to mark the page of the book he does not read on the train. He has come to rely on the Polaroids more than he presumed he would, liking how he can stare into her grey eyes and she cannot look away, cannot blink. He inspects every one of her features, guesses at the way they pull together to give her each of her expressions.

He wonders who else has hoarded photographs of her and whether they realise what they have given up. There is so much to find out, always more to discover.

He knows that what he is doing is wrong. And he knows that she is displeased. No, more than that. She does not respect him. But she does not understand him either, and this gives him hope because one day she will — people can learn. He is doing this out of love. The joy he feels when he comes home to her is so immense as to be terrifying. He can no longer remember what it was like to be alone in his apartment, cannot recall any reasons he would like to be so. Everything in his life is tied up with Clare. Each day he tries to show her who he really is, and he knows that one day, not too far away, she will see him properly.

Clare feels like she is not existing. But the toothpaste tube is getting flatter, the bin in the kitchen slowly filling up, her hair is getting longer, and all of these things remind her that she is. It comforts her to think that at some point someone will come looking for her. It frightens her to wonder how long this might take and who it might be. She supposes it will be her mother. Clare had been carefree with her correspondence home while travelling. At the time it felt blithe, but now it seems foolish. She has sent only two postcards to her mother since leaving Australia, one just days before she arrived in Berlin. She imagines her mother receiving each one, absent-mindedly reading the back and attaching the card to the fridge, where it gets covered by takeaway menus and bills. It will be months before her mother realises she has not heard from Clare, longer before she thinks to do anything about it. If her father was still alive he would come to look for her — that's what fathers do.

'My mother will be looking for me, Andi.' She watches him for a reaction, but he gives nothing away. If she was describing the situation to someone else, she would suggest that his body stiffened at her words, but this is conjecture.

'She'll be wondering why I haven't been in contact with her.'

'No, she won't.'

'Yes, she will. She will be expecting to have heard from me by now.'

'She has heard from you.' He does not look at her. 'You emailed her.'

'No, I didn't,' she retorts, but even as she says it she feels like she must be lying. He is so certain, and her voice is whiny. *Don't be so pathetic*, she tells herself. *Don't be so useless.*

'Yes, you did. I sent her an email on your behalf.'

'How did you get her address?'

'It was in your phone.'

Dismay engulfs her. He has thought about this more than she gives him credit for. She thought she had him figured out. She had made the decision to keep quiet, to not aggravate the situation, to let him come to the realisation that she is not going to flee. But even as she enacted this plan (it doesn't even deserve the name, she is aware of that) she knew it was naive, for she cannot escape. Having searched every aspect of the apartment, having worked at the door lock with every implement she can find, and having scrutinised every step of Andi's routine, she knows that there is no way out — not within her control. She has been marking the passing days by turning down corners of *Anna Karenina*. It is a long book. Yet she still harbours hope that something will happen, that her mother will arrive to fetch her. Mothers do not leave their young unattended. But this knowledge worries her more than it comforts her.

'But won't Mum think it was strange that you emailed her? She doesn't know you.'

In the prison of the apartment, the familial moniker sounds rude, like swearing in a church. And that one intimate word, 'Mum', brings it all crashing back for Clare. This is actually happening to her.

'I set up a new email account for you, and I emailed from that.'

She takes a slow breath. She holds it in her lungs and releases it as quietly as possible. And then she takes another. She tries to ignore the saliva pooling in her mouth, the way her shoulders attempt to hunch together as if to protect her heart. She will not feel the fear her body is trying to feed her. She breathes again.

He is not going to let her go. This is not an accident. He has thought of everything. No one is coming to save her.

'You emailed her?'

He nods. 'I wanted your mother to know that you are okay.'

Okay. But is she? The only thing about this situation that felt okay was that she would eventually be leaving. But now she knows — *she knows* — that this is bigger than just her and him. He has thought of everything.

'But I'm not okay.'

He crosses the room to stand in front of her. She watches his nostrils enlarge; his chest rises as he draws in a large breath, taking in her careful silence and keeping the air from her. Her heart begins its drum roll, and she clenches her teeth, tries not to let any more words escape.

'I thought you would be grateful, Clare. I did it for you.'

'This has nothing to do with me.' The words are out before she can check them, and they leap into a scream. 'This is your own sick fantasy, you fuck! I'm just a prop, a doll.'

His open hand smacks across her left cheek, and her head drops in surprise. Before she has even lifted her hand to her face, he slaps her again, his other hand coming down across her right cheek and throwing her off balance. She stumbles backwards against a chair and reaches for it blindly. But it evades her, and she falls to the floor, the chair's wooden legs kicking at her own.

'Don't you *ever* speak like that.'

Her teeth are overly large in her mouth, her eyelids swim pink currents across her eyes, and she waits for something else, something much worse. He lifts the chair from beside her, her foot coming free and dropping to the floor.

'It's *all* about you.' He puts the chair back on the floor; its feet whine in protest as he pushes it into the table.

'What about your mother?' She will not let this one go. 'Your father? What do they think of you?' The words fight for space in her mouth, and pain sprouts from her body. She is on her hands and knees on the floor but she will not retreat. How bad can he make this? She wants to taunt him until he snaps; she wants for this to be over. 'Do they know *you're* not okay? Do they know what kind of person you've become?'

'You know nothing about my mother.'

'That's because you never say anything! Who are you, Andi? Where the hell have you come from?' She stands now, tries to ignore the heat engulfing her face. 'Don't you have any family? Any friends? Isn't there something you should be doing other than this?' She gestures at herself, drops her hands to her sides.

'No.' He shakes his head at her. 'There's nothing as important as this.'

And she knows then that it will never end. This is all there is.

He catches a glimpse of his reflection in a mirrored column. His skin appears green-hued under the fluorescent lighting. Tungsten lighting, Clare had explained to him. Or is it the other way around? Does tungsten describe incandescent bulbs? He must ask her again, pay more attention. Either way, the strip lighting makes him appear ghostly.

He stands in front of the department-store directory. *Unterwäsche*. Underwear. There is nothing listed. People push by him, shaming him with their unfaltering strides, shopping bags demonstrating their morning's success. *Damen*. First floor.

On the escalator he stares again at his reflection, trying to imagine how he appears to a stranger. Friendly? Aloof? He cannot tell; he looks like himself. On the top step of the escalator he stumbles, the mirror mocking him with his own surprise. He regains his composure and walks through the ladies' clothing department until he sees pyjamas, then underwear. Where to begin? He wishes Clare was here to help him. Reaching out, he touches a bra and recoils at the stiffness of the lace.

'Can I help you?'

The whites of the assistant's eyes are startling, her smile pasted on.

'Something for your girlfriend, perhaps?'

'Yes.'

'What size is she?'

Surely there can't be too many to choose from. 'Medium?' He shrugs. He doesn't want to cup his hands — it seems crude. He tries to think of something that would be the same size. Does it matter that one of her breasts is bigger than the other?

'Is she tall or short?' asks the assistant.

He holds his hand to his shoulders, looks at it, then lifts it higher. But that's almost as tall as himself and he knows the top of Clare's head very well. He lowers his hand. 'About this?'

The question hangs there. How can he not know? He should have asked her for her size; he had just assumed that he would know the right ones when he saw them. He throws his gaze around the floor, a forest of metal trees waving bras and knickers at him like flags.

'Maybe you can bring her in here? She can choose something she likes and she can try the different sizes?'

'Oh no. It's a surprise.'

The assistant looks pleased. 'I see. Well, perhaps you choose a set, and if it is the wrong size she can bring it back in.'

'Yes, I can bring it back.'

Her smile turns quizzical.

He corrects himself. 'Yes, she can bring it back, that's right.'

Some of the sets are the colour of flesh; the bras look like breasts hanging in row upon row, their nipples blurred away for propriety's sake. There are cream breasts, black breasts, ones in tartan, polka dots and stripes. He chooses a set that is pink and orange — it is exactly like a festive flamingo. He wants her to be beautiful again; he wants her to think that she is.

She doesn't like to get her face wet in the shower. Instead, she ducks her head to the left and to the right. Put your left shoulder in, put your left shoulder out. Put your left shoulder in and shake it all about. She turns her back to the taps and lets the water fall on her head. Keeping her eyes tightly shut, she turns again and cups her hands in the stream. Takes a deep breath and splashes her face. She lathers up with the soap, rubs it about her face then rinses it off, blowing ferociously through her nose to stop inhaling any soapy water. Since she began talking to Andi again, she has been showering three times a day, sometimes more. It is the only place in the apartment where she doesn't feel trapped, where she feels she is existing of her own volition.

She dries herself quickly standing on the bathmat. The mirror has fogged up, but she does not mind; she does not think she will recognise herself. She pulls on her underwear and reaches for her bra. The elastic has lost its cheerleading snap and instead it curls, set in waves like an old lady's perm. Tiny matted balls dull the synthetic fabric, and she casts it aside. She puts on one of Andi's shirts. Anything else seems excessive — she'll only have to take it off when the day ends or when she showers again. The fog has dispersed, and her reflection catches her staring. She looks sad. But is she? Her reflection smiles at her. She smiles back. It is a simple exchange.

From the living room, the sky gives nothing away. She braces herself against the kitchen bench and lunges, stretching one leg and then the other, her calf muscles pinching at her legs, complaining about their lack of use. She puts on a record, delighting in the amplified crackle of the dust. She listens to the end of one song, the start of the next, and at a particularly spectacular riff she punches the air in exuberance. She laughs aloud, realising that she has become one of those people who express their emotions even when no one else is in the room. As though there might be film cameras about, paparazzi to chart her happiness.

Climbing into her perched position by the window, she makes herself as compact as possible so none of her creeps over the edge. It is not very comfortable, but she fits. It is amazing how much space people insist on for themselves. The need for high ceilings and cat-swinging rooms. She wonders how long she might last in this position and twists around so she can see the clock face. Half past four. Was there anything she meant to do before Andi comes home?

She looks out the window. Nothing has changed in the courtyard below, and for this amongst other reasons, she is beginning to doubt the existence of time. Her watch, an authority on the subject, supports this view; its hands refuse to move, but she is yet to take it off. If she just glances at her wrist, she is reminded of all the other places she has been when needing to know the time, when it actually mattered. She hugs her knees, curls her toes and concentrates on taking up as little space as she can. She is neither small nor large. Not tall or short, fat or thin. She abides by the law of averages. She imagines that in the actual world, the one where everyone else lives, she would take up very little space. She does not go to places and court attention. She is in the thoughts of very few people. This comforts her. Celebrities take up a lot of space. They exist for many other people — it must be hard work. But she exists for just one, and while this can be exhausting in itself, she is glad that she is small and inside and sitting, knees drawn up, on this particular windowsill. That she is taking up no one's thoughts, she is not weighted down by anybody's expectations. As long as she does not move from this spot, none of that will change.

'Hey, Clare! Look what I got!' He calls out to her from the hallway, the door slamming shut behind him.

She waits to hear the familiar click as he turns the key and the lock slides into place, and she twists round to see Andi hurrying towards her.

'Look.' He proffers a bottle of wine.

She accepts it, not sure why he is so excited. It's a shiraz. Then she realises. An Australian shiraz. 'Where did you get this?'

It's a Rosemount — cheap. It makes her think of house parties in Brunswick backyards, people crowded around fires burning in washing-machine drums, lemon trees holding court from the fence line. Sipping shiraz from plastic cups, the smell of burning red gum.

'I found it at the supermarket. Not the Aldi, the other one. You know the one just over the river?'

She stares at him. Holds his gaze until he looks away, realising what he has said. She has no idea where any supermarkets are. Prick.

'Anyway, you mentioned you liked shiraz so I thought I would get a couple and maybe we can get a pizza?' He takes the bottle from her hand and puts it on the table. He leans down to kiss her on the cheek, and the body that is no longer her own allows it. And her impostor thoughts let her feel glad that he is home, the bringer of wine that reminds her of Melbourne and of another time.

He falls onto the couch beside her; his jacket smells like traffic exhaust, and she inhales. She wants to be outside. But she wants to be right here, too.

She pulls away from him and gets up from the couch. 'I'll get a bottle opener.'

She didn't think she would remember the taste so well. It's heavier than the Chilean wines. Probably not a suitable wine term, but the first adjective that comes to mind. Not fruity, not spicy. Heavy.

'So how was your day?' She sounds ridiculous, a bit player on a suburban stage.

'It was okay, but slow. I had two classes sitting exams so it was a very quiet day.'

'Fair enough.' She takes another sip of wine, tries to picture Andi standing in front of a class of teenagers and commanding their attention. She is jealous of those students and the shared nuances of conversation that can only be achieved when people are speaking in their first language. His English is less stilted now than it once was. She would like to think this is because he is more comfortable with her. She suspects it's because he initially pretended to be less fluent than he was, did not want to seem a threat. Even so, she feels he is considered when speaking to her. Reserved. It makes her uneasy, as though his thoughts are being censored.

'What about you?' he asks. 'What did you do?'

She stands looking into the courtyard, immerses herself in the vista as though she has never seen it before. Nothing ever happens in the courtyard. Nothing ever happens in the apartment. It is the same, day after day after day. But still she stares out the window, as if there is something to see, hoping that something will change. The television tower watches her watching, springing into view whichever direction she looks, dripping with bonhomie like a loyal Dr Seuss character. It used to worry her, this waiting and lack of action, but now that she knows her thoughts are elsewhere and that time is elastic, she has lost any sense of urgency.

'Clare?'

She does not want to answer his question, to prise apart this world with her truth. But she does not want to lie. So she tells him what she did, the real her, not the one who spends her days moving pot plants and cutting letters from newspaper headlines. What she would do if she was out of this mess.

'Oh, you know, the usual.' She turns and faces him, leans against the sill. 'I went into the city and did some shopping. Stopped by the library then caught up with a friend for coffee. Then we went for a walk through the gardens, even though it was freezing.' She looks straight into his eyes, dares him to question any of this. 'And then I figured I still had a few hours left before you came home so I began work on a new photographic series, one that uses time lapse.'

He says nothing, and they stare at each other until time — so elusive to her, so deftly chartered by him — breaks free again and barrels forth.

'Oh, Clare.' That expansive, disarming smile.

She understands how true that description is now. His smile makes her put the safety catch back on; she feels the unused bullets drop to her feet.

'You know this is how it has to be.' He widens his eyes at her, performing innocence.

She turns back and watches his reflection in the window. It lifts its arm in a toast. It is not smiling, it is not focusing on anything. It walks towards her, catches her eye, her own reflection, and becomes Andi again.

'Come on, baby. Let's enjoy the wine.'

And why not? Where would she rather be than with a man who wants her so much he is dedicated to never letting her go? Sometimes it seems like a dream. And since it sounds so ridiculously clichéd, she swats the word 'nightmare' away before it lodges itself in her mind.

'Are you sure you don't want a tree?' He can see the listing snow outside — it turns to slush as quickly as it falls. 'It's not too late. I could still get one at the market.' He rubs her feet as they lie in his lap. They are so soft, bear none of the calluses of his own.

'Nope.' She looks up at him. 'I haven't even got you a present.'

'You don't need to get me a present. It's enough for me that you are here.' He lifts her foot to his mouth. He wants to kiss her toes, but she gives her leg a shake, and he lets it go. 'Besides, my present will be fun for both of us.' He hopes he is right.

'Did you get your parents anything?' She puts her cup of coffee down on the floor, stretching out her foot and curling her toes into the palm of his hand until he begins massaging again.

'Of course I did.' He had told his father that he was going away for the Christmas break; he wanted to spend the entire time with Clare, without interruptions. Every day, every night. His father had not minded, seemed almost amused that Andi had made a point of telling him. But Clare thought it was selfish, that it was uncaring not to spend Christmas with his family.

'What did you get?'

'I bought my father an Amazon gift voucher.'

'A voucher? For your dad?' She draws her foot back. 'You can't get him a voucher. A present is supposed to show that you thought about the person you're giving it to. If I had ever given my father a voucher, he'd have been insulted.' She puts her hands to her temples as though beset by a sudden headache.

He does not say anything. He does not want to talk about her parents.

'Actually, Dad would not have even known what to do with an Amazon voucher. I don't think the internet was around when he was alive.' She scrapes her hair into a ponytail and twists the ends under so it holds together in a knot.

'Your father isn't alive?' The words are out before he can stop them. How come he does not know this?

'He died when I was ten.' She looks at him, raises an eyebrow.

He does not know whether to believe her. Why has she never mentioned it before? 'You never said.'

She shrugs. 'You never asked.' She gets up off the couch, picks her coffee cup from the floor. 'You better not have gotten me a voucher.'

Her teasing smile offers him relief. She is not upset — it is just an oversight. But he feels as though he has made a mistake; he wonders what else he does not know about her.

'No, not a voucher.' He follows her to the kitchen. She stands with her back to him washing out her cup. He wants to hold her, to tell her he is sorry about her father; he cannot imagine losing his own. But everything about her screams *don't touch*. The only movement is in her elbow as she swirls the cup about. He feels like they might stand here forever.

'Do you want your present now?'

She rinses out the cup and puts it in the rack. She does not turn around when she speaks. 'It's still early. How about we play backgammon for a while?' She swivels her head slightly, lets her voice fall over her shoulder to him.

He nods. 'I'll set it up.'

It's a game she has taught him. At first he found it disorientating, the board expunged of numbers and letters. But he has grown to love the measured way the markers skip from one spike to the next, like stout gentlemen stepping out in the evening. Clearing some books from the coffee table to lay out the board, he notices the pile of Polaroids.

'You think you're still on your winning streak, don't you?' She takes a cushion from the couch and drops it on the floor by the coffee table.

'You bet,' he replies. 'Are you saving these for something?' He picks up the Polaroids, fans them like playing cards. Over a dozen Clares stare at him with one eye, the other obscured by the next photo.

'Maybe.' She puts her hand out, demanding them, and he passes them over. 'You don't want them, do you?'

'No.' He only needs one photo of her when he's not here — the most recent. He had not thought about what she does with the ones he discards.

'Do you want to go first?' She passes him the cup, smirks. 'You'll lose anyway.'

They play as the day folds, getting up only to turn on the light, change a record, pour more wine. She wins six times in a row before he gives up.

'Okay, that's it. Time for your present.' He pulls himself up off the floor and heads to the hallway. He takes the key from the safe and unlocks the front door. He picks up her present from where he has left it on the landing and goes back into the apartment, where he puts the present on the floor so he can lock the door again, put the key back in the safe.

'Close your eyes, I have not wrapped it,' he says as he returns. He holds it to his chest as he pauses outside the door to the living room. 'Are you ready?'

When he enters the room, she is standing by the table. She looks like she is about to cry.

'What's wrong?'

Her lips are pursed, and she is blinking rapidly. 'I heard you unlock the door. I thought you were going to let me go.' She takes a deep breath. 'I thought that was my present.'

He does not know what to say; he had not given it any thought. The landing was just the best place to hide the present, somewhere she would never go.

'No, this is it.' He nods at the case in his arms. When she doesn't say anything, he brings it over to her, puts it on the floor. In her hands he places a set of tiny keys. 'Merry Christmas.'

They both look at the red suitcase. Its sides are battered, its corners scuffed. She looks at the keys, and then at him. Impatient, he snatches the keys from her hand and bends down, stabbing one into the lock on the case. The first catch releases and he presses the second one then lifts the lid. Inside nestles a piano accordion: its marbled red body embraces the light, its keyboard pearled like the inside of shells.

She lets out a little sound — it could be a guffaw or a gasp, but he doesn't want to ask.

'Apparently, it's quite easy to play, and I got some books,

there are some different ones, and you can try and see how you go.' His words jump on top of each other in his rush to get them out. He stands up, takes a step back.

She crouches down, runs her fingers over the grille, traces the diamond shape printed on the closed bellows. 'It's beautiful, Andi.'

He lets go of his breath. She edges closer and lifts the accordion from its case. He reaches down to pass the leather strap over her head, and she bends to let him before standing back up.

He found it in a second-hand market weeks ago and kept circling back to the stall, trying not to show too much interest, lest the woman refuse to haggle. His desperation must have still been obvious though, because he ended up paying more than it was worth. But it was just so beautiful and — in the way its purpose and workings were so visible — captivating.

Clare undoes the leather belt that holds the bellows together, and the accordion sighs open. Tentatively pressing down on the keyboard, she draws the ends apart, a wheezy note leaking out into the apartment.

'Oh, Andi, it's so funny. It's like an animal. It sounds like it's snoring!' She presses the bellows together, pulls them apart, the notes mangled but somehow kind.

'I only wish my snoring was so musical.' He is so pleased she likes it, so relieved he got it right. His mother used to play the piano accordion. She would squeeze out nursery songs and folk tunes, his father looking on bemused. Andi had always been enchanted by the instrument, but when he tried to play it, his arms would get tired so quickly that his mother would work the bellows, tell him which keys to press to eke out a tune.

Clare cannot manage to draw anything recognisable from it, but she does not seem to care.

'It's such a beast, Andi!' She strides around the room, dragging miscellaneous notes from the instrument and laughing at her own incompetence. 'But so fun. Thank you!'

And when she reaches up to kiss him, the accordion asserts itself between them, digging into his ribs. It's just like hugging his mother.

She is used to waiting. When studying photography, she had become adept at setting up lights, redirecting glare. Making one time of day into another. When she began photographing buildings, it was entirely different, because they want to be lit by the sun. And so she would wait: for the sun to appear, to disappear. For clouds to lighten or darken the sky. For the contrast, the heaviness in the air. She would wait for the buildings' lights to come on as dusk fell, revealing everything within.

And now she waits again, trying to catalogue the minute changes that distinguish one day from the next. With nothing else to spend her time on, she cashes it in. What she would have once given for this time! She disposes of minutes and hours with abandon, and in return she acknowledges two distinct phases: when Andi is at home; and when he is not. There is no motion. Time no longer passes, it just changes from one present to the other. She feels guilty. She had always been taught that time is precious; it is not to be wasted and cannot be hoarded. It is something that everyone must attend to and nobody can escape from. It favours no one, holds no vendettas. And now, all of these truths have ceased to be.

In the beginning (that has a mythical resonance, it makes her feel she is living within a tale), she tried to enforce time. But then, realising that there was no end point and that she did not know what she was counting towards, she stopped. Now she attempts to track the passing of space. She moves objects about the apartment, tries to see if they will take up more or less space if they are upside down or in the opposite corner of the room from where they began. She stacks books into towering ziggurats and waits to see if they will fall.

She becomes intensely aware of movement as she is the only source of it. This makes her uneasy, surrounded by things that will not move without her intervention. She watches the plant for hours, trying to see the moment that it grows, or whether it will acknowledge her in any way. But it does not reach out to embrace her with its leaves; instead it stretches towards the window, as intent on escape as she knows she should be. For company she leaves a record spinning in its final groove, the speakers hissing quietly. She becomes afraid that without time, and without movement, she will freeze. She cannot sit still: her right foot develops an insistent jiggle. It jiggles of its own accord, and she watches it jerking away at the end of her leg and wonders if it is really a part of her.

Is time a dimension or a state? It seems important to clarify these things, now that she knows they can cease to exist. She longs for the *World of Science* encyclopaedia her father gave her on her tenth birthday. It held so many answers. *Time is … Space is …* It would give units, definitions, parameters. It would take the questions out of her hands and make them the prerogative of someone more able. *Andi is … Clare is …* She tries to compose definitions that adequately explain her current situation, but she cannot settle on even the most basic of certainties. Does he love her — is that why he has done this? — or does he hate her? But she dismisses the question as soon as she asks it; the matter of Andi's love is an illusion, a red herring that steers her away from any useful conclusions about her situation. She cannot ever know the answer, cannot know what occurs in his mind, any more than she can be certain of what happens in her own. She certainly doesn't love him, but does she hate him? Neither word seems to describe the situation as it is. Every thought is so influenced by the locked door, a definite that she cannot change, that they do not seem like her own. They are constructed thoughts, made by her body to pass the time, to function throughout the day in this small space, but they do not belong to her.

She harbours a growing suspicion that the loss of her own thoughts, her inability to track time, and her vague experiments in the existence of space are all going to have a negative effect on others. Space and time are absolutes that one is not supposed to question, let alone neglect. She is sure her skewing of their existence will have consequences and she wants to be prepared. She supposes that her lost thoughts must be out there somewhere, being had by somebody else. Thoughts on photography and architecture, identity and purpose. All of those thoughts that she once knew so well, that she has carried with her throughout her life, but which have been displaced by current circumstances. She was not made for thoughts of confinement and escape, inadequacy and fear — she was never supposed to be in a place like this.

Is she going mad? She asks the question of her reflection in the mirror, but it does not answer, it just repeats her question like a schoolyard bully. 'Am I going mad?' it mimics, and she turns away, goes back to tracking space and making movement. If she is asking the question, she cannot be going mad. She is just suspended. Time stands still when you are in love, that is what the songs say, and her new hijacked thoughts tell her that this is true. As the turntable turns and the ziggurats fall, she waits for Andi to come home.

'I think you would like my father,' he says.

His own words surprise him, but as he says them he acknowledges their truth. His father would like Clare — it would be nice if they could meet.

'You should invite him over,' she says. She lunges forward and folds towards her feet.

He waits until she is upright before he answers. 'You know I can't do that.' He wishes she wouldn't make him spell things out. He doesn't like telling her what they can and cannot do.

She shrugs, twists on the balls of her feet and lunges again. He had bought her a book on yoga positions, and it is open on the windowsill in front of her.

Last night, when he met his father for a drink, he had almost mentioned Clare. He was trying to think of ways to describe her when his father pulled a piece of paper from his pocket and laid it on the table. His mother's name and a phone number were scrawled in blue ink surrounded by cubes and hatched lines — his father's familiar scribbles.

'She wants to see you, Andreas. She asked for your details, but I didn't give them to her. I told her that you would phone.'

'You shouldn't have.' Thoughts of Clare had fled his mind. He put his beer glass down on the note; condensation soaked the paper and made the ink bleed.

His father tutted in disapproval and retrieved the paper. 'She'll be here in summer. You can't avoid her forever.'

'Why not?'

His father drained his glass and stood up. 'Because nothing lasts forever. Why do you have to make things more difficult than they already are?' He held the piece of paper out to Andi and, when he refused to take it, placed it on the bar. 'She had her reasons, Andi. She was more sensitive than most. She couldn't tolerate the way things were.'

'Everyone else could.' He could not understand why his father had capitulated so easily.

'Just because some people — some of us — accepted the way things were, it doesn't mean it was the right thing to do. Your mother had principles. She couldn't take the easy option.'

'She left!' Andi was astounded. 'She didn't have to deal with it anymore. How was that not easy?'

His father shook his head. 'You have no idea what it was like. Call her. You'll regret it if you don't.'

Andi opened his mouth but had not said the words. He watched his father prepare to leave the bar, all elbows and edges as he put on his coat. He knew all about regret.

'If things were different you could meet him,' he tells Clare. 'It's just a little difficult right now.'

She does not answer, and he wonders whether she is counting under her breath, making him wait. At times like this, he is affronted by her immediacy, the way everything in the room seems caught up with waiting for her to say or do something.

'Do you think about me when I'm not here, Clare?'

'Sometimes.'

The word pops up from between her legs, and he catches it gratefully. 'Only sometimes?'

She straightens up, lifts her arms. 'Only sometimes.'

'What do you think about me?'

This time she does not pause before answering. 'The usual things. I wonder what you think of me. What you were like as a child. When I will see you next. How we met.'

He nods, pleased with this. Sometimes he feels as though she is his imaginary friend. That she appeared from some other realm and lurched into his life. They know none of the same people, nothing of each other's worlds before they met; they know each other only through the stories they tell. And she could be lying to him, she could be making it all up. He would never lie to her. But he has no one to check her identity with — she could be anyone.

'I think of you all the time,' he says.

She does not answer, sits herself on the floor. He can see a faint flush of bruise across her lower back, almost like a tan, and he knows it is from doing sit-ups on the wooden floor. It is as though she is becoming an overly mature fruit, too sweet and about to turn. It excites him that he is the only person who will see her body change like this.

'I know you do.' She nods as she says this.

He does think about her all the time. He worries that she will not be there when he returns, though every time she is, it reminds him of what a huge mistake he has made, one he can never rectify. By the time he reaches the bottom of the stairs each morning, he is worried about whether he remembers her correctly.

'What about your mother?' She balances on one foot, trembling with the effort, the other leg stretched in front of her. 'If things were different could I meet her, too?'

'I don't think you would like her,' he says. He cannot quite imagine how that meeting would go.

'Why not?'

He tries to explain the way things are. 'She's not very nice.'

'What do you mean?' Clare has stopped her stretches.

'Well, for example, when I was five years old she left me at childcare … I loved going there. To me, an only child, it was such an exciting world of friends and games. But one day, my mother was late and I had to wait with the receptionist, who was annoyed at having to stay back. I really needed to go to the toilet and finally I couldn't hold on anymore and I wet myself. The receptionist didn't even say anything, she just stared at me.'

Clare sits cross-legged on the floor, listening. 'What did your mother say?'

'Nothing. My father came eventually and he went to lift me onto his shoulders to carry me home, but then he realised what had happened. I remember so well that walk back to the apartment. I had to run to keep up with my father and my trousers chafed at my legs. All I could smell was urine and I thought everyone was laughing at me. I was so angry at my mother for leaving me there.'

'But that was years ago. And I'm sure she didn't mean for that to happen.'

'But it still did.'

Clare stands, lifts both arms then bends to touch her toes. 'She probably had a reason for being late.' Her voice is muffled against her knees, and when she stands her face is flushed. 'I'm sure she didn't just forget you.'

Of course she hadn't forgotten him. Perhaps it would have been easier if she had.

'Her grandmother was ill. She had taken a train to Hanover to visit her.'

'To the West?' She stops stretching. 'I didn't think you could just leave like that.'

The West. It still sounds like a make-believe faraway place, somewhere that no one ever actually got to, and no one ever returned from. Why did he think Clare would be able to understand what it was like back then?

'Some people could. It wasn't so hard. It wasn't how you think, Clare. People went to the West and came back all the time. It wasn't a prison.'

As soon as the word is out of his mouth he wishes he had not used it. But she doesn't say anything, just salutes to the window and bows before the television tower.

'I have two things for you today, Clare.' He comes in from the hallway, his hands behind his back.

'Only two?' She is getting frustrated with his gifts. She has been hoping that he will tire of her. That their relationship will become like any couple's — that they will grow apart, differences irreconcilable. And he will unlock the door. But his enthusiasm for the situation shows no sign of waning. It has become almost a teasing joke between them. *When will you open the door? When you are ready to leave.* So now she answers with a note of contrariness and waits to see what will happen.

'Clare, you're such a pessimist. Most people would be happy if someone brought home two presents a day.'

'Most people would be happy if they were not locked in an apartment all day.'

Annoyance crosses his face, but he banishes it, and she is relieved. Some days a comment like that will make him so angry that he will stop speaking to her, pretend she is not even in the room. It is not nice to be invisible to the only person you ever see.

'We're not going to keep talking about it. You know it's better this way.'

She stares at him, daring him to look away, but when he readily does so, her frustration flares. Does he not see her?

'So, left or right?'

She hesitates. She does not care. 'Right.'

'Good choice.' He hands her a paper bag and she sits at the table to open it. Inside is a book of paper models. *Great Buildings of the Communist Era*. She flips through the book to see that each building has been rendered flat so they can be punched out of the card and built, a little city of aspirational architecture.

'Andi, it's incredible.' She cannot contain her delight. Some of these buildings she has seen — her favourite television towers amongst them — others she has never heard of.

'Look at this.' She points out the Wedding Palace in Tbilisi, Georgia. Its walls curl in on themselves while maintaining a vertical line and somehow it suggests worship, without indicating of which god, or whether any is necessary at all. 'And this one's like a concrete game of Jenga.' She shows him the

Roads Ministry stacked on the banks of the Mt'k'vari River.

'I thought you might like it.' He smiles at her. 'It even has the Palast der Republik.' He takes the book from her and flips through the pages until he finds the one he is looking for and hands it back.

She recognises the building immediately, its tinted windows reflecting nothing, looking more like sheets of copper than glass. She wonders whether it has been completely dismantled by now. It takes her back to the day after she met Andi, the day she had decided it was time to leave Berlin.

'What was in the other hand?'

He stoops to where he has put the other bag and gives it to her.

It's heavy for its size — it feels like a grenade. It's a bizarre association because she has never seen a grenade, let alone held one, but that is the object which comes to mind, and she wishes for a moment that this is what he is giving her: a way out for both of them. Would she? But when she opens the bag, she finds a tin of leatherwood honey and knows that even if she lobbed it through the living-room window, the most damage it would do is broken glass, perhaps a sticky mess in the courtyard below.

'Where on earth did you get this?' She rolls the tin in her hand. The paintwork, with its red and yellow lettering, is so familiar to her. She remembers the honey from childhood breakfasts — it has such a distinct taste. 'They only make it in Tasmania.'

He shrugs. 'I found somewhere that would order it for me. Can I taste it?'

She feels like her childhood has caught up with her and she

does not know what this crossing of timelines might mean. Andi returns from the kitchen with a teaspoon and prises open the lid. The smell is immediately recognisable; she takes the spoon from him and digs it in. The honey has a creamy consistency, almost buttery. It wants to be spread, not drizzled, and as she licks it from the spoon she is transported back far away and long ago.

'It's delicious,' he says, running his tongue over his lips. 'I've never tasted anything like it.'

'It's just so particular, it's —' She searches for the right word but he cuts her off, his lips pressed against hers.

She should pull away; she knows that she should. She feels as though the Andi she first met has come back, that the door isn't locked. It's like that very first night before everything went so horribly wrong.

'I can't do this.' She pushes him away, wanting only to pull him back towards her. Instead she directs her words to the teaspoon in her hand.

'Do what? What do you mean?'

'This. I can't … This is all wrong, I shouldn't be here.'

'But where else would you be?' He puts the tin on the table and takes both of her hands, his eyes imploring. 'It's just me, Clare. It's always been me.'

And because she wants to believe him she kisses him back. Because maybe if she gives him everything he wants, he will set her free. And maybe it will stop her feeling so terrible, as though she is going to cry at any moment. Within minutes they're on the couch, his hands under her clothes. And she tells herself to stop, that she is doing the wrong thing. She cannot have sex with a man who is keeping her prisoner. But she doesn't stop; she is just so thankful that something is finally happening to make this day different from all of the others. And as he feeds his hungry hands all over her body, it feels to Clare just like before, which is exactly where she wants to be.

He crouches down, one hand on the floor to keep his balance. Clare has taken each of the Polaroids he has discarded and pinned them to the wall. They trail each other, Monday to Friday, along the skirting board. He is surprised to realise that he can remember taking each one. The one where she is sipping from a yellow mug was a Thursday. He was teaching senior students that day; he remembers looking at her photo as they role-played job interviews. There is one where she is in profile — the coffee pot had started steaming on the stove just as he took the photo, and she had looked to see it wasn't boiling dry. The thought of all the photos that will follow the ones already here pleases him.

He stands and goes to the safe to retrieve his phone and the key. He does not want to go to work; he never wants to go now that she has come back to him. Her body is something new every day — he cannot get enough of it. He is still surprised every time she lets him near her, every time she draws him in. He takes the Polaroid camera from the shelf. She is still sleeping, but he needs his photo.

Usually he would wake her to stare bleary-eyed into the lens, but this morning he turns on the bedside lamp, lies down next to her in bed with the camera between their two faces, and takes the photo. She does not wake. He stands by the bed, waving the square of film as it develops. The photo is dark, and one eye is lost to the pillow, but it is still unmistakably her.

He puts the photo in his pocket and takes hold of the sheet, pulling it to her ankles. She sleeps on her side, one knee bent to her chest, the other leg trailing as though she is skipping. There are red lines down her thigh, and he bends to look more closely. When they had started to sleep together again, there were no lines. He is sure about this: he drank in every part of her, everything he had missed. They have appeared sometime since, straight cuts on both legs, skimming the surface of her skin but deep enough to bleed.

He does not know what to say to her about them. He mentioned them once, and she said they were scratches from her nails — that she gets itchy in her sleep. He did not believe her, but could not figure out what else would have caused them. He is certain they are deliberate. There are five of them, each one a different length. Somehow, he feels responsible even though that is ridiculous: she has done this to herself. He reaches out to touch them but does not. He knows how they feel — like impostors, they do not belong to her skin. Is she trying to make herself unattractive to him? He covers her with the sheet, switches off the lamp.

Clare is not the person she thought she would be. She is not her real self; she has become some other being. Her camera bag in the corner reminds her of what she was like before: in charge and confident. Capturing the world and putting it away. Now she spends her days in an apartment, dressed in a t-shirt that smells of this new self, tired knickers and a pair of woolly socks. There is no reason to wear more, to put clothes on only to take them off again. She turns the heating up and does star jumps to keep warm, huddles beneath blankets on the couch or sits on the floor, back against the radiator, wondering if it is possible to cook her insides.

How long since he locked the door? How long since she gave up on her silence? She endeavours to continue her soft approach. *Don't mention the war*, she repeats to herself as she waits in the apartment each day. *Don't mention the door*.

She is surprised by the audacity of her own body. It slips through the days, barely seeming to change, but then when she looks at herself in the mirror, she sees she is different. Her finger healed long ago; no hint of bruise remains, though sometimes when she tries to play the accordion, her hand held to attention for too long, she feels a stiffness in its joints. She instructs her body through her yoga exercises, and it complies without argument. The lines on her legs appear and change with each day, the only reminder that she is real, and she waits for Andi to take issue with them.

When she doesn't think about the walls closing in, she feels as he tells her to — she feels okay. They have had nights of mayhem, sitting up until sunrise, passing joints and drinking wine. Standing tall in the apartment, up on the couch as if it was a soapbox, telling long stories, making speeches about the state of the world. They talk with fondness about the past, about how they met and who they used to be. They do not talk about the future. They talk about music and films and food. At night his warm body is a comforting antidote to the days of loneliness. She thinks about leaving, in the manner of going places, but not about escaping. There is never enough time to think about it all properly before it is tomorrow and the next day and the next, and soon it will be the day that Andi relents. He will reward her fidelity, realise that he has nothing to fear and that he can unlock the door.

When he brings gifts, mostly she feigns appreciation. Often the item is useless: a knitted scarf, a moisturiser mixed with sunscreen. One time he brings home strawberries, but she does not touch them. They rot and sink into each other in their punnet, their fermenting smell evidence of their demise, and eventually Andi throws them in the bin. Everything is back to normal, but for the door, which remains locked.

She composes a polite unsendable letter to her publisher explaining why she will be late with the book.

> *Dear Daniel,*
>
> *I hope this letter finds you well. I am writing to let you know I have, unfortunately, been delayed in Berlin. A young man I met on a street corner captured my heart (and later the rest of me), and I am afraid I may not be able to keep to our agreed schedule.*
>
> *I have taken many interesting photographs that I think you will approve of. The concrete-block housing in Warsaw and on the outskirts of Riga were fine examples of modernism stripped bare of illusion, but my imagination has really been fired up by the television towers, those undeniably phallic salutes to the possibilities of communication. While Berlin's own will be familiar to many, the most beautiful was definitely the Jested tower in the Czech Republic. It shoots right out of the mountain top, as though it might blast off at any moment. There are even glass 'meteorites' set into the building's concrete core, as though the whole thing just crashed to Earth.*
>
> *Anyway, please excuse my tardiness. I really am very sorry*

that I won't be able to meet our agreed deadline. I would like
to reschedule for the future, but I'm not sure that would be
feasible either.

Best wishes,
Clare

To her mother she composes apologetic emails:

Hi Mum,

How are you? I am well. Well, not really. I suppose I am
okay (I would hate for you to worry), but I've kind of gotten
myself into a situation and I am hoping you can help. You
see I met a boy, well, a man really, and things happened (I'm
sure you can imagine what), and now I seem to be stuck in
his apartment — he won't let me leave.

I did ask him for some sort of compromise: we have talked
about it at length and tried to make it work but we just seem
to disagree on fundamental things. I know you think I can
be too picky but I promise you this is not one of those times.
I should never have gone home with him in the first place
and I promise I won't do anything as stupid again, but if you
could send someone to come and get me out I would really
appreciate it.

Hopefully I will hear from you soon,
Clare xx

Clare imagines what Andi writes in his emails impersonating
her and she tries to think of ways she can hijack these, tell him
what to include and use them to alert someone to her situation.
But whenever she tries to clarify what exactly her situation is,

her thoughts get muddy, petering out amongst the daydreams.

She spends her listless days wishing she knew where she went wrong but knowing that she would do it all again; she cannot imagine a life without him, a life where strawberries were not her favourite fruit. And so she admonishes herself for these daydreams — the unsent emails and the playing out of the moment of her emancipation — because they are a pointless exercise. He has tied up all the ends so completely that until he changes his mind, there is only this particular life.

And there is relief in this. She lets her thoughts travel in this direction, too jaded to chase them back to sense. There is some liberation in this being tucked away, not partaking in the world. Her mind is able to wheel free, not preoccupied with trying to frame the next photograph or look for the least obvious shot.

Some of the lines on her thighs have healed, and she traces their silvery tracks with her fingers. They remind her of raindrops racing down windows, traces of their very selves left behind. She wishes that she was made of glass, that anything could run so easily across her surfaces. To be so fragile, though, would be like leading a life very hung-over. Unsure of the weight of things. She would have to be careful not to land too hard, not to be startled. Yet if she is glass then perhaps her scars are cobwebs, not raindrops. Forgotten threads crisscrossing over her legs, holding her knees to her hips like puppet strings. But she dismisses the thought: she is tired of her mind hiding truths from her. For the scars are not whimsical metaphors or veiled landscapes; they aren't like anything at all.

'Lie down on the bed.'

He likes the way her words are clipped and authoritative. It is as though she has cleansed herself of all emotion, left it piled in the back of the wardrobe to be rummaged through when she is after something special. Emotions for all sorts of occasions.

He lies on his back and waits. She takes a sip of wine and puts the glass on the bedside table, and he catches her hand in his own, pulls her to him. She kisses him with her eyes open. They stare at each other, too close to see anything. She lifts one leg over his stomach — she tastes of red wine — and when she pulls away from him, he feels the cool air rush in between them. He tugs her back down, and they fuck as if it is a fight. She claws at him. He groans. He wants to throw her from him and pin her down all at once. The wine makes the whole world seem soft. He does not feel like he will ever come.

And then it is over. The sweat lifts and cools from his body, and he rolls over to look at her. She flinches. He does not know why. He reaches for her, his hand on her thigh, and he can feel the welts that run up her legs. 'I told you to stop doing that.'

She tries to pull away from him, but he holds firm.

'You should not do it, Clare. It's not right.'

The cuts on her legs have been multiplying. She had told him she did it to measure her pain threshold, as though it was a normal thing to do. Why would she want to be bringing more pain onto herself? The situation is difficult enough for both of them as it is.

'If you do it again, I'm going to have to punish you.'

She snorts air through her nose, dismissing him.

'I won't buy you any more tobacco.'

'Fuck off.'

But she offers the expletive without feeling, and he knows

that he has won. She won't cut herself again. Almost as much as the cutting, he hates that she smokes. It reminds him of his mother, that same smell enveloping her person as if she has come from somewhere more exciting, that there is somewhere else she would rather be. The fragrance clings to Clare's fingers; it follows him wherever he goes.

'What is the worst thing I could do to you, Clare?' He props himself on his elbow, head in his hand. He uses his other hand to untangle her hair. A length of it is trying to creep into her mouth; some strands are ensnared in the intersection where her top and bottom lips meet, and he tugs them free. What a beautiful place to be.

'I don't know.'

'Well, I would never do it. Whatever it is, I will never do that to you, Clare.'

She moves her head as though to nod, but the action is stunted, swallowed by her pillow.

'This is perfect,' he says. She turns away from him, reaches for her wineglass. 'This. Us,' he continues, answering her unasked questions.

The room is imbued with Clare. The whole apartment bears the mark of her, deliberate and accidental. Her books discarded on the floor. The Polaroid gallery. The marks on the wall, like river pebbles, that he could not understand until she told him she had been doing handstands, her feet propped against the wall. He pictures her like this, upside down, face red and buckled like a root vegetable, arms shaking.

'It's incredible, Clare. Our entire world is here, in this space between you and me.'

He is everything to her. She could not be without him.

Out there the world is fractured and multiple, but here it is singular. He feels steady, like he has finally stopped striving for something.

Years before, when he was living in London, he would call his father late at night, and the silences they had always shared would hang between them over the darkened continent.

'You should travel some more, Andreas,' his father had said, when Andi told him he would be returning home at the end of the academic year. He could hear the turn of a page, the distracted pause as his father marked his place. 'There are so many places I would have loved to go at your age.'

'So go now,' he retorted, but his father simply laughed, incredulous. His father's life was amongst his books these days; he travelled in the manner he always had, through stories. It was as though the borders had never been opened, and Andi wanted to reach down the phone line, rip the book from his father's hand and throw it far enough away that he would have to at least leave his armchair to chase it down. Little chance — he could not even chase his own wife.

But Andi had not wanted to travel either, longing only for the emptiness of Berlin's streets. He had always thought his city was as bustling as any other, until he went to London to practise his English and soften his accent. There the chain stores volleyed people about as though they were trapped in a pinball machine, bumping them from one high street to the next. Every surface seemed to be covered with a price, the curled elegance of the pound sign semaphoring from every bit of advertising. He was relieved to return to Berlin; the familiarity soothed him.

Berlin was the only place he felt at peace, the only city where he knew there was no chance of a serendipitous encounter with his mother. He could never understand why, when she left, she opted for somewhere entirely new, a world so different from what she knew. But as he could never understand why his father let her leave, her destination was irrelevant.

'Are you glad you stayed, Clare?'

She finally looks at him, and he passes her a smile.

'Are you?'

'Am I glad?' She asks his question, repeats it. 'Am I glad?'

He holds his breath, waits even though he knows the answer. She looks so different from when she first arrived. Her hair is longer, and her skin more pale. Her freckles have relented, leaving her face ashen.

'What else could I have done?' She arches her eyebrows with this question, and his mouth pops open, expelling his held breath.

'Anything. You could have … gone somewhere else.' He suggests this alternative delicately, unsure what mood she is in today.

'I suppose,' she agrees. This is a good sign. 'I could have gone home?' Her rising intonation incorrectly tacks a question mark to her statement. Like a *Get Well Soon* helium balloon it lifts the sentence, sets it free.

'But you didn't have a home,' he reminds her, offering ballast. 'You just had a storage unit.'

'True.' As she ponders this, he begins to wonder whether he should have just stayed quiet. It is a conversation performed on pointe, and the strain of getting to the end is causing him anxiety. 'But I could have gone back to Australia.'

He pictures Australia as an immense sports field ringed

with burning trees. In the middle, its sails catching the sun, is the Sydney Opera House, and on its steps stands his mother. She waves at him, takes a bow. She is everywhere that he is not.

'Well, I'm glad you did not go, Clare. I would have been lonely without you.'

She raises her glass. 'And I, you.'

'To remaining,' he toasts.

'Remains,' she returns.

'Take off your clothes,' he says.

'No.'

He seems surprised. She is a little herself. It would be easier to just do what he asks and not think about it. How much does he want it? She wants a measure — what kind of currency are they dealing in here?

'Clare, come on.' He laughs. He is laughing at her. He seems incredulous at her reluctance.

She feels a smirk's ugliness creeping across her face. 'You have already seen everything my body has to offer.' She pauses. 'And you are not the only one.'

She does not know why she says this. She hears her voice coming to her ears as though it is someone else's. She talks like him now. There is uncertainty in her words; she is speaking English as if it is her second language. She has lost her contractions.

He moves to the bed. He reaches down and strips it of its sheets. As he bundles them up and tosses them to the floor, she cannot help but smile. Line-en. He always calls them line-en, rhyming line with mine. It makes sense yet it is wrong. He is wrong, and this gives her pleasure.

'Take your clothes off.'

'No.'

'I won't wait.'

She knows that he will. He will wait. He stares at her, but she does not move.

'Clare.' He thrusts his bottom lip out, a sulky child.

'Fuck you, Andi.'

Does she say it? She cannot be sure. Her disembodied voice is like a radio presenter's. She stands, tries to catch his eye, but he won't look at her. He lifts his hand, then pauses. He loosely holds his wrist, turning his hand this way and that. Is he going to slap her again? Is that what he is going to do? He holds his own hands, twisting them as though he cannot quite believe they are his. Or perhaps he is admiring them. It is difficult to tell.

Her cheeks feel larger than her whole face. They seem to be the beginning and end of any sense of existence right now. She waits for him to slap her, and when he does not move, she pulls her singlet over her head, drops her underwear to the floor. She steps out of it and stands, naked, waiting. Her cheeks tingle.

As he walks towards her, it is as though every sense she has ever known has returned. Her body picks up the vibrations of his footsteps; she clenches her cunt in anticipation. He lifts his hand, and she flinches. He cups her face in his warm palm and holds it there, inspecting her.

When he lets go of her face, he reaches to the floor and picks up her discarded clothes. She sits on the edge of the bed and waits for him to push her back. He does not. She lies back and waits for him to kneel astride her. He does not. His footsteps walk away. She can hear clothes being bundled up. The buzz of a zip being drawn closed.

'I'm going to the laundromat.' He leaves the room.

He had never expected to know obsession. It is something that other people are afflicted by. People who are not so strong, people who drift. Obsession is something to cling to when the ordinary world is not enough. And yet here he is, his mind full of her. The way she walks, the way everything she says sounds like a question. And what it's like to fuck her. He is surprised by how much time he spends thinking about this. Sometimes he catches himself in the very act, her body moving beneath his own, and he wonders whether it is just an exquisitely vivid daydream. He knows her body so well, the way she arches to reach him, her desperation as she holds him inside her. And he finds himself wondering how to be sure he is not dreaming; he wants to pinch her and see whether she wakes up. When he runs his hands up her inner thighs, feels the welts under his fingers, that's when he knows she is real.

This obsession has rendered him useless. He is unable to think properly about work and about his day-to-day necessities. It has stripped him of all purpose. He is conscious, every moment of the day, of her waiting. Waiting for him to come home. To come to bed. To sit beside her. He feels like each individual minute is documented by his need for her. And hers for him. Look at her, curled up on the couch, her head resting on the arm. Look at her pale legs, shiny in the light, soft at the edges where her skin blends into the shadows. Look at her, pulling a strand of her hair, twisting it around her finger and letting it fall loose before picking it up again.

The day he first saw her, he was alone, and she was alone in the same place. He thinks of her standing behind him in the bookstore. Walking home, her hand in his, and then drifting about his apartment as he cooked her dinner. And now they will never be alone again, on the same street, in the same store, in an apartment room. Here they are, months later, as familiar with each other as with their own reflections.

He hates that he slapped her, frightened her. He does not want to do it again. He cannot pretend it was accidental: he did it twice and he thought about each one. What makes her think that her mother is any different from his? She isn't going to come looking.

When he wakes in the night, he is immediately aware of Clare sleeping beside him. What comes next? This situation is not nice. It is not comfortable. When he is out in the world and not with her, he imagines Clare beside him. What would she make of that person's odd outfit on the train? Would she choose the hard or the soft cheese at the deli? At school he is aware of talking about her too often. 'When will we meet this mysterious Clare?' his colleagues ask. What would she think of them? They of her? Her constant presence in the apartment is exhausting. His yearning for her when they are apart is more so.

But he wishes he had not hit her. It felt so fucking good, that's true, to make her understand, but that is not the person he is. He cannot think about that — it was a mistake. There is no need for her to be afraid of him. He has done everything possible to ensure they both know what to expect each day. That is what is so perfect about the situation: they each know where they stand.

He gets up, and she goes back to sleep. He showers while she lies with her eyes closed, enjoying the warmth of the sheets, the knowledge that she has nothing to do today, no reason to get up. As her body stirs she draws herself from under the covers. Some mornings she joins him in the shower, others she does not. He takes her photograph, leaves. And then begins the waiting. She walks from room to room, trying to catch the sun moving, dangling her feet in its pools, hoping to spot something changing. She takes yesterday's Polaroid photo and pins it to the wall. She cuts letters from the newspaper and assembles English words. She picks up the piano accordion and pulls and pushes it, emitting noise rather than tunes, mournful wails that match her mood. She plays to the plant and to the television tower. She never plays for Andi.

For weeks the jigsaw, another gift, has stood untouched in a plastic bag by the bookshelf. She does not think she is the kind of person who makes jigsaws. When eventually she decides that perhaps she is, she closes her eyes and draws the box from the bag. Keeping her eyes closed, she opens the box and places the lid face down on the floor, next to the table. She does not want to know what the puzzle is of. She is so starved of intention that she needs an extra incentive to impel her to completion.

She tips the pieces onto the table. Jigsaws are light, all cardboard and air. They are not a popular form of entertainment anymore — they just don't offer enough. She suspects that jigsaws seem insubstantial in a world where everyone wants value for money; they want weight in their purchases, as though lightness is a flaw. But in people, weight is a flaw. She enjoys cataloguing the contradictory nature of humans. It's comforting. She lifts her hand, and it stays aloft. She drops it back to the table. Her own hands seem to weigh nothing; neither does her head. She places her elbow on the table and rests her head in her palm, trying to release its weight from her neck and shift it to her hand. But it won't be separated: it refuses to be heavy.

Pushing her chair back from the table, she regards her legs. She lifts one and lets it drop and then lifts the other. They each hit the floor with a satisfying thump, but still they don't feel as though they have any heft. She prods a thigh with her finger and when she removes it, the skin reluctantly shifts back. It does not spring; it is as though there is nothing beneath it. She is empty. She goes to the kitchen and takes a knife from the drawer. It feels heavy, as though it might be important, and she thinks of Chekhov's advice. She wishes there was a gun on the wall, but there is not, just this burden of a knife that she keeps returning to.

She sits herself back in the chair. The jigsaw pieces crowd the edge of the table, and she wants to be rid of them. Knife in hand she scoops the pieces towards herself; they fall from the table edge like lemmings. Some of them land lifeless in the ditch between her legs, others rain to the floor. They weigh nothing; she can hardly tell that they are resting on her and she opens her legs and lets the pieces fall further. As she presses the knife into the skin near her knee, she expects to hear a sigh of air being expelled into the apartment, lifting her fringe as it pushes past. When Andi returns, she imagines he will find her hollowed-out skin draped over the chair like a deflated balloon.

But there is no air, only a bright bead of blood that builds and builds as she pushes the knife down. It looks as though it will hold its spherical shape forever, then it bursts and rushes down the side of her thigh. She pulls the knife towards her and the stream increases. She is careful to cut straight: she does not want to run into any of the other lines, already permanent. It feels like a paper cut; the pain sings up her body, becoming an itch in the tips of her fingers. But no, she lies, it doesn't really feel like anything at all. The blood drips onto the jigsaw pieces. It is exactly the same temperature as her skin. She may not be heavy anymore, but at least she knows she is warm.

She wonders what would happen if —. But she stops herself. Andi does not couch his comments in perhapses and what-ifs, and she wants to be as certain. Maybe it is a language thing, this directness, but even so, it is refreshing when considered next to the over-analytical and fatuitous speeches of so many people she knows, including herself. (*Knew*, she corrects herself. People she knew.) The unfinished sentences, the misuse of prepositions, the nouns lazily disguised as verbs. She longs for complete sentences, for direction and narrative advancement.

Her days and nights feel more real than any have before. Here, in Andi's apartment, she is living a distillation of her former life. She is, for the first time, living in the present because there is nowhere else to be. Her past and future are far from her reach; she is free from their obligations.

She waits for the blood to congeal, marvelling at the way it copes with being out in this new world, and then she puts the knife back on the table and begins picking up puzzle pieces from the floor and laying them out.

From now on, whenever she takes out the puzzle, she also

takes out the knife — it lies on the table as she shuffles the puzzle pieces about. The pieces catch at each other, and she breaks them apart. She siphons off the edge pieces, hunts for the four corners. The puzzle is a palette of indigos and blues; bright oranges and yellows gleam from the pieces' surfaces. In time she discovers that it is a picture of the Sydney skyline, a view she is not as familiar with as Andi might have supposed when he bought it for her. It is the tiles of the Opera House sails that give it away. She should keep a diary of such moments of recognition. The moment when a place feels like home, when a song becomes familiar, when a lover becomes known, moments that cannot be had again.

The cuts remind her of how, in the space where her blood meets the air, her body still belongs to herself; that Andi may be in charge, but he has not seen her body do this. She stalks about the apartment half-dressed, her legs bare so that she can keep an eye on each line she has made, make sure they are healing in order. She pulls on jeans before he comes home, and if he feels the lines beneath his hands in bed at night, he does not say a word.

In the quiet of the apartment, putting the puzzle together, she is satisfied with the dull cardboard click of the pieces fitting in place, their edges feathered from use. When Andi is due to return, she breaks the puzzle apart, puts it back in the box. She does not want to leave it out, to have him chart her progress or idly shuffle the pieces about of an evening. She does not want to finish the puzzle. What would she want then?

'I was the age you are now when you were born,' his father calls up to him. Andi is standing on the kitchen table, taking down the lampshade, and his father is on his hands and knees, looking for one of the screws that has fallen out. The last one refuses to be released. No matter how much Andi rattles it and tries to manoeuvre the shade free, it sticks fast. His arms are burning with fatigue, and he does not answer his father.

'We hadn't really discussed having children. Your mother was so much younger than I — there was so much time. So, really, you were quite the surprise.' His hands brush in wide swathes across the lino floor as though he is feeding chickens.

Andi gives a grunt of acknowledgement and watches his father inch across the kitchen, a blind man looking for the point of his story. Turning his attention back to the ceiling, Andi sharply nudges the lampshade with the heel of his hand. The third screw lands with a tinkle on the floor, and his father pounces on it.

'A good surprise, I hope?' He drops his arms, and blood rushes back into his fingers. He waits for his father to clamber to his feet before passing him the lampshade.

'Of course.' His father holds the shade in both hands like an offering. 'I always wanted a child, you know, ever since I was young. I think it came from not having any brothers or sisters. Do you feel the same, Andreas?'

'No.' He reaches up to unscrew the light bulb. He had always wanted a sister, a miniature version of his own mother. When other boys would run home from school, leaving their sisters to dawdle along in packs behind, he imagined that he and his sister would walk in step, sharing everything. She would be his shadow; they would be a full-sized family.

'I suppose when you meet the right person, then you might

want children. Are you seeing anyone?'

Andi and his father swap light bulbs, old for new. Should he tell him about Clare? His father would like her; he would see that there is something different about her. He would ask questions about her travels and where she comes from, and he would listen attentively, more questions at the ready. Andi pictures them deep in conversation, food untouched, while his own cutlery taps out a lone jig on his plate.

'No, I'm not seeing anyone.' He screws the new light bulb in place and sticks his hand out for the lampshade. In a way, he regards children as a public shame. Left behind as a reminder of broken marriages, their faces are a jumble of borrowed expressions, serving only to haunt parents with memories of the partners they could no longer tolerate. If Andi had not existed, it would seem distasteful that his father had never quite managed to let go of the memory of his mother — an unhealthy obsession with the past. But Andi's existence makes it okay for his father to hoard a junk room of her belongings, to eagerly anticipate her letters and, now, to unabashedly look forward to her visit.

'Well, I'm sure you will find someone soon enough. These things happen when you least expect it.' His father offers up two of the screws, pinched between the thumb and index finger of each hand like miniature maracas. 'But I have one piece of advice for you, Andreas.' He holds on to the screws, not letting go of them until Andi looks him in the eye. 'When you find her, don't let her go.'

'I won't, Papa.' He directs his assurance to the lampshade as he twists the screws back into position. His father has become so sentimental in his old age; perhaps his mother has, too. He puts his hand out for the final screw.

'Especially, if you do have children. That's when you really need to hold on.' His father passes him the screw and looks at the spent light bulb in his hand as if unsure of how it got there.

Lampshade secure, Andi jumps down from the table, landing beside his father. He has an urge to enclose him in a hug, but as he lifts his arms to do so it seems ridiculous, and he pats him on the shoulder instead. 'I'll do my best,' he says, and they both look at the cloudy light bulb, wondering what to do next.

As her eyes adjust to the darkness, Clare can make out the grey square of window on the wall. In this light it impersonates a blackboard — she wants to practise her handwriting on it, form cursive letters that swoop and join without grace. The wardrobe squats to one side of the room, resentful of the bed taking centrestage. A collection of mugs and glasses huddle on the bedside table, refugees from the kitchen.

'Clare?'

She directs her gaze towards his voice but cannot make out his face in the dark. Glancing back to the window she catches the shine of his eyes and the outline of his tousled hair in her peripheral vision. She looks towards him again, and he disappears, her eyes unable to coax his shape from the night. She looks away, and he returns, head propped up by his hand. This elusiveness does not concern her: he always makes more sense when she is not considering him directly.

'Mmm?'

'Are you awake?'

He must know that she is. His night vision is better than hers. He can probably make out the features of her face. Without trying to alter it, she wonders what expression she is wearing. She cannot feel her lips straining — she must not be smiling. Her top and bottom teeth are touching; perhaps she is pouting. Lately she has been more wary of him, unwilling to incite his temper and hesitant to make her presence felt. But he was so remorseful, and so attentive with his apologies, that she has lowered her guard a little, her resolve has weakened. In short, she does not know how to feel, does not know how to behave. What is someone supposed to do in this situation? She is sure she is getting it wrong.

'Yes. Are you?'

'Yes.' He drops his head back to the pillow. 'I cannot sleep.'

A gust of air escapes the sheet and passes over her face. It travels so fast. Doesn't it know there is nowhere to go?

They lie on their backs, staring at the ceiling. She can make out the light globe now, hanging like a ripe fruit on an oversized stalk. *Glühbirne*. Glow pear. It makes so much sense that she grins. It seems a shame that he isn't looking at her to notice. He likes to see her happy.

'Me neither.'

They sigh in unison, happy to share their disgruntlement.

'I used to try and imagine you,' he says. 'I would lie alone in this bed, knowing that one day I would meet a woman I could fall asleep beside every night. And I would try and imagine what she would be like.'

'Was she anything like me?' She wishes, just once, to sleep alone for one whole night, starfished across the bed.

'No,' he replies. His voice play-acts surprise. 'She was not like you at all.'

She does not believe this. Most women are much the same.

'I had no idea what you were like. But now that you're here, I cannot imagine not knowing you. Isn't that strange?'

She has become aware of his heat. It has made itself distinct from the rest of the atmosphere. A glaze of sweat lounges between her breasts and around her crotch. She would give anything for a breeze to sweep away the stillness, stir his pulsating heat back in with the surrounding air. She yanks the sheet from her body, and for a moment, as the sweat evaporates, cool teases her body. He takes the sheet and waves it back and forth so that it billows above their bodies like a parachute.

'It's too stuffy in here for sleeping.' He lets the sheet settle and reaches for her hand. 'Come on.'

In the living room, he switches on a lamp, puts Nina Simone on the stereo. At the window she lights a cigarette, takes a drag and stubs it out. The television tower is unaffected by the misty rain that clings to the city. Clare is disappointed: she'd hoped that it would droop a little.

'We can make a whole town,' he calls out from where he sits on the floor. The book of Soviet architecture is open before him, and he is punching one of the flattened buildings from its moorings on the page. She crouches down beside him, and he plants a kiss on her shoulder. She watches as he tears the cardboard along the perforations, careful not to lose any tabs. He has chosen the Palast der Republik. Its shape could not be more simple, and in only a few minutes it stands on the floorboards like a grand shoebox.

'Your turn.'

She flips through the pages. She chooses the hideous People's House in Bucharest. Too big for one page, it is drawn across a gatefold — it will dwarf all the other buildings. She folds along each of the lines with precision, tucks the tabs neatly into slots.

'They had to build the central staircases three times,' she tells him. Her memory takes her back to the pimply tour guide, his Adam's apple bobbing up and down above his red polyester tie, his skinny arms pointing at the twin staircases like an air steward indicating exits. 'Apparently Ceausescu wanted to be able to walk down one flight, while his wife walked down the staircase opposite, with them looking into each other's eyes the whole time. But his wife was taller than he was so the workers had to change the height of his stairs so she wasn't looking down on him and so that they still arrived at the bottom at the same time.'

'It's always the short men that make trouble,' he says, laughing. She does not agree.

They carry on making the models until there is nothing left of the book, and the floor is littered with buildings. He has mixed mint juleps, and as the morning sun breaks into the room the dregs of mint in the jug and discarded glasses pass green shadows across the miniature metropolis. She watches the way Andi lines the buildings up with the floorboards, creating diminutive streets and boulevards. He looks to her every now and again, as though seeking her approval, and she finds herself giving it willingly. She recognises the emotion that loops itself about her ankles, climbs her legs to her hips, aims itself at her heart. She is content. But it is a feeling so close to happiness that she shakes it loose and goes back to bed.

Clare's accent is atrocious; it makes him want to laugh.

'*Ich möchte ein Kaffee, bitte.*'

'*Nein, ich möchte ein-*en *Kaffee, bitte.*'

'*Einen.*' She repeats his emphasis, smiling. 'Because it's accusative, right?'

'*Ja, sehr gut.*' He stands up from the table and bends to kiss her forehead. 'A coffee it is, or would you prefer a beer?'

'Hmmm … perhaps a beer. I've already had two coffees today — I'm pretty wired.'

'A beer it is then, we can't have you climbing the walls.' He heads into the kitchen and takes two beers from the fridge. He feels as though this day could go tumbling on and on, and he would never want it to be tomorrow.

'So you're quite good at teaching German. Is it easier than teaching English?'

'I don't know about easier,' he replies, returning to the table and handing her a beer. 'But I definitely find it preferable.'

'Why's that?' She takes the beer and clinks it against his own.

'Because I get to teach it to you.'

'Right answer.' She smiles. 'But I'm confused — how did you learn English? I would have thought they only taught Russian at school?'

'We did learn Russian, it was compulsory. But, to be honest, no one was really interested. English was offered, and even though nobody thought the Wall would ever come down, it seemed obvious that English was going to be the more useful language.' He sits and traces his finger, wet with condensation, around her hand. She has such lovely hands. 'And I suppose it was because of my father being an English teacher — though he was more interested in the literature than the language.'

He remembers his father sitting in his reading chair, lamp on and book open in his lap. He was always reading English books, but Andi never asked what they were about. Novels, he assumes, but cannot be sure. These days his father buys all of his books online and is amazed by the speed with which they arrive.

'There's a book on absolutely everything, Andi,' his father told him, enthused. 'You type in any topic you can think of and someone will have written a book on it.' It is as though his father has only just discovered a world outside of his own.

'That's how they met, my parents. He taught her English at university.' Andi takes a sip of beer. 'Once dinner was finished, they would sit at the dining table and read stories and poetry in English and German to each other.' He has not thought about it in a long time, but when he describes it, he can almost hear their voices.

'My mother's accent was nowhere near as strong as my father's,' he recalls. He didn't recognise it then, but he knows it now. She probably has no accent at all anymore. 'I suppose she was quite a bit younger than him when she began learning. Well, she was always quite a bit younger than him; he's more than ten years older. Was it the same with your parents? Or were they the same age?'

When she doesn't answer, he realises she is probably thinking about how long it has been since she has seen her mother, how her father is of no age now. He makes these slips every time he loses himself, allows himself to think that things are working out okay. Every time that locking the door behind him each morning seems like the most normal thing to do in the world, and when he cannot remember what it was like to fall asleep alone.

'Perhaps she always felt he was too old. She left him —'

'The same age,' she interrupts him. 'They were born in the same month and the same year.' She looks at him and smiles. 'They always had a birthday party together. Mum would make Dad a cake; he would buy her flowers.' She pushes her chair out and stands. 'I'm going out for a walk.' She leaves her beer on the table, and he hears her grab her jacket from where she has hung it next to his in the hallway. There is the sound of the bedroom door closing, and he knows she won't come out until it's dark.

She wonders whether he shows these photographs to anybody.

'Look at me.'

She looks at him.

'Smile.'

She does not smile. Andi presses the button, and the camera flashes its response. She blinks, and he takes the Polaroid that slips out of the camera and shakes it in the air.

'I'll be home late.' He continues to shake the photograph, addressing Clare's foggy apparition. 'Is that okay?'

She nods, and her image surfaces on the Polaroid film, nodding in unison with Andi's shaking hand. He takes yesterday's photograph from his diary, puts today's in its place.

'Your hair is getting long, Clare.' He studies the two photographs before closing the diary, leaving one image on the table. 'I'll see you later, baby.'

He kisses her on the lips. She kisses him back. She does not want him to leave. He leaves.

She wanders to the window, rolls a cigarette, lights it and waves it in front of her face. She does not inhale. She wishes the tobacco would make her thoughts spin faster, but it does not. The cigarette smoke butts up against the closed window, searching for release as it does every day. She returns to the table and picks up yesterday's photograph. Her hair *is* getting long; she will need to cut it soon. She looked happier yesterday. Was she?

She takes the photograph to the bathroom and compares it to her reflection in the mirror. She looks the same. But she cannot be the same. She is a day older and she is no longer just herself. She is pregnant.

She holds the Polaroid next to her face, and her eyes flick from one to the other. She tries to catch her similarities out. Or her differences. In the photograph, she is not looking directly ahead; she is looking to the left. She had been looking at the table when he took the photograph yesterday, trying to see whether the newspaper headline had a 'c' in it. She needed a 'c'. In the mirror her reflection stares straight ahead without fail. She cannot catch it out.

She stubs her cigarette out in the basin and walks back down the hall into the living room. Taking a drawing pin from the tin on the bookshelf, she reaches up to pin the photo to the wall. She started from the skirting board, the Polaroids evenly placed, crawling up the wall like ivy on a lattice. She has grown up past her own waist, beyond her head. She has not counted how many replicas of her populate the wall, but if she should reach the ceiling, she will begin again, filling in the gaps. Each image looks identical to its neighbours, but if she looks at one from the bottom and one from the top, she can see they are quite different. Her hair a little longer, her skin a different colour. The faces from long ago don't look like her at all. Or is it the faces at the top, the more recent ones, that are unfamiliar?

She steps back to survey the wall. It is like a line-up, a gallery of mug shots. What sort of crime does she look like she has committed? She does not appear drunk and disorderly, perhaps just a little dishevelled. The gallery regards her with reproach. It's his crime, she pleads with them. But she knows that it is hers, too. The jury waits for her justification, expressions inscrutable. Her face has become thinner. That's what it is. And her freckles have faded. But which one does she resemble the most?

She looks down at her legs. Her thighs are lined with silvery scars. Her shins are hairy, and the skin beneath is dry. What did she use to look like? Tears well up in her eyes, and the heat of shame creeps up her neck. She takes a deep breath. Why can't she remember what she looked like? She lifts her arms, examines her hands. They look like her hands. But have the freckles faded there, too? And her muscles? Did she use to have more muscle? She flexes her leg, watches closely. Her muscles flail beneath the surface of her skin then fall back in relief.

She lifts her t-shirt, looks at her stomach. She tries to imagine it growing, the skin stretching, and she cannot. All she can think of is the baby trapped, desperate to get out. Her periods, so regular, have stopped. She feels ill in the mornings. She wants there to be another cause, but she knows that there is not.

She runs into the bathroom. She strips off her clothes.

Her pubic hair has grown. She looks in the mirror. Are her shoulders more stooped, less? Her eyes appear panicked — is she? She turns around, tries to catch her back in the mirror. She can see the pink flush of a pimple rising on her shoulder. How many of those has she had and not noticed? It suddenly seems imperative to document herself. She doesn't want to change, but she knows that in the coming months she will. She doesn't want to forget what she looks like.

She understands, now, the photographs Andi takes. She thought it was sweet at first. 'I want the most up-to-date picture of you with me every day,' he had said. 'I want to be in love with the you of right now, not yesterday.'

In the living room, she takes the Polaroid camera from the shelf. It has been a long time since she has held a camera, and this one feels like a toy. It has a rainbow stripe running beneath the lens, and the word 'Presto!' flags the red button. Her own cameras are still in their bag. They are useless here — no darkroom, no computer. Which is why Andi had been so pleased when he came home with the Polaroid camera. 'It just makes total sense,' he said. 'It takes the photo, and there it is.'

She holds the camera with both hands and aims it at her feet. She presses the button, and the bulb flashes. The paper pushes out from the slot. She bends over further and takes a photo of her knees. It will be upside down, but she does not think that will matter. She straightens up a little and takes a photo of her faded pubic hair. Her stomach, which appears just the same as it always has, so calm on the surface. Her breasts that look as though they belong to someone else. As the photos spew out, she tosses them on the table without looking at them.

With one hand she takes a photo of her other hand. Her elbow. She swaps the camera to her left hand and does the same again.

She aims the camera at her arse, presses the button. At the backs of her legs, which is less successful. How to photograph her back? She tries a few possibilities, waves her arms around fitfully. She takes one photograph from below, one from above. She photographs the back of her head. When she is done, she realises she is cold. But she is no longer panicked.

She showers, rubbing soap all over her body. When she dresses, she is thankful that her body disappears beneath the clothes, avoiding further scrutiny. At the table, the Polaroids have all been exposed. She still cannot tell if she has changed, however, because she has nothing to compare the images to. But at least she has this record. She gathers up the photographs; they are such a little stack and yet they are her entire body. She stands in front of the bookshelf and wonders how to choose. Eventually she closes her eyes and picks books at random from the shelf. Into each one she places a Polaroid body part. For Klimt she offers up her breasts — she thinks he would like that.

As she puts the books back on the shelf, she reviews her invisible work with satisfaction. Swinging her arms, she walks to the window where the television tower greets her.

'Hello,' she says. Her voice is unfamiliar. It sounds different when she is alone from when Andi is there. 'Hello, tower.' She sounds a little forlorn.

She wonders what she sounds like to Andi. People's voices never sound to themselves the way they do to others. She knows this from the message she recorded on her own voicemail. Her recorded voice sounds lower than — lower than what? Lower than it should? Lower than it sounds to her? What is more true: the sound of your voice to your own ears or to someone else's? What would it be like to have company, other than the plant? Someone to answer her questions, to listen to her voice and tell her if it sounded wrong.

'Is this my voice?' she asks herself aloud. 'Or is this my voice?' And when she finds herself waiting for an answer, she shakes her head. 'Fuck, I'm going mad.'

She is lying on the floor, staring at the ceiling. He crosses the room to the stereo. There is no record on the turntable, but the volume is turned to the max. It's like being inside a conch shell, surrounded by the sound of the ocean. He switches off the amp, and the whisper and crackle of the speakers is silenced.

'Clare?'

She has not moved. She lies on her back with one hand behind her head. The other lifts a cigarette to her mouth. She holds it there, near her lips.

'Yes?'

She is dressed in one of his t-shirts and a pair of her own knickers. Two grey woollen socks cling to her feet.

'What are you doing?'

She lifts one leg, places her foot flat on the floor. Stubs her cigarette out in the teacup beside her and puts both hands behind her head. 'I'm waiting.'

He stands next to her, his feet by her bent elbow. 'What for?'

She looks at him, indifferent. 'For you, Andi. I am waiting for you.'

'Well, you can stop now.' He steps over her, one foot on

either side. He offers her a hand, but she does not reach to grasp it. 'Come on, Clare. Get up.'

She doesn't. This annoys him. He nudges her with his foot.

'Clare.' He tries to keep his voice friendly. 'Clare, come on.'

She won't move and she won't look at him. She won't acknowledge his presence.

He kneels, one knee either side of her. Holding her gaze, he undoes his belt buckle and his jeans. He is already hard; he wants to make sure she knows he is here. He leans forward and puts one hand by her head, uses the other to pull himself free from his underwear. It is an awkward movement, and it irritates him to think that she will have noticed this. Still she has not moved.

He leans down and kisses her neck. Moving his knees further apart, he settles himself down onto her. He cannot see her eyes now and he is glad. He closes his own. He pulls her knickers aside with one hand and finds her wet.

'You were waiting for me,' he whispers and he enters her quickly, thrilled with the way her body welcomes him. He pushes against her. His knees are uncomfortable on the floor, but her body is giving. And, too quickly, he lets himself come; he does not try to slow down, he just lets everything go and falls onto her, spent. He lies there, waiting for his breath to catch up to him, listening to the silence of the apartment, and then he stirs himself, lifts up off the floor. He moves to one side of her and stands, doing up his jeans.

She looks at him, and he realises she has not moved from her original position. Her hands are still behind her head.

'What?' He throws the word down to her, petulant.

'Nothing.' She brings herself up into a sitting position and reaches for her papers and tobacco. He kicks them out of the way, knocking her hand with his shoe.

'Ow!' She pulls her hand back with a yelp and shakes it, as though trying to surprise the sudden pain away. 'That hurt!'

'You should not smoke so much.'

He wants to pick her up and throw her from the room but he will not. He will not be a part of this anymore. What is wrong with her? She is not the way she promised to be. He slams the front door as he leaves.

He walks to the river, sees the arc of the Ferris wheel above the trees. As he crosses the bridge he is almost running — he cannot get far enough away. He only slows when he reaches a park. From a bench, he watches children pull themselves onto the play equipment and hurl themselves down the plastic slides, shouting to each other.

'I can do this faster than you!'

'You can't catch me!'

He cannot take his gaze from these children. He notices the way they don't look at each other: they are too busy concentrating on their own trajectory, thinking about what to grab hold of next, what leg to use to launch themselves from a platform.

He must stop staring: people will think he is strange. He leaves the seat and walks away from the playground towards the trees. He lowers himself tentatively to the ground, wonders whether it is damp or just cool. Stretching out on his back, he laces his hands behind his head. He can still hear the children shouting, one of them bossier than the others. He thinks of Clare lying like this on the floor of the apartment. Is she doing it now as she waits for him to return?

Sometimes when he comes home, he unlocks and locks the door as quietly as possible and takes his shoes off in the hallway. Then he steps slowly towards the bedroom and slips inside it. He stretches out on the bed, inhales its familiar smell of sex and washing powder and closes his eyes. He feels like he is alone and no one will disturb him.

'What are you doing?' She inevitably finds him there.

He'll open his eyes warily. 'Nothing.'

He lies on the grass with his eyes closed. The sun has already gone down, and he hears parents calling out to their children, telling them it is time to go home.

'Hurry up, Klaus!'

'Why?' The little boy answers back to his mother.

'Because it's time to go home.'

'Why?'

'Because I said so.'

'Why do you get to make all the rules?'

'Because I'm your mother.'

'Why?'

'Because I love you.'

He hears the thud as the little boy jumps from the play equipment and lands on the ground. The sound of his impossibly light footsteps as he runs across to meet his mother.

Cooling tears pour down Andi's cheeks. He squeezes his eyes as though to stop them, but it just makes them run faster. The stream of tears trickles to his jaw, first the right side and then the left. He swallows and, clenching his teeth, pulls himself up into a sitting position. He hugs his legs, as though to reassure them, as though they are the cause of his crying.

The playground is deserted. He can see the bright blobs of

colour as the children disappear into the dusk, running ahead of their parents. He would like to go with them. To have someone else be in charge, to be gathering him from the playground, putting him in his pyjamas and depositing him in bed.

He is still crying. He is surprised at the tenacity of his tears, they who have arrived unbidden and refuse to go away, though he does his best to ignore them. He has not seen Clare cry in a long time. Either she has become very good at not crying, or she does not have a reason to cry. He is not sure which is the better reason.

He shivers — the ground feels more wet than cold. He should go home. She will be waiting for him.

'Why?' he imagines her asking.

'Because I love you.'

'That's your answer to everything,' she will retort.

'Because it's true,' he will say. But still he does not want to go home.

Once she has decided that time no longer exists, she feels relieved. The sun will rise and set: this is true. But even this has little effect on her because when she wants light, she turns on a lamp, and when she wants twilight, she switches the lamp off.

During those long hours of time when Andi is not there, she thinks about him. She thinks about him so often that in her thoughts he is more present than when he is actually in the apartment with her. At these times, Andi is the subject, and she is not sure what this makes her. Semantics don't leave much room for feeling.

Bed has become her favourite place to be. Lying against

Andi's warmth she feels at peace. Dreams come to her, parading through her mind like a travelling circus rolling into town. In bed she thinks of people she has not seen in years, of places she is not sure she has ever been. As she drifts off to meet these dreams each night, she thinks that things are not so bad. That wherever she was, she would be dreaming; and no matter who was lying beside her, her dreams would remain the same. Of this she is certain: they are her dreams.

When she is not anchored to her dreams, she finds herself focusing on Andi and having to face the fact of her imprisonment. She tries to avoid this because she hates to see him struggle to articulate his reasons for doing this. She feels sorry for him even as she needles him with plaintive questions. And yet she carries on asking, waiting for the moment of desperation when his eyes lock with hers and he finally answers.

'Because I love you, Clare.'

There is reason behind the madness.

In return, she catalogues the reasons for which she loves him. She does, doesn't she? He loves her. He looks after her. And he has gone to such great lengths to have her here. There is something admirable in that; not many people would try so hard.

In the evenings she stands back watching him. Like an audience she follows his every move, tries to read the symbolism of his actions and offers feedback only when required. When pleased, she is vocal; when disappointed, she stays polite. The conversation that they carry out at these moments is stilted. He asks her questions, and she answers them correctly. She likes to be as neutral as possible while she observes him. She is fixing him in her mind, so that at other times, when he seems less like Andi, she can remember him.

He will ask how her day was, and she will answer. She will ask him how his day was, and he will answer. She will ask more involved questions, and he will continue answering. It is like any conversation that people have under normal circumstances. They will both make jokes, usually about words and pronunciation. He will teach her the German word for things, and she will repeat it. He will smile at her when she repeats it correctly, and this is the smile that she will remember when he is not himself. He will stop what he is doing, look up at her, right into her eyes, and smile. She tries to coax this smile into existence as often as possible. She wants as many in reserve as necessary.

Once time has disappeared, patterns emerge. Andi comes home. (She has taken to calling the apartment 'home', because that is what it feels like. Home is where the heart is. She supposes there is an element of truth in this but she is unwilling to explore it further.) Andi comes home. One of them cooks. If it is her turn, he alternates between watching her from the kitchen doorway and standing at the stereo, choosing what record to play next. If he cooks, she sits on the bench, trying to entice smiles.

After they have eaten, they settle in the living room. They are like two dogs that have turned and turned, trampling the grass before they lie down to snooze. They sit in the living room and talk. It is these conversations that surprise her the most. They are always different. She is not sure where the new material comes from, considering. It is as though a package arrives every day, and they open it together. They talk about people. Places they have been. Opinions they have had about these things. They talk about characters in books and, tentatively, about their families (usually as though they are characters in books — with slight irony), offhand and at arm's length, and she wonders how effective hands and arms are at keeping things away.

It is at these moments that she forgets the door is locked, and she suspects that he does, too. These times are like the nights before things became as they are, and her love for him surges forth, and she feels like the boy with his finger in the dyke. Much better than feeling like the boy who cried wolf.

'How did you know it would be like this?' she asked one night.

He looked at her, quizzical. 'That what would?'

'This. Us. How did you know that if I stayed, then things would be like this?'

'It is like when a tree falls in a lonely forest. If there is no one to hear it fall, it does not make a sound. I needed you. I did not want to fall in silence.'

She understood then that he was afraid. And that he knew how wrong all of this was.

'But it's not all about need,' she had said.

'What else could there be?'

Often now she sees that he is trapped within himself and wonders whether he is actually ill, whether his mind has betrayed him. She had thought that perhaps he was cruel or selfish. Or too earnest, overly enthusiastic for his cause and, in the excitement, forgetful of others. Most explanations she applies to Andi involve the traits of small children. She wonders whether his unreliable mind is tipping him into psychosis, somewhere she won't be able to follow. She does not know whether this makes it better or worse. And if this is the case, then is it love that she feels? Or is it sympathy? Are they not the same thing?

She wants to help him, to tell him that it will be okay, that she understands. And maybe she can help him. Because while keeping her locked in this apartment is wrong (she does know that, she reminds herself of it every day), perhaps she can make it right. If she can help him not to fall, then maybe she is doing good, and this is right. And if this is right then she does not have to worry anymore. She does not have to make it right by getting out because she is helping him to be okay.

At night, when he is quiet, she reaches across in bed, holds herself to his back. 'You'll be okay, Andi. We will be okay.' She wonders why okay is all people ever seem to reach for. 'We will be better than that. We will.'

She makes promises she hopes she can keep. She is the boy with his finger in the dyke, indeed. She saw the trickle of water and she has stepped in to plug the hole. She will save Andi from himself, from falling in silence, and she will keep back the angry waters.

'Do you want to have a child, Clare?' he asks.

She pauses, spoon to her mouth, and her eyes widen, making room for the fear that fills them. He can see it, rolling in across her irises like a settling fog.

'A child?'

He finds her doing this so often lately. Repeating what he says as though she has never heard the words before. Waiting for him to fill in the gaps, tell her what they mean.

It annoys him, this repetition. Why is it that he has to supply everything?

'Yes, a child.' He does not want to play her games. He just wants to speak directly. It should not be so difficult.

'I've not really thought about it.' She drops the spoon to her bowl, and it makes a gentle smacking sound against the stewed apple.

'Yes, you have. Everyone has.' He doesn't want a discussion, he wants an answer. 'You have that contraceptive thing in your arm. You must have thought about children.'

'Well, I suppose I have.' She takes another spoon of apple. 'No, Andi. I don't want a child.'

He watches her finger the contraceptive rod that sits at her bicep. It disturbs him when he feels it, alien beneath her skin, but she seems unperturbed by it.

'I think *I* do.' Even as he says the words, he does not know if they are true.

She takes up her bowl, walks across the room to the photos of herself. 'I don't really think it's a good idea, Andi. I don't really think it's the right time for that.' She speaks to the Polaroids; he can see her head shaking as she consults each one.

'But it's the perfect thing. We would be a family.' He can see it now. Walks to the park collecting autumn leaves, reading picture books in the evening. He tries to ignore his mother in the background, laughing as she kicks up leaves or reaches out to turn the page of the book.

'How exactly would that work, Andi?' She leans her back against the wall, her multiplied face reiterating all the words. 'Would you let the child out of the apartment? Or would they have to stay here, too?'

Why must she always come back to this? Those are just details, they could be worked out. Just as he worked this out, just as he managed to make everything the way he wanted.

'It's not about that, Clare.' He crosses the room towards her, takes the bowl and puts it on the floor. Then he holds her hands, pulls her forward, away from the crowded wall. 'We would be making something perfect together, something new.' He kisses her lightly on the lips, imagines how a baby's skin would be even softer. He fingers the rod where it nestles against her muscle. It would be so easy to remove. All it would take is a little cut.

'Are you trying to replace me?' She squeezes his hands, leans into his gaze.

For a moment he thinks she is making fun, waits for the crack of her smile.

'Are you?' She shakes his hands again as though wanting to dislodge an answer, and he pulls free from her grasp.

'Of course not.' He turns away.

'You could keep the child and let me leave …' She follows him across the room to where he sits on the couch. She crouches beside him, and her butterfly hands tap across his cheek.

'No!' He bats her hand away, and when she doesn't move, he gives her shoulder a gentle shove so she topples to the floor where she bursts into laughter.

'It won't work, Andi.' She giggles as she sits up. 'You can't just make another to add to your collection.'

'Shut up, Clare.' He steps over her and leaves the room. Why does she have to make things so difficult?

She does exactly as he says and lies down on the bed. She does not want to argue with him. She is not afraid, but she does not want him to be angry with her. She wants only to keep rolling through these days without friction, glancing off the soft surfaces of each morning and night and waiting for the time she will no longer be here. She wants to tell him that she has decided to stop: that she will not cut herself anymore because she is afraid of what it might do to the baby. But then she would have to tell him about the baby.

She has a gift for causing him frustration; she is trying to keep it in check. He stopped bringing her tobacco (as though he knew she should no longer be smoking), but then her fingers had nothing to do. They wanted to be holding something, needed to be busy. When he saw the latest red line on her thigh, as if a cat had scratched her amongst the scars, he had been so much angrier than she had ever seen him. His face becomes red when he is in a fury, two spots, high on the cheekbones. She likes the way his face reacts so readily to her actions, but she soon feels remorseful, as though she is taunting an animal that cannot contain its very self. It is not a nice thing to anger someone.

She stares at the ceiling. In Melbourne, her bedroom was white with a yellow ceiling rose, as though the sun never set. The first time she went to the Tate Modern, there was an installation that recalled this in the turbine hall. A semicircle, high up on the far wall, was reflected in a ceiling of mirrors, where it became full, an orange harvest moon. People were lying on the ground and looking up at themselves, waving their arms about as if making snow angels. They were forming shapes with strangers (because patterns cannot be made alone);

like synchronised swimming teams they bent their arms and legs, crossed their limbs on top of each other. She wishes she had an audience here, to be only one amongst many.

When she feels the cool note of metal on her thigh, her thoughts swerve back to the present. She cannot see the line it leaves but she knows well its mark. She wonders if he is using the same knife that she does.

'You like it, don't you?'

Surely she does not. But her body betrays her. The goosebumps pop, and she shivers. Or she shivers, and the goosebumps pop. Her body acts the same way it does when he runs his fingers across her lower back, brushes his lips against her neck. It reacts the same way it always has for any man, which would once have made her feel like a pre-programmed robot. Now she feels like she is malfunctioning. But she does not think she cares. Because it is not her body anymore. It is his. She is relieved she made this decision: it leaves her mind to think on other matters.

Stroking her face with one hand, he runs the knife along her inner thigh from her knee up to her crotch. He has had to spread her legs to do this, yet she feels no shame about her graceless pose. His hand blurs at the edge of her vision. She is amazed at his certainty: he wields the knife like he has done this before. Her neck hurts from watching him so she lets her head fall back on the pillow, throws her gaze back up to the ceiling. She could project a ceiling rose. A different one for every day. Maybe she will ask him for a projector. He could film the sky during the day and bring it back to her, scatter it in pixels across the ceiling.

He draws the knife along her leg again, steadier this time,

and she clenches her knees, hisses a sharp intake of breath. The sting is high-pitched; she can feel the warm trickle of blood meeting the air and running down her leg. Tears form, but she does not want to cry. Instead she grits her teeth. It hurts more than when she does it herself. It is just one more way in which her body is siding against her. A sob threatens to engulf her, but she will not let it. She can still be in charge of this. She has to be strong; she has someone else to think about now. She pictures the patterns she would make on the ceiling, if only there were mirrors and members of the public to help her out.

'Open your eyes.'

She does not want to but she has learned to obey. He is holding a mirror in front of her face. His elbow pins her to the bed, like a stake.

'Keep them open. I want to show you what you look like when you come.'

He swiftly pulls the knife up her leg; it stings as her misbehaving body is opened to the air. She watches the girl in the mirror, tries to stare at her straight-ahead eyes as they spasm. He is probably right: she probably looks like this — she would not know.

She waits for the release of air, but it does not come. It is as though he is dismantling her body, laying out her parts on an oil-splattered tarpaulin with plans to one day put her back together, a smoothly running machine. He throws the knife to the floor when he stands, the sea-grass matting dulling its expected clatter.

'If you ever cut yourself again, Clare, I will cut you, too. Every time you do it, I will do one to match. You cannot keep changing yourself like this.'

As he leaves the room, he slams the door behind him. The light globe quivers on the end of its cord. If it fell down, would it burn her? She shuts her eyes and concentrates on her stinging leg, the warm blood trickling to the mattress. She stands from the bed, the blood drying like knotted string against her legs, and follows him into the living room.

'You shouldn't do that to me.'

'You should not do it to yourself.'

But it isn't the same. How can he not see that? She hates him for taking this away from her, for proving that she is nothing but blood inside.

'It's not yours. It's not your body. I can do what I want.'

'Is that what you want? To destroy yourself?' He tries on an incredulous expression but it is ill-fitting. He gestures towards her legs, dismissiveness leaking from his fingers. 'Is this what you want?'

She looks at those fingers, wishing that she, too, could be so sure, so direct. She shakes her head.

'You're just seeking attention,' he says. 'But you already have it. Do you think there is any room in my mind for anything but you? You're all I think about. It's making me crazy!'

She feels sorry for him; he finds all of this so difficult to understand. 'I'm going for a walk.' She waits for him to contradict her, but he does not say anything, so she returns to the bedroom and closes the door.

If she had a projector she could beam entire forests onto the walls. She would dress up in layers, wrap a scarf around her neck and pace against projections of birch trees in a Baltic winter. Strip down to a singlet, cover herself in sunscreen and project gumtrees for an Australian summer. Instead she throws herself on the bed. Lying on her back she leans her legs against the wall. She will never smell either of those trees again.

She cannot feel anything different beneath her hand. She always wondered why pregnant women stroked their bellies, even before the bump had formed. And now she knows. It's the waiting to feel something growing. She refuses to be surprised; she will be ready for this. The tiredness, the nausea. Did she think it would never happen?

Her breasts grow with each day. She can feel the weight of them: they wish to distance themselves from her; they pull towards the bed as though there is somewhere else that she should be. She will be able to lie on her back until the baby's weight becomes too much. And then she will lie on her side.

When she stands, her head spins, and she waits for the blackness to pass. She finds the rod in her arm, pinches it between her fingertips. They do not last forever, a few years at most, and now she has proof of the work it was doing all that time, while she thought she was alone. Something she never will be again.

Despite the persistent company of the child growing inside her, she feels an increasing loneliness. Her days in the apartment have become even more listless. The projects she had established to keep her mind busy have fallen away. The newspapers are piling up with their headlines intact; the jigsaw remains a jumble. She finds herself becalmed, as though tides are coming neither in nor out, and there is nowhere for her to catch hold and moor herself.

She wants to blame him for getting her pregnant, though she knows it was only a matter of chance. Or a matter of time, which she has long since stopped believing in. She does not want to tell him, but how can she not? Has he noticed the untouched tampons in the bathroom cabinet, her changing body?

The plant has begun to accuse her of infidelity. *It was just me and you*, it seems to say to her. *You weren't supposed to bring anyone else in to our days. There's not room for more.*

She has tried to ignore the plant, but it keeps hassling her. Its leaves rustle with disapproval every time she drops her hand to her stomach. She has taken to putting the plant in the bathroom each day, returning it to the living room before Andi comes home. When she goes to the toilet, she throws a towel over it, blocking its views, and she wishes the weight of the towel might reprimand the plant enough to give her peace. But when she lifts the towel, its leaves seem to unfurl even wider, feeding on their disappointment in her. As she hoists the plant in her arms, balances it on her hip and kicks open the bathroom door, she is aware she holds the plant as she will hold the baby. Close by, a secure grip. Not letting it get away.

He rolls over, throws the covers back and traces his hand across her shoulder. She continues to sleep. She may as well be far away, and it irritates him that he is not privy to her thoughts.

'Dreams are only ever interesting to the people having them,' she says when he asks. He pleads with her to tell him what goes on inside her night mind, but she refuses. He is afraid she is dreaming of places he has never been to and that he cannot know. Are they places that she would rather be?

'Is it Australia you dream of?'

'I've told you, it's nothing. The beach, cliffs. I often dream of a jungle and swinging from vines, like they do in cartoons. There are no real people in my dreams, no meaning. They're just thoughts, Andi, left over from the day.'

But one night she woke suddenly, sharply puffing as though in a race. 'I dreamed my teeth were falling out. All of them. And even more than I had. They just kept coming, filling up my mouth, and I had to spit them out. They were spilling all over the table, cascading between my fingers.'

Holding her, he asked for details, eager to climb into this tiny piece of her thoughts. But she had little more to say, her fear subsiding as quickly as it had arrived. Eventually she drifted back to sleep, and the following day she said nothing of it.

Listening to her quiet breaths beside him, he is jealous; he rarely dreams. Instead he often lies in a state of restless wakefulness, his mind ticking over, his body begging to be left alone. He does this now, holding her body against his own as though to infuse himself with her peace. When it does not work, and she does not wake, he gets out of bed and goes down the hallway to the bathroom.

He has begun to think of life without Clare. At moments like this she is so far away from him that her physical presence is more torturous than comforting. He knows that he should release her, of course he does, but he is worried about what would happen next. She would tell the police, and he would go to prison. This is what would happen in such a situation — it is only right. And while he cannot quite abide the possibility, it is life without Clare that troubles him more than life in prison. It would not be enough, the sending of letters, the waiting for visiting hours. It would be so much worse than the long days spent at work, with his eagerness to return home. Would she visit him? But he dismisses this thought. She loves him; she would visit.

In the brightness of the bathroom light, he inspects his face in the mirror. There are dark moons beneath his eyes, and his skin seems loose, as though his skull is shrinking away. He looks more like his father every day, gawky and flustered, as though constantly being taken by surprise. He fears that, let free from their little world, she will forget to exercise the love she feels. And he will be left like his father, alone but for the memories of better times. He cannot let her go.

He has earned Clare's love; he made it happen. Perhaps this is where his father went wrong. He expected love to simply be something that arose, fully formed, between two people. And when his wife left, it was as though that very thing had been stolen from him and there was nothing available to fill the void. If his father had paid more attention, Andi is sure that his mother would not have gone missing. Nothing should be taken for granted.

He turns off the bathroom light, goes back to the bedroom. He slips under the covers and takes her in his arms.

'Clare?'

He knows she is pretending to be asleep.

'Clare?'

He kisses her neck, rubs his hand over her hip.

'Mmmm?'

'Clare, I want to talk to you.'

'I'm sleeping.' She wriggles as though to accentuate her sleepy state.

'What are you thinking?'

'I'm not thinking, I'm sleeping.'

'Clare …' He pulls her towards him, rolls her body into his. Her eyes open slowly, look at him, shut.

'I want to talk to you.'

They don't talk as much as they used to, and he worries about what comes after silence. For some time there seemed to be nights when they couldn't stop fucking in order to talk. Or talking in order to fuck. And now they don't do much of either, and he wonders again whether she is real; he fears that he has been taken in by some elaborate game. Has he tired of her?

'Don't you want to talk to me?'

Her eyes open again, regard him with disdain. 'No, Andi, I don't want to talk to you. I want to sleep.'

And there it is: he feels the anger twist inside him, a catapult ready to fire.

'Well, it's not always about what you want, is it?' He holds her by the shoulders so she cannot roll away. The light from the hallway is still on, and it makes her hair a red halo around her face. He waits for her to emit a growl like a storybook lion. But she stays quiet, and her eyes stay open. He feels her body stiffen; she is making herself harder and more difficult to embrace.

'Okay, I'm awake. What do you want to talk about, sweetie?'

Sweetie. He lets go of her shoulders, turns away from her and waits. Her hand creeps over his chest, nuzzles into his folded arms, searches for his own hand and holds it. It feels like a burrowing creature.

'Andi, what's wrong?'

Her other hand searches in between his neck and the

pillow, her fingers stroke his cheek. He wants to turn and kiss them but he does not.

'I was dreaming about the snow,' she says. 'I was dreaming about the snowman we made when I was very young and we went to the top of a hill that was near our town. The snow was in patches, you could still see the grass everywhere, and it probably had all melted away by the next day. But we gathered enough to make a snowman, and in my dream it was even bigger than me.'

He can picture the snowman, its belly leaning into the ground, its crooked smile. 'What were the eyes made out of?'

She pauses a moment before answering. 'Gum nuts. And his mouth was a gum leaf.' She cuddles up close to him. 'Maybe we can go to the snow one day?'

Her voice is loud in his ear. He wants to go to the snow. He wants for all of this to be over. He is tired of the care he must take, of the way time refuses to acknowledge their very existence. Nothing has changed or gotten better, it just stays the same; and he wishes he was not caught up in all of this, that he could be free to come and go as he pleases.

So then he tells her about his childhood, talking about snow as it is to her, an imaginary element, not the grey trampled slush he wades through on the way to work in winter. He tells her about tobogganing with his mother, her legs around him, forming a shell like a car body; her squealing voice above his head as they tore down the hill. 'Faster, Andreas! Fast as the wind!'

And he had worried he couldn't make it go any faster, but she did not seem to mind, and when they got to the bottom of the run she was laughing so much that she fell off the toboggan, her legs still wrapped around him, bringing him with her into the snow.

'You must miss her, Andi?'

He is calmed by her voice and he does not want to disappoint her. 'Of course.' But the truth is, he does not miss her. There is no point missing something when you cannot have it back.

'How old were you when she left?'

He thinks about not answering, about feigning sleep. He thinks of all those boxes stacked in his father's spare room with no address to send them to. Belongings that his mother didn't want and his father didn't want to part with. He still has the scrap of paper his father gave him with her phone number, its plus sign indicating an international location; he has not called the number, he does not want to know what country she lives in. But it is almost summer. Soon she will be in Berlin, and he feels as though his world is folding in on itself. He has become an adult, but she has remained the same; she is still mother to his five-year-old self.

'Five,' he says at last.

'What? That's so young.'

'I told you about it.'

'When?'

'I told you about how I waited at childcare that time,' he replies.

'What, when your mother caught the train to visit her grandmother?'

'Yes.' He wonders why he hasn't explained it before. It all comes out so easily — it doesn't seem like such a big thing now. 'That was the last time I saw her.'

He hears her intake of breath. 'She never came back?'

'She went to visit her grandmother and she stayed.' He rolls over so he is facing her. Her eyes don't leave his face. 'She always wanted to leave East Germany. My father says that was her only chance.'

'But why didn't she take you with her? Why didn't you all go?'

'We couldn't all go. They only gave her a visa to visit the West because she left us behind. A husband and child, it was like insurance. They thought she would return.' His mother used the Wall as an excuse, a reason to never return; and his father used it as a reason not to follow.

'Did your father know? Did they plan it together?'

It was a question Andi had never needed to ask his father: the answer was as obvious as the boxes piled in the spare room, waiting as if one day she might return to unpack them.

'My father is pathetic. He just let her go.'

'But did he know?'

'She left him a note saying her grandmother was sick, she had gone to Hanover, that she would be back in a few days and to pick me up from childcare. He didn't know she wasn't coming back. He even thought she might after the Wall came down. He didn't hear from her again. And still he waited. Until now.'

'Until now?'

'She's coming to Berlin.'

'When?'

'Soon.' Andi turns away from Clare and stares at the ceiling, tries to make out the light fitting in the dark. He blinks rapidly, counting, not letting the tears leave his eyes. 'I'm not going to see her.'

Clare doesn't say anything, and he wishes that she would.

'I don't even know her. She's like a stranger.' He rolls over to face her, kisses her on the nose. 'Unlike you. I know everything about you.'

Each day she thinks of new things to show Andi when he comes home, an attempt to take his focus away from her, from her changing body, which is courting disaster. It begins with the books: she lines them up according to the colour of their spines, with height as the second defining category.

She perfects her handstands up against the wall. It reminds her of lunchtimes at school when they would tuck their dresses into their knickers and cartwheel about the yard. There was so much freedom in being upside down, and it was something the boys were never able to do. She dips her hands to the floor and kicks her legs up, but the first few times her legs flail and come down, one after the other. At first she was too tentative: she was not used to flinging her adult body about. But now she just throws her hands down, flicks her legs up behind and lets them hit the wall. She stays there, feels the blood rushing to her face and her arms begin to quiver. Her head against the wall, she arches her back and, finally, when she can hold no more, she lets her feet drop to the floor with a thud.

She handstands in the middle of the room, maintaining her balance as she counts to five, then eight, then ten. She walks about on her hands: quickly at first, the momentum jolting her along, but as she gets better at balancing, her hand steps become slower and more certain.

She practises the handstands every day until her heels

have marked her upside-down height on the wall. Her heel marks look abandoned, and she wonders about Andi's mother, wonders about her own mother, a world away. Why has she not come to find her yet? She has so many questions to ask her mother. It would be awkward to discuss this situation with her, and she doubts that she ever will. But she runs through conversations in her head, answers herself as she expects her mother would. She asks her mother whether handstands would hurt the baby. Her mother laughs and wonders why Clare would be doing handstands anyway.

When her mother has dismissed each of her concerns, Clare removes all the teabags from their tin and puts them in a saucepan. She pours hot water on them and watches the tea steep to a dark brown. Using Andi's toothbrush she paints with the tea mixture on the wall. It does not take very well: it trickles to the ground. She carries the bowl back to the kitchen and adds cornflour to the tea, stirring quickly. Back in the living room, she draws fighter jets on the wall with fire shooting from their engines, bombs falling onto the ground below. She draws spirals of smoke rising from the floorboards and pilots floating to the skirting boards beneath parachutes. It is the same kind of picture her sister used to draw when they were young. She, on the other hand, would draw landscapes, a river winding through the hills, a sun in the corner of the page beating down. Everything in perspective, leaning with commitment towards the vanishing point. She would pepper the landscape with a cottage, cloudy sheep, a train track, a reed-edged pond, all the requirements of country serenity. But those storybook pictures are too static for the apartment; she wants things that move, so she paints two-dimensional

Roger Ramjet planes with bubble windows and wings bent with speed.

In the bedroom, she paints a rainbow across the wall above the bed. She makes a green-tea mixture and one with tomato sauce, but even so the rainbow is quite dismal and she thinks the baby will be disappointed.

He wants to hurt her. He wants to be rid of her suffocating presence. These urges build slowly. He wakes and feels her body by his side. He slides his arms around her and runs his hands over her breasts. She is soft and giving and pliable, and he enters her from behind. She moves in time with him, and when he comes, he wants to push her away. It is too easy. He wants to know where the borders are, how far he can push.

When he returns from work, he moves about the apartment, checking to see what has changed during the day. He considers the paintings on the wall. They are horrific, naive as a child's, and there is something malicious about them. They are brown and green, faded colours of camouflage. He will wash them off; he should make her wash them off. Whichever way he looks, he can see something of Clare's. His apartment has nothing to do with him anymore, and he wants to box up all of her belongings, stack them in a corner and paint his walls white again. He stands in front of the Polaroids, pinned out in a grid, and looks at her. He brings a chair from the dining table to the wall. Stepping up onto it, he sees her latest photos at eye-level. Her face has become more square. He goes back to the hallway, picks up his bag and gets out the photograph he took of her this morning. He compares it with the her of now.

'You've cut your fringe.' He feels the blood rush to his head. Sometime between when he took the photograph and now, she has cut her hair. He was at work all day with an inaccurate photograph. 'You made yourself different.' He tries to keep his voice steady. He holds up the photograph. 'I take this photograph of you so I know how you look every day, and you made yourself different.'

She nods, slowly. The different hair nods, too.

'Fuck, Clare! All I ask is that things stay the same. Why would you do this to me?' He grabs her arm, forces her to look at the Polaroid. 'See! This is how you looked this morning. This is how I thought you looked today. And when I come home, I find you are different. Why are you doing this to me?'

'I thought it would be nice. A surprise. I thought you would like it.'

'Show me! Show me how you did it. You got the scissors from the kitchen, didn't you.' He marches into the kitchen, holding tightly to her wrist. He pulls open the cutlery drawer, grabs the scissors. He can see a red hair caught between the blades. 'And then what? You went to the bathroom?' He strides down the hallway and he can feel her jerking along behind him.

'Andi! Andi, it's okay. I can show you. I can show you!'

He pushes her ahead of him into the bathroom and switches on the light. He wants to see exactly what she did, wants to know what she does when he is away.

'Show me what you did.' He throws the scissors down into the basin. They clatter about and come to rest. He can see stray hairs in the basin, some embedded in the soap. Hairs that should still be on her head.

She picks up the scissors. With her free hand, she brushes

her hair forward. 'I just wanted to trim it a little,' she says, her voice wavering. 'So I got the scissors and cut like this.' She mimes cutting a straight line across her forehead.

'Why didn't you ask me, Clare? I would have done it for you. You can't just go changing things like that. There are reasons for everything — you should know that by now. This is not just about you.'

She does not look at him; the scissors hang in her hand. 'It's just hair. It will grow back. It doesn't matter.'

He steps forward and grabs the scissors. Standing behind her, he puts one arm around her body and forces her to face the mirror. His body is pressed against hers; his left arm comes up under her arm and his hand holds her chin. He takes in their reflections, their heads side-by-side. He is pleased by the way his body easily covers hers; she is so much smaller than him.

'See how different you are? See how it changes the way I look at you?' He stares at the reflection of her wide eyes. They are focused on his moving lips. He regards her fringe, her naked forehead. He would never have cut it that way — it looks too blunt.

He flips the scissors open and lifts them to her face. 'When your hair grows to this line, then I will cut it for you.' Her body tightens in his grip. He picks a point on her forehead, presses the blade of the scissors into her skin.

'Andi!'

He pulls the blade quickly, and the skin puckers then gives way. In one smooth action he glides the scissors across her forehead. Blood wells in the shallow cut, and he is surprised by how smooth the bone of her forehead feels beneath the scissors.

He drops the scissors into the basin and watches her reflection. Tears slide down her cheeks, and the blood gathers in one place and swells. He stares at his own reflection. He looks the same as he did this morning after he had brushed his teeth. Her body is shaking, and he pulls her to him.

'Don't cry, Clare. Don't cry. I was just showing you that there are rules. There have to be.' He holds her close, drawing his fingers through her hair. She shudders; her tears must be coming to an end. He lets her go, grabs her hand. 'Things don't need to change.' He kisses her on the forehead; her blood is sticky on his lips. 'I love you the way you are. Don't do these things to yourself.' Giving her hand a gentle squeeze, he walks out of the bathroom.

This cannot go on. She gets herself up from the floor and stretches. She rolls her shoulders, first one and then the other. They roll more smoothly when she does it backwards than forwards. Joints click and rub inside of her. She wonders whether this is normal but decides it does not matter. Normal or not, it is how it is. Her body appears to be shrinking when it should be growing. Her calf muscles have disappeared, and her knees tremble when she stands up. She tries to stand on one foot and she wobbles.

She is not sure how long she has been in the apartment. The sunlight is brighter than it used to be, and it rains less. But when it does, the rainfall is more substantial. She knows the difference now between showers and downpours. Rain and sleet. The sky is often blue: it must be nearing summer.

She knows it would not be so difficult to find out. She could look at the dates on the newspaper, but she chooses not to. That is a lie. She deliberately avoids them, goes out of her way to fold them over, make them go away. She does not want to know if the halfway point has happened or is still to come. If she is to be here forever, there will be no halfway point. She lifts one arm above her head and then the other. She rises on her toes. She can only stay stretched a few seconds before she falls forward. She tries it again.

The doorbell rings. She did not know there was a doorbell, but she recognises its sound immediately. Who has come to visit her? She drops her arms and crosses to the stereo to turn down the music.

The doorbell rings again. She turns off the music and waits.

'*Andreas?*'

A woman's voice floats in from the hallway.

'*Andreas? Bist du da?*'

She walks down the hallway quietly. She stops at the front door.

'*Andreas, ich bin's, Ingrid. Ich bin's, Deine Mama.*'

She feels sick. Andi's mother. Her stomach is heavy, and she feels as if she is going to throw up. She puts her hand to the door as though to open it, but of course she cannot. She withdraws her hand, lays her head against the door. It makes a little thud, and hearing this, Andi's mother's voice takes on a sense of urgency.

'*Andreas? Hallo? Ist jemand da? Hallo?*'

'Hello.' The word is out of Clare's mouth instantly, an unsolicited hello enough to elicit a mimicking response.

'*Hallo? Würden Sie mich bitte hereinlassen? Ich bin Andreas' Mutter.*'

'*Tut mir Leid, aber ich spreche Englisch*.' Apologetic, she hopes Andi's mother will realise the conversation is futile and leave. He will not want to see his mother, of that she is sure. She cannot stay here; she cannot be here when he returns.

'You speak English? Is this where Andreas lives?'

Andreas. The name keeps coming back; it is a stranger's name. Would a man by the name of Andreas be less complicated than one called Andi? She cannot talk with his mother — he will be furious. But she cannot lie.

'Yes.'

Silence.

'My name is Ingrid. I'm Andreas's mother. Can I come in?'

'No, I'm sorry, you can't.'

It is a truth. She is pleased with this; she has not compromised anyone.

'You can't let me in?'

'No.'

'Are you Andreas's girlfriend?' A pause. 'His wife?'

She conjures a wedding where this woman and Andreas's father would be weeping tears of happiness in the pews, sharing congratulations and hugs with her own mother.

'Yes, his girlfriend.' The term is foreign on her tongue.

'I'm sorry, I do not mean to be rude.'

'That's okay.' She is surprised at the lightness in her voice. She sounds almost cheerful. 'I'm his girlfriend.'

'That's nice. I mean, I'm happy that he has a girlfriend.' A pause. 'What's your name?'

'Clare.'

'Clare. That is a lovely name.'

'Thank you.' She is pleased with how this conversation is

going. She has not said anything wrong.

'Clare, when will Andreas be home? I would really like to see him. Can I wait for him inside?'

'I'm not sure when he will be home. You can't wait here.'

'Why not?'

She thinks about going back to her seat on the windowsill and asking the television tower exactly what she should do. She cannot remember what she looks like today. It is probably not how Ingrid expects her to look. She is not wearing much, and is certainly not wearing the right thing to be meeting Andi's mother. She cannot unlock the door.

'It's just not a good idea,' she says. 'We don't have visitors.'

Ingrid takes some time to respond.

'Well ... perhaps you can tell him that I came by? I won't be in Berlin long but I would very much like to see him. And I would like to meet you properly, Clare.'

She thinks she would like to meet Ingrid. After all, she is a mother. And Clare has lots of questions for a mother right now. But perhaps it would be better to just ask her own.

'I don't think he will want to see you, Ingrid. And I can't promise to tell him you visited. I don't want to upset him.'

'But he's my son, Clare. I want to see him.'

'I know.'

There is silence on both sides of the door. She wonders what time Andi will be home. She runs her hands down the glossy panel of the door, wonders if Andi's mother is doing the same.

'You haven't seen him since he was a child, have you?'

Ingrid takes so long to answer that Clare wonders if she has left.

'No. It's been a long time.'

The silence pours out, and she savours it — it is so nice to share something with another person.

'It was difficult then, with the Wall and … and how things were,' continues Ingrid. 'It wasn't how I wanted it to be.'

'But you left him behind?'

'Yes.' Ingrid sighs, and Clare would like to reach out for her hand.

'I think you should go now, Ingrid. I don't think it's a good idea that you're here. He's still quite upset that you left, he doesn't want to see you.' Her words run on, she is speaking too much, she shouldn't be saying anything. Andi would be so angry if he knew.

'Clare, is everything okay?'

And Ingrid sounds like her own mother, her words swollen with concern, her voice creeping around the edge of the door and streaming towards Clare to bestow a kiss on the cheek. She cannot talk; her throat is closing over and her eyes are too big for her head.

'Clare?'

She cannot speak with his mother anymore. She is going to say something wrong and she cannot imagine what might happen next if she does.

'It's okay.' Her small voice whispers, and she reins it back in, builds it up and throws it out again. 'I'm okay, everything is okay.'

'Well, as long as you're sure.'

She says nothing.

'Clare, I'm going to leave Andreas a note. It has my details so he can contact me. You don't have to say anything, you can just give it to him.'

She listens as Ingrid searches around in her bag for a pen. She can hear the words scratched out on the other side of the door. A scuffling below and the paper is pushed under the door.

'I'm going to go now, Clare.'

'Okay.'

A pause. 'Take care, won't you? Hopefully I will see you soon.'

'Goodbye.'

'Goodbye, Clare.'

She takes the piece of paper into the living room. Ingrid has written her name, the name of her hotel and its address, her mobile number and her email address. So many identifying items. *Lieber Andreas, manchmal muss man weit weg gehen, um der Liebe willen. Es tut mir leid. Ich liebe Dich, Deine Mama.*

She folds the paper in half and puts it between the pages of a book. In the bedroom she lies back on the bed. It is late in the day, and the ceiling is the same colour as the sky. She shuts her eyes; she wants to sleep.

She dreams about her own mother. That she has come to Berlin to find her. She knocks on the door and apologises. She calls out. But when Clare opens the door, they have nothing to say. She gives her a perfunctory kiss on the cheek, asks her if she has any bags, or a coat. They stand in the doorway staring at each other, waiting. The hallway light goes out, and when Clare steps outside to join her on the landing, her mother is not there. She switches the light back on, looks about the landing. She leans over the banister. Nothing. She goes back into the apartment and shuts the door.

It is dark when she wakes, and Andi is not yet home. She gets up off the bed. She walks quietly to the living room and takes Ingrid's note from the book. She thinks about rolling it up into a cigarette she won't allow herself to smoke, letting the words burn and float up to the ceiling. They would become impregnated on her fingertips, and when Andi kissed them later, wrinkling his nose at the smell, she would not have to tell him about the letter.

When the train stops at his station, he does not stand up. Others get off, the doors clang shut and the train moves on. He sinks further down into his seat, his knees touching the empty bench opposite. He is more like his father than ever. His father, who is probably right now sitting at home, pouring coffee for his mother, doing everything he possibly can to please her. He imagines his father showing her around his apartment, clearing books from the armchair or couch so that she may sit. He wonders whether his father will show her the spare room, ask her to take away the boxes of her things. But he knows that he will not. Instead his father will show her the boxes, want to lift the flaps and filter through the memories with her. And his mother will watch from the doorway, perhaps she won't even step into the room, and she will feel nothing but sorry. Not that she went, just that she came back.

The train stops at the next station, and Andi sits up but does not stand. He left work early. The students are on holidays, the exams are marked. Yet he does not want to go home; there is nothing for him there. The train moves on. It is not Clare, it is him. When he sees her, he finds his anger grows. It grasps hold of every thought, and rips it out of his hands. He has no idea of what he is doing; each day is so much like the one before that he feels compounded. His hands want to grab her, to shove her out of the way, to push her up against the wall and make her disappear. There is nowhere to exist without her anymore; every fissure of his mind waits for her. It is as though he cannot act except in retaliation.

When the train stops again, he gets off. He has never been at this station before. Clare has never been here either. It may as well be a different country. As he climbs the steps to the street he looks at his watch: his diversion has taken only minutes from his day, and there is nowhere to go but home.

The Polaroids of Clare reach almost to the ceiling. She has to get on a chair to stick the new one up each day. She pushes the pin into the wall. She looks at the recent images that show the line across her forehead. It is angry and dark on the first image and the next. Then it becomes broken, dotted like a 'cut here' line around a voucher. As the images progress, the line fades to pink. If she looks in the mirror she knows she will see it: a line of slightly smoother skin skirting her eyes like a horizon, but it does not come up so clearly on the Polaroids. Film can be forgiving like that. But she knows the line will never completely disappear.

She usually sticks the photo up in the morning but not today. It is late afternoon: Andi will be home within the hour. He comes when it is light now — the days are longer. She gets off the chair, ignoring the dizziness that accompanies her everywhere and walks to the window.

Suicide is something other people do. But now she sees no alternative. She can feel her body being pushed aside, making way for the one that is forming. She cannot bring somebody else into this. She folds herself up on the windowsill. She smells. She is not wearing any socks — it is her concession to the weather. Just a t-shirt. Knickers. He likes her best that way. 'I like to see as much of you as possible,' he says. 'I can see clothes on anyone.' She likes herself least this way, but it matters little. When she looks at her scarred legs, she is disgusted, repulsed, pleased. She is none of these things and she knows that she should be. She looks at her legs, and she is not even sure they are still her own.

She feels the panic rise. It is so familiar now, the way her stomach twists and turns and the saliva builds in her mouth. Her visual focus narrows, and her armpits prick with sweat. She should not be here. She needs to get out. She cannot get out; there is no way out. She will have to die. She cannot commit suicide. She does not want to die. She is pregnant. She cannot be pregnant. She does not want to leave Andi. What the fuck is wrong with her?

'What the fuck is wrong with me?' She tries the words out aloud. They drift away, unanswered. She leans her head on the glass. The ground is five storeys below. It could be one; it could be twenty. She cannot get out.

'I belong here.'

She wants someone to argue with her, but they don't.

'He cannot live without me.'

No response. She looks down at her pale legs, lined with scars.

'No one will recognise me.'

She walks down the hallway to the front door, touches it, turns and walks back to the window of the living room and touches it. She repeats this over and over, as though she is swimming laps in a pool. She feels increasingly faint, and this is what she wants. To fall over and have it all disappear. Finally, she stops at the front door. It swims up before her, white in the gloom of the unlit hallway. She twists the handle, pulls the door and it opens.

Clare stands with her hand on the door knob looking into the hallway. The safe sits, as she imagined, by the wall. The rest is dark, just a gleam from the varnished banister. She steps onto the landing. The concrete floor is cold beneath her feet. She does not take her hand from the door. It is instinct, to not let a door slam, to not be locked out.

When was the last time she tried the door? She cannot remember. In the beginning she would try it many times a day. As Andi left and then throughout the afternoon, waiting for him to come home. And then she stopped trying; it seemed such a futile gesture. But how could she have ever considered it so, when now the door is open? She feels cheated. How long has he been leaving the deadbolt unlocked?

She must leave. She cannot leave dressed like this. She steps back into the apartment, goes to close the door. She does not trust it so she props the door against her foot, reaches into the hallway and picks up the safe from the landing. She goes back into the apartment, carefully placing the safe between the door and the jamb, preventing the door from closing fully. She must hurry: he will be home soon.

She runs into the bedroom, tugs her backpack from the wardrobe. It looks so ridiculously bulky. She leaves it and pulls on a pair of jeans. Next to her backpack are her boots; it has been such a long time since she wore them, they feel like they belong to someone else.

She keeps stopping what she is doing to look at the door, checking it is still propped open. In the living room, she picks up her camera bag, slings it over her shoulder. Then she puts it down again. She moves the chair over to the wall of Polaroids, climbs up and, without hesitation, pulls one from the wall. Behind it is a folded piece of paper, and she lets it fall to the floor. It is the letter from Andi's mother. She should have given it to him days ago. *Sometimes you have to leave in order to love.* She had translated it with the aid of Andi's dictionary, shuffling the words about to decipher Ingrid's intention. She thought it was such a terrible thing for a mother to write to her son that she could not bear to pass it on. She wanted to save him from the pain, because she knew that she could. She unfolds the letter and leaves it on the floor and puts the Polaroid in her jacket pocket. The television tower blinks at her. Hurry, hurry. She grabs her camera bag and runs down the hallway.

She pulls the door wide open, still amazed that it has become a moving object, and steps through. She is out. She goes to move the safe aside to let the door slam shut, but she has a moment of fear that she will be locked on this other side, and she lets the door rest ajar. The stairwell is inky. She runs her hand along the wall, feeling for the light switch. Nothing. She waves her hand up and down, broad sweeps on the cool concrete. Nothing. Hurry, hurry. She skitters down the stairs in the dark, stumbling, catching herself on the banister. At the bottom, daylight leaks in through the outer door, and she wrenches it open, throws herself into the courtyard. The linden greets her, a glorious technicolour green, and she is across the yard, through the other door, the passageway and into the street. She turns left. There are people. She is outside. She begins to run, her bag banging awkwardly against her as she sidesteps the people who have no urgency. At the intersection she looks to her left, and there, the television tower. It blinks at her, a friend. Its red and white lights switch on and off — nothing changes their rhythm — and she heads towards it gratefully.

Her ankles threaten to give way on the cobbled streets. She keeps looking in the wrong direction for oncoming traffic; she is afraid her instinct will lead her in front of a vehicle. She wants to slow down but she cannot, and she knows people are looking at her strangely, but she is running and she is getting away and she cannot stop. Her breath is short, and she keeps staring at people, expecting them to be Andi, surprised when they are not.

When she finally makes it to Alexanderplatz, her lungs are burning, her legs shaking. The square is filled with people, their hands grasping shopping bags, lifting takeaway coffees to their mouths, holding mobile phones. They are oblivious to her, and she wants to be one of them. She slows to a walk; she is breathing heavily. She skirts around the department store and sees the S-Bahn sign. Inside, the shopping mall is cool yet the air is close. She joins the crowds jostling down the stairs to the platform and lets herself get sucked up by them and ferried along.

He won't know where she is. He will worry; she should have left a note. And then she catches herself, realises what she is thinking. She is free. She will not see him again. She knows what she must do. She is away.

Ingrid's steps slow as she reaches the top of the landing. Each tread feels familiar, the import of her previous visit having committed this stairwell to her memory. She had asked Andreas's father about Clare. Who was this girlfriend of their son? He had said little. He had not met Clare, and Ingrid suspects that until then he had not even heard of her. She has received no response to her note and has spent over a week distractedly wandering the streets of Berlin, trying to evoke memories as often as she tries to discourage them. She did not want to pressure Andreas, did not want to force herself upon him, but tired of waiting, she has returned to his apartment, decided once more to surprise her son, and do more than talk to a haunted voice through his front door.

She arrives on the top landing and lifts her hand to knock before realising the door is propped open.

'Andreas?'

No sound comes from the apartment.

'Clare?'

She wants now to put a face to the voice, wants so desperately to hear soft footsteps coming towards her. Has Clare left the door open for her? An invitation? Is she circumnavigating Andreas's refusal to see her?

She knocks on the door, calls out the names again. Nothing. She pushes open the door and goes into the apartment. It appears to be a safe that is holding the door open, the kind used by small businesses for petty cash and kept in a desk drawer. Resting the door back against the safe, Ingrid calls out again.

'*Hallo?*'

But she is alone in the apartment. Sound bumps off the hard surfaces and sinks into her body. It is a reception she knows well. She walks down the hallway, passing the bathroom and the bedroom. She cannot resist looking into the bedroom, though she feels there is something sordid about a mother seeing where her grown son sleeps. The bed is unmade: white sheets cascade to a floor of sea-grass matting. The curtains are closed, but she can make out a backpack staggering out of the cupboard — it looks like a person slumped there.

At the end of the hallway, she turns into the living room. Summer light floods through large windows framed by white curtains. There is a mural painted across one wall: aeroplanes and parachutes, the kind of thing you paint to amuse a little boy. Does Andreas have a child? Does she have a grandchild? She looks for further clues, wants to know what sort of person he has become. She expected his apartment to be dark and enclosed — the light and the IKEA furniture surprise her. She had wanted him to be miserable. Bright cushions recline on the couch and armchair, records are scattered on a coffee table. She can smell cigarettes in the air, and she hopes that Andreas or Clare will return soon, that they have just walked to the shops or a nearby park.

She crosses the room to the window. Looking at the view seems the only legitimate activity for a stranger waiting alone. She is reminded of her own apartment in Berlin so many years ago. The windows were much smaller, and the television tower further away. But it was the same, in its way, and she is glad that she and Andreas have shared this at least.

She hears a thud. Is it the downstairs door closing? Her heart lurches, and she turns from the window to face the living-room doorway. Where should she stand? How will he react to seeing her? And then she sees the wall.

From skirting board to ceiling, the wall is covered in a grid of Polaroid photographs. It looks like an art installation, each photograph pinned in strict formation with its neighbours. They are all the same image — no — they are all of the same girl, and she knows instinctively who it must be. She moves towards the gallery, aware that footsteps on the stairs are mimicking her own. There are so many photos, perhaps two or three hundred, and in each one Clare regards her. She smiles and she grimaces; she looks into the distance; she looks at the floor; and she looks through the window to the television tower as though greeting a familiar friend. But no matter where her gaze falls, in every single photo she has been captured. Towards the top of the wall, one Polaroid is missing, and Ingrid stands on a chair to look at the ones on either side, urging them to give a clue to Clare's absence.

The footsteps arrive on the landing, and then she sees. The photo to the left of the gap shows Clare with long hair. In the photo to the right she has a fringe, and an angry line is carved across her forehead.

'Clare?' he calls out as he closes the front door.

As she climbs down from the chair, Ingrid hears him turn the key in the lock.

'Clare, are you in there?' His footsteps follow his voice down the hallway.

She turns to meet her son.

ACKNOWLEDGEMENTS

Thank you to everyone who has helped me along the way with this book. To my parents, Annette and John, who have always been supportive, as have my sisters and brothers, Stephanie, Alexander, Hannah, Bridget and Nicholas. To my friends for giving me permission to retreat. Particular thanks to Anna Egan, Naomi Saligari and Emma Wakeling, who read early drafts and gave honest and helpful feedback. Thanks to Franka Tuchelt, Damian Lentini and Tobias Titz for their help with all things German. And many thanks to Alanna Egan for the hours spent discussing this book, and for reminding me why we write.

With thanks to everyone at Scribe, who are absolutely delightful, in particular to Nicola Redhouse and Ian See. And the most particular and heartfelt thanks of all to Aviva Tuffield, whose intelligence and astute questioning made this a much better book — and me a much better writer.